HOLE
IN THE
WOODS

Jennifer Graeser Dornbush

ALLY PRESS

Mercy and truth have met each other.

Justice and peace have kissed.

Psalms 84:11

"Jennifer Dornbush flips convention on it's head as she seamlessly weaves forensic procedure, investigative intuition, and suspense into narrative form."

"*Hole in the Woods* is powerful, painful, and completely compelling. I loved it."

"I liked the book all the way to the end. The ending was a surprise to me!"

"There's nothing more frightening than the truth. Inspired by the brutal real life murder of Shannon Siders, Jennifer Dornbush's novel is a taut and gripping tale of justice finally served. Having grown up in the same county as Siders, Dornbush brings an insider's perspective to a cold case and the community it shatters."

"A haunting and gritty tale of a real cold case murder that is sure to keep you up at night."

"Jennifer Dornbush's HOLE IN THE WOODS is nothing less than an act of courage. Evocative fiction. Part elegy for innocence lost, part redemptive tale of hope winning out. This book ensures the dead have a voice in the living."

Tom Bernardo, *Writer and Producer of Amazon crime drama BOSCH.*

"Hole in the Woods is a great and worthwhile read for a very worthwhile cause. Definitely hope to see more like this from Jennifer in the future!"

Lisa Kaplan , *JD, FBI Special Agent (ret.)*

"Rife with suspense, Hole in the Woods will keep you guessing until the end. An engrossing must-read for fans of the crime genre that will chill readers to the bone."

Tosca Lee, *Award winning New York Times best selling author*

"Hole In The Woods is a gut wrenching, physical force. The story is powerful, involving a young girl who is raped and tortured. Author Jennifer Dornbush blows the doors off conventional thrillers. I would read it again, but the terror is all too real and I need my sleep.

Don Bruns, *USA TODAY Best Selling Author*

"This tale will drag you inside and never let go. A remarkable thriller you will not be able to put down.

DP Lyle, *Award-winning author, lecturer, story consultant*

For Bob, in memory of his daughter,

Shannon Siders.

*And for the countless loved ones who are still
waiting for answers, for justice, and for peace.*

Prologue from the Author

E ven though we grew up in the same county in west Michigan and were born the same year, I only came to know Shannon Siders through her death.

Shannon was a bit of a wild child the summer of her murder. Her father, Bob Siders, describes her as sowing her wild oats-- testing the limits. Like many teens. But, as Bob says, just before Shannon was killed, her wild days were starting to wind down. She was coming to a cross roads in her life and a big part of the change was her boyfriend. They had fallen in love. Serious talk of marriage was on the table. Days before Shannon was murdered, he left for a new job in Ohio to start saving for their future. Bob liked this guy and was rooting for the relationship. He was a positive influence on Shannon. A high school drop out, Shannon started discussing the possibility of getting her GED. Her dad's constant nagging "to get a job" were starting to sink in. A friend of Shannon's had gotten her a promising interview for a clerk position at the local grocery story. But she never got to apply because Shannon went missing the night that her friend went to tell her about the job.

The summer Shannon was killed I was also a carefree teenager, working at a floral shop in the next city over, hanging at Lake Michigan with my friends and prepping to leave home for college in Chicago. Sometimes I wonder how many times our paths crossed that summer. Were we buying a snack at the same gas station or tubing down the Muskegon River just a few hundred feet from each other?

I didn't know Shannon went missing one late July night. I only first learned about Shannon's death when her body was found by a hunter three months later in the Manistee national forest near a landmark named the Hole in the Woods. My father was the county Medical Examiner at the time and he told me a few details about the case. He determined after examining her remains that Shannon had suffered a brutal death, disturbing details that I wouldn't find out until sitting in on the trial some 25 years later.

This was a shocking event for our rural, tight-knit community. It cast a dark cloud on our rural county. Shannon's story is the kind of story parents and their daughters have nightmares about. Its tragedy and horrors are universal. Shannon's story is the kind of cautionary tale that gets passed down between young women from in high school hallways to college dorms. And that's probably why it stuck with me all these decades.

I kept up with the case as it unfolded in little layers for 25 years... through newspaper stories, documentaries, and finally attending the three-week trial in the spring of 2015. I desired justice for Shannon just as much as anyone in my county. We all wanted to believe that some day her killers would be found and put away. We wanted her story to be complete and her family to have catharsis. We all wanted order from this chaos. We wanted good to win over evil for her. We wanted to see right come from a very wrong situation.

And we got our wish.

After decades of persistence and hard work, justice for Shannon came. This triumph, however monumental, doesn't erase the pain. Her father and mother, family, and friends still grieve Shannon's absence. "It doesn't seem to ever get any easier," Bob Siders admits.

It was Bob who kept her case alive. He worked tirelessly for twenty-five years to force her case in the public eye and fight for justice. He says he wants Shannon's story told so that law enforcement and people like him can see how important it is to never, ever give up! He wants to encourage others in this situation to have faith and keep fighting the good fights to solve cold cases. He's living, walking proof that restlessness and persistence and hope can lead to justice.

In our world of constant "bad news" and fear mongering, we need to know those bleak stories don't always end bleakly. Here is a story that didn't end up as bleak as it could have. Here is a place where the selflessness and charity of an imprisoned criminal emerged to give an innocent girl justice and a father a measure of peace. Here is place where light was shed in darkness.

Jennifer Graeser Dornbush

Please note that the events portrayed in this fictional work do not completely reflect the documented facts regarding the Shannon Siders case. However, I have tried to retain many investigative and forensic elements in tact as much as possible, proving that old adage that truth is stranger than fiction. The characters and locations in this novel are all fictional, except for the "Hole in the Woods," which refers to a local name for a large clearing surrounded by a densely populated wooded area of the Manistee National Forest in Newaygo County.

Chapter 1

RILEY ST. JAMES

E very investigator I've ever known has that one type of case they struggle with. The unforgiveable sin. The faces and places change as the crime scene rewinds over and over in sweaty nightmares. Maybe it's infanticide. Animal cruelty. Elder abuse. Burn victims. Drownings. Suicides. Torture. It's different for everyone.

If you're lucky, you can get another investigator to take your assignment. But usually, you have no choice with it. Departments are short staffed and you aren't paid to be picky. Time is fleeting and so are the criminals. Suck it up and pray it won't stick with you when you put your head on that pillow. You want sleep. You fear sleep. You avoid sleep. You try to force sleep. After two hours, you take a third Ambien and wait for it to kick in, chasing it with a shot of whiskey. And lie there another two hours until the gray light of morning seeps out the edges of your room darkening blinds. Headache numbing the base of your neck, you drag yourself into the shower. You kick the demons back under your bed. They need to rest up for another night of torture.

You soon discover that you work these cases with a doggedness you don't have for your other cases. And the universe sees that and you get rewarded with more and more of them. Just to gnaw away your sanity.

Find the criminal. Make the arrest. Attend the trial. Hope for fair sentencing. Life in prison. Satisfaction? Yes. Justice? Yes. Closure? Never. Trace the deep lines on the brows of the victim's family. They weren't there a few years ago. They etched themselves into the flesh the moment they got that call. Trawling deep, gnarled trenches in the faces of loved one. They grow more creviced as the case drags on. Closure. Never.

No amount of confessions, jail time, or penance will ever be enough retribution for the act committed.

And in the dark recesses of your soul, you pray, you beg the very God that gave that a-hole life, that he doesn't have some crazy death-bed conversion. Because you want to be certain he'll burn in hell.

Chapter 2

GRABLE

Detective Kevin Grable hears Misty Beckett's pitchy voice demanding to see him. Right now. She has a fresh, hot tip on the Nina Laramie case. It could be *the* tip to solve the murder.

"Grable?!" The middle aging, receptionist leans her belly roll over the glass window sill partitioning the lobby from the bull pen. She juts her floppy neck in Grable's direction, "Misty's here."

"Yeah, I heard," says Grable.

Grable ambles from his desk to the small, wood-paneled lobby of the Derby police station with its stiff pleather seats and yellowing white walls.

"How ya doing, Misty? You get your hair colored?"

"One of the Nina Laramie Murder Facebook followers, who calls himself… or herself… GreatWhiteNorth… or GWN as I call them, contacted me directly through Facebook messenger and told me that

Nina's killer snuck into the funeral home before she was buried and left a confession note in her coffin."

"And this is just coming to light now. Twenty years later." Grable shakes his head at Misty.

"It's not surprising. Social media makes people feel anonymous," says Misty.

"We have an anonymous tip line. Why didn't GWN call that?"

"Everyone knows you cops trace those calls."

"That's not true." Grable is all too familiar with Misty's string of conspiracy theories surrounding local cases, and part of him was pleased she had shown up to interrupt the monotony of his day.

"What are you gonna do?" She pops a small bubble in her gum between her teeth.

"What makes you trust what Great White North is telling you?"

"GWN was one of my first followers when I set up the Nina Laramie Murder Facebook page three years ago. GWN is constantly replying to posts that other people leave. And posting things about Nina's life that only her close friends would know. So, like, I'm pretty sure it's someone from here. Probably someone from our high school. I just think it's legit."

"Okay, interesting. Can you send me the message?"

"Already done. Check your inbox."

"Why do you think GWN is doing this now?"

"Nina's anniversary. It's twenty years next week Nina was found at the Hole in the Woods."

Grable mulls it over. As much as he hates to play into Misty's self-created, cyber-celebrity, the logic of it strikes a chord. As a detective, he's looked into far more obscure tips than this one. "I'll take a look. Thanks, Misty."

"I'll keep ya posted if anything else weird shows up." She winks and snaps her fingers at him as if they're gal-pals.

"Counting on it."

"You'll never know if you don't dig up the body." Misty slings her handbag over her shoulder. "Are you gonna do that?"

Grable shrugs. He can't even imagine the community and press hoopla he'd stir up digging up Nina Laramie's twenty-year-old corpse. Not to mention the great displeasure from the family.

"Do you like my new hair color? It's called Autumn Flame."

"Suits you. Always starting fires."

"Very funny." But it's not to her.

Grable waits to pull up her message until every last strand of Autumn Flame disappears out the door.

Chapter 3

NINA, 1989

They drove me to the Hole in the Woods. Not home. Like I asked them to. That shoulda been my first clue. They said there was a party out in the woods. Said there were people they wanted to meet up with. I said I wanted to go home. I needed to take my dog out. And my Dad would be coming home from work in a few hours. I make him breakfast before he goes to bed.

We drove deep into the woods on a dirt two-track, turning off onto a long sandy drive that led into the hole. It was called Hole in the Woods because of the large clearing of trees surrounded by woods. To the left of the drive is a pond and further up there's a fire pit where us kids met to party.

There was no party tonight.

There was no one at the Hole in the Woods at all.

They parked the car near the huge fire pit and we got out. Empty beer bottles and plastic cups littered the ground. Parties had gone on there over the weekend. But it was a Monday night. I had never been to a party on a Monday night. Monday's were for hanging at the gas station.

The moon was full that night and you could see really well through the trees. One of them twins said how romantic it was and didn't I think so. Can't remember if I said so. I was starting to wonder what the hell we were going to do out here.

I asked them if they brought any wood so we could start a bonfire. The air had dropped ten degrees since dusk and dew was forming on the ground. There was no wood. I said I was going to wait in the car where it was warmer.

The other twin grabbed my hand and jerked me over to the hood of the car. He told me to get on the hood and look at the moon with him. I didn't like the way he treated me. It made me nervous. But I slipped onto the hood when his grip tightened on my arm. It was then he leaned over to kiss me. A sinking gut feeling kicked in. Something was off. He knew I was with Adam. I pushed him away. Told him I needed to get home. Take care of my dog, Tucker.

He didn't like that. Pinned me down and said me he was going to kiss me and to let him. Or there'd be trouble. He pressed down hard. His teeth bit into my lips. A warm sensation leaked onto my lips. I tasted blood.

I wriggled away and in the moonlight and I caught a look on the other one's face. He wanted me, too. They had planned this all night.

My heart started racing and a flash of heat surged through my body, coming out my pores in a damp sweat.

They exchanged glances and the Evil passed between them. The one closer to the fire pit started toward the car. The one on the hood next to me let go for a second to unbuckle his belt.

I slid out from under him, off the hood, and ran into the woods. Just ran. Not sure what direction. Just hoping to find a road or a house or a field or somewhere to hide in.

I heard their footsteps pounding behind me, snapping fallen twigs with their heavy steps. Why couldn't someone turn off that damned moon. They could see me plain as day. I glanced back. They were in pursuit, but stumbling over logs. Sluggish. Disoriented.

At that moment I realized it was possible that I could out run them. They had been boozing and doing drugs all night. I was alert. Sober. I had an advantage. I kept going, leaping over tree branches and praying I wouldn't trip. Thin tree limbs snapped back at me, whiplashing my face as I breezed past them. I didn't even try to shield myself.

Chapter 4

RILEY ST. JAMES

I was recently appointed to detective on a cold case team, along with a dozen other officers from around the state. We have over sixteen hundred cases in our statewide database, dating back to the early 1800's if you can believe that. The twenty-year-old Laramie case was top of the list. An egregious rape and murder. A teenager in a small town, bludgeoned and left for dead in the woods. It was mine to have. Sarge insisted I was perfectly matched for this challenge. Fresh eyes. A woman's intuition. It would require every ounce of finesse I had learned in my forensic statement analyst training. In other words, I know how to talk to people without pissing them off. I know how to get them to confess. I know what to look for. I know how to listen and read between the lines.

Sarge never brought up my own history with rape and assault. That was eighteen years of water under the bridge and a year in therapy ten years ago. You man up and move on, whether you're ready or not. And you always tell them you're ready. No pussies here.

Patrol policing, which I've been doing the past ten years, doesn't put you in touch with too many rape cases. I've managed to pawn off most of my sexual assault cases to co-workers. Have a car fatality? Suicide? I'm on it. Just don't send me to a weeping, shaking girl whose sparkling brown eyes that have been exchanged for a hollow, black stare.

I pack up my belongings and sublet my downtown apartment to a co-worker's daughter and her boyfriend. Cold cases can take a long time. Our strategy as a cold case team was to imbed in the area where the crime occurred and live among the community. You gotta earn trust. Ears to the ground. Break the codes of silence. People always know more than they let on. People talk to each other. Not to the police. Eventually. You'll crack it. You just have to be in the right place at the right time. And you can't do that from a high rise in Detroit looking at your computer screen and combing through a stack of decades-old chicken scratched case reports.

I have never been to Derby in my life. Never even heard of it and I've lived in Michigan since I was born. Derby lies a six-hour drive north from Detroit. Northern Michigan. Not as far up as the UP. That's Upper Peninsula. Which I've only visited twice in my life.

Unlike the southern part of the state, which is flatter farm land, northern Michigan is a dense wooded topography peppered with small towns. People here don't want to be bothered or hassled. Live and let live. Turn a blind eye lest you get your own plucked out in the process.

Derby County is what I would consider on the bigger side of small town. Close to 20,000 population. Looks like it's pretty modern as far as small towns go measured by the fact that they have a McDonald's, Taco Bell, Wal-Mart, and a Kentucky Fried Chicken. Signs of civilization. Not a great civilization. One addicted to mediocrity and ease of living.

I drive in and boy, does it look just like it did on Google Earth. There's a small downtown with a string of buildings that lines two blocks. Wiki said it was settled in the early 1800's by loggers. A library bookends one end of downtown. Yup. Quaint. And a new gym and spa bookends the other. A bank. A health food store. I passed a larger grocery store and a bowling alley on the way in. There's an old-timey four-screen theater. Down the road is a decent sized hospital. A bakery that caters to big-boned farmer's wives and hearty mid-western appetites. Hey, that's what Yelp said, not me. Yelp also told me that there is, and I quote, "a truly hipster brewery boasting a meat and vegan menu."

I'm not a vegan, by the way. I love a thick medium rare porterhouse. Loaded baked potato and deep, rich glass of red wine. Little bite of cheesecake for dessert. Stress and late nights don't allow me to tamp down my sweet tooth.

I pull up to the house I rented. Sight seen only from a realtor's website and Google Earth. I'm pretty geeked about it since I've only ever lived in an apartment in the city. I wanted to be close enough to walk into town. It's a four bedroom. And of course I don't need all that room, but it was the only property available this close to Derby central and at half the rent I pay in the city. I'll have to install a few security measures, including an alarm system and video surveillance. I don't mess around.

It comes with a nice big yard, maybe half an acre. Front porch. With a rocker. All I need now is some chewing tobacco and my shotgun. And I should fit in just fine. It's a stereotype. I know. But stereotypes exist for a reason.

When I unpack and go out onto the front porch the first thing that strikes me is that it's so quiet.

So, so quiet.

Who knows, maybe I'll be here long enough to get a dog.

I see there's an old rusty grill out back. Fingers crossed it works. I make a mental note to pick up a steak at the store.

So quiet.

My ears are ringing from the silence. I haven't been in such a quiet, wooded area since college.

Chapter 5

NINA, 1989

I ran til I wanted to puke. I am not athletic. I tried out for track one year. The coach let me in out of pity. Or maybe my Dad had something to do with it. He was trying to keep me in school. I liked hanging out with everyone. But I couldn't run worth a darn. And track meets made me nervous. I usually skipped those and went to my friend's apartment to watch soaps.

My breath was so hard in my ears that I couldn't hear anything else. I dared to glance back and saw that there was no one chasing me. I slowed to a jog until I spied a clearing and ran towards it. To my left, coming out of the woods was a long, narrow two-track under the power lines. The grasses were tall under there because it was mid-summer and everything was in peak growing season. The grasses came up to my mid-thighs, which made it challenging to run at any speed.

I kept debating about diving back into the woods for a little cover or just staying on the path. I could find some help there. My pace dropped to a fast walk so I could catch my breath. My t-shirt was soaked in sweat. The light sweater on top of my shirt clung to my back. My new Ked's were no longer white. I think it's almost funny now how concerned I was about my shoes. I reached for my necklace to see if it was still there. It was. I felt for the three pearls on the chain. Fingering each one. Mom had given it to me for my sixteenth birthday. They were real pearls, too.

I was like a scared doe, twitching at every sound and scanning the woods. I moved into a light jog again. My body was shaking and my legs felt weak. I wanted to cry. I wanted to scream. But I just kept jogging, massaging a hand under my right ribs to relieve the side ache.

The two-track through the power lines was a series of small hills, up and down and up and down, like a kiddie rollercoaster. Nothing here was flat. And my energies were being consumed quickly. I had just run up one of them when I saw twin dots of lights ahead.

Who was it? Who else would be out here? Maybe it was some other kids just riding around looking to party. Help. They could help me! Should I flag them down? Should I let it pass? Should I run back into the woods? Should I hide? I was paralyzed with questions when I saw a car crest a hill up ahead. Headlights blinded me. I was spotted. I heard the engine rev and tires peel out on the sandy road, trying for traction.

Wait. No.

They were headed right for me. Fast.

Their mustang dove into a valley in the road, bottomed out, and then crested the next little hill.

I turned around. I don't know why. And started running down the road. Away from the car. It was a move based on instinct. Not smarts. I should have darted into the cover of the woods.

In seconds the engine was at my side. I felt the bumper tap my calf. I started to veer off the two-track into the grassy area. I made a sharp right towards the fence and tripped over a log half-sunken into the ground.

Going down my only fear was that the car would run over me. I sprung to my knees and pressed up with my hamstrings when I felt a metal object thwump the back of my head. The force rolled me off the road and into the tall grass. I inhaled the plume of dirt that swept over me as the car went by.

Choking and gasping for air. I tried to rise and figure out what had just happened. The car was about fifty feet ahead of me. Red brakes lights glowed. Then, white reverse lights. I couldn't get up.

It was coming back. Back to get me. The Evil.

I willed myself onto my hands and knees.

I reached for the air trying to pull myself up.

I scrambled to my feet and stepped towards the woods. My head was bursting with bitter tasting pain. Like chewing nails.

I took a few wobbly steps. Tried to adjust my eyes, but things in front of me were blurry.

I could hear them brake hard. Gears slamming into park. There was yelling. Shock waves vibrated through my brain.

Car doors opened. Slammed closed. A trunk creaked. Metal clinking.

I kept moving as fast as I could. By feel. By shape. I dodged trees. Zig zagged back and forth. The reverberations in my head dizzied me. Every fourth step I stumbled. The pain in my head was shooting back and forth from one side of my skull like arrows being launched at one second intervals.

I knew I was an open target. I reached for my mother's necklace. *Help me, Great Spirit.*

Blackness edged my peripheral vision.

Chapter 6

RILEY ST. JAMES

I am not much of a drinker anymore. When I'm at a bar I order soda water with a slice of lime because it looks like an alcoholic drink and people don't keep pressing to buy me a drink. I've found that if I tip the bartenders well, or show them my badge, they don't care about losing the sales. They just wanna keep me happy and keep me around for safety's sake.

Tomorrow's my first official day in the office.

Tonight, my personal assignment is to get to know some of the locals. People talk when they drink.

Plus, I don't want to be alone tonight. It's too quiet in the house.

Looking around there's a scattered crowd for a weeknight. An older couple at a table eats burgers in red plastic hot dog baskets overflowing with French fries. A group of three guys play pool in the back corner and keep an eye on a football game. A scrawny gray-haired fella picking his teeth nurses a glass of whiskey at the bar. I take a seat at the other end of the bar and wait to see what transpires.

The bartender appears from the kitchen with a plate of fried fish and places it in front of the scrawny guy. She swaps out his empty glass for a new one. And a chaser of Coke.

"Hey there, what can I get ya?" She calls out to me.

"Start with a club soda and lime."

"You got it." She's mid-forties, brown hair in thick blonde high-lights, and wears an oversized sweatshirt to hide a tubby tummy. Skinny legs with big, broad feet stuck into imitation Ugg boots. She lays down a cocktail napkin and sets my drink on top. "Anything else? Food?"

"Oh, no, I'm good thanks. What's your name?"

"Joyce."

I extend my hand. "Riley St. James."

"Oh, I know who you are, Detective St. James. And I know why you're here in Derby."

"Word travels." I'm a little surprised.

She leans in to me a little. "Hey, I'm glad you're here. And I hope you arrest the assholes who killed her."

"That's what I intend to do."

Assholes. Plural. She's already got it pinned on the Newton twins.

"You probably already read the files?"

"Yeah." I've scratched the surface.

Her eyes travel across the bar to a group of guys at the pool table.

"You sure I can't get you a burger or something? On the house."

"That's very generous, but I'm not really hungry."

"Take a rain check then. Come in anytime you want."

"Thanks, Joyce. How long have you been working here?"

"Since I was seventeen. I basically inherited the place from the previous owners."

"You get a lot of business?"

"I get everyone. Even those I don't want," she smiles and I get the feeling she can handle it.

"Corner on the market," I joke.

"You wanna know anything, you come to me."

"I appreciate that." And I do. Greatly. "Call me Riley. Please." I have a good, friendly vibe from Joyce and wonder if she might become one of my main information hubs.

Joyce slips away from behind the bar to clean burger baskets and bring another round of beers to the older couple at the two top on my left. While she does, a man at the pool table comes over and leans on the bar next to me wafting of faint body odor and cigarettes. He doesn't look directly at me. He speaks to Joyce as she rounds the corner back behind the bar.

"Joyce, can I get another round?"

She glances up with a look of disdain and she slips the dirty dishes into a plastic dish bin under the counter. She reluctantly starts to pour a fresh beer.

"Come on. Don't glare at me like that Joycie," he teases her.

"I want you guys outta here after this round. Got it. Or I'm calling the cops."

I'm not sure what kind of customer service is going on here, but it doesn't seem to rile this guy up. He kinda gloats in it.

"On what grounds, Joycie? We ain't causing no trouble." His smile is yellowed. I'm close enough to see the plaque build up filling the space between each tooth. He's got a bowl cut hair style Literally, as if he put a bowl on his head. "I ain't afraid of Kev. What's that limp dick gonna do?"

She hands him a beer. "Last call." She holds out her hand for his money.

He pays her and moves an inch closer to me crossing into my personal space.

"You hear they're gonna dig up that girl's body tomorrow?" he says to me.

Sirens go off in my brain. I want to draw him in. "Is that your best pick up line?"

"Just a conversation starter."

Okay. I'll bite. "No. I haven't. What girl?" I play dumb. Joyce looks over and I wink at her with one eye. She gets it and keeps her trap shut.

"You're not from here, are you?"

"I am now."

"Where from?"

"Cleveland." I lie.

"What are ya doing in a dump like Derby?"

"Fresh start." I give him a little smile, hoping to earn trust.

"Running from the law? Or a boyfriend maybe?" He swigs his beer.

I try again, ignoring his questions. "So, what's with this girl they're digging up? Enlighten me."

"They found her in the woods back some twenty years ago."

He looks over at his buddies. Joyce hasn't moved her eyes off him. And that gives me pause. He still doesn't look at me.

"That's it? And?" I egg him on.

"And, I dunno really."

"You sure as hell do know." Joyce hisses from across the bar. "You know the story damned well. Don't act stupid. Go ahead, tell the lady." She's daring him.

The guy inches away from me. I can finally inhale without smelling his stink. Still not looking me in the eye. "I don't know. Just heard rumors is all."

"What kind of rumors?"

"That some cop killed her and dumped her body in the woods."

"Some cop?" notices Joyce rolling her eyes.

"Gimme a break. There was no cop that done that," Joyce is seething at him. Definitely some bad history here.

"There's no evidence to prove that it ain't either," he says. "There's no evidence at all."

I nod and give Joyce a look that lets her know I need to do some work here and she heads back to the kitchen.

"She's just still pissed at me cause I broke up with her ten years ago," says the man once Joyce is out of sight.

"Oh, you two used to date?"

"Almost married her."

I nod. And press my agenda. "No evidence, huh?"

"Her body was just bones when they found her. That's it. There's no way to prove nothing." He almost sounded proud about the fact.

I nod again and go silent. It's a tactic I use a lot to get people to fill in the conversation gap.

"Twenty years and no one's said anything to anyone?"

"Maybe there's nothing to be said," he says.

I shrug. "What do you think about this dead girl?" I want to see how he reacts. He doesn't even flicker an eye lid.

"I don't think about her much at all."

"You brought her up."

"Just trying to make conversation, lady."

"Odd conversation starter."

"It's biggest news we got around here."

"You seem to care." I want to use her name, but I can't. I can't let on that I know.

"What makes you think I give a shit?" He shrugs. "She was a friend of my cousin's."

"What was she like? She mean something to you? You date?"

"Nah. No. Told you I barely knew her."

I swirl my straw around the lime slice sending it to the bottom of the glass. I watch him take down half his beer.

"You wanna get outta here?" he says, glancing my way, but not facing me.

"And do what exactly?" This is not an unexpected turn.

"Take a drive."

"What's there to see around here? In the dark?" I know exactly what he's after, but I want to see him play it through.

"Just drive. That's just what people do around here." He's getting agitated. I bet he's an angry drunk.

"What's to see?" At this, his left eyelid twitches.

"Just around the county. Over the dam. The lakes."

"It's late. Don't you have a job to get to in the morning." I test him.

"Hey, nevermind, then." I've crossed some sort of line. He slides his mug towards the edge of the bar table. It stops just short of crashing down into the barkeep's sink.

"Have I said something to make you angry?" I ask calmly.

"You're hard to deal with."

"Am I?" I flirt with him, making sure I'm looking into his eyes. He continues to have a hard time looking back at me. "You seem like the kind of guy who likes a challenge." It's so cliché, but it works every time.

"I like to watch a woman struggle." He laughs. It creeps me out. I've pushed all the right buttons.

"You sound like the kind of man who's used to getting what he wants." Again, so cliché. But men like this are base.

"I am. I do." He glances around me.

Scumbag. He rocks back and forth on the edge of the bar, eyeing the shelf liquor. Nearly five minutes we've been talking and he still hasn't looked me in the eye. I keep my gaze on him.

"You haven't even asked me my name."

"Come on, don't be a little bitch."

Line crossed. Game over.

"Bitch isn't my name." I'm firm this time. And he turns his gaze straight into mine.

I see it. Right away. Unmistakable. It's there in every one of them I've ever dealt with. The Evil.

I keep steady, although inside my gut has just turned to jelly. "I'm not what you're looking for tonight."

Joyce shuffles up with a glower. "You're beer's gone. Now you need to be too."

He slides off the bar stool, "Your loss… Bitch." I let it go. He doesn't look at me. He saunters towards the back where a couple buddies throw darts at a board.

"Piece a work, huh?" Joyce says. I nod.

"He seems pretty interested in this case."

"He should be. He was with her the night she disappeared. That asshole's the number one suspect. Solomon Newton."

After a minute I see Solomon head for the back door, lighting a cigarette as he slips out.

"How often does he come in?"

"Now and then."

I watch what I say because I don't want to sound ignorant, and I haven't read through all the files yet. There are literally hundreds of interviews recorded.

"He was questioned, but the cops never made an arrest."

"Why not?"

"Isn't that why you're here?" says Joyce filling up three mugs of beer at the tap and trying to field an order being shouted at her from the bar.

"What's he drive?"

"Black Ford 150. Same as his brother."

I glance back over to the darts. Solomon has come back in and joined a couple more guys in a competitive round. Patrons start to spill in from the back doors.

"My only other waitress cancelled on me last minute," Joyce says leaving her station behind the bar to wait on a six top of couples who have just sat down in the dining area. I leave Joyce a generous tip and slip out the front and head around back to the parking lot. I see the black Ford 150 in the back of the lot and I take down the plates.

Then, I head for home on foot. I hover my hand over my pistol while I walk. It's only a quarter mile to my new dwelling, but I'll take a round-about way and keep an eye on my surroundings. I don't really think he'll come after me. He's too damned lazy and drunk.

But never, ever assume you're safe. I learned that the hard way.

Chapter 7

NINA, 1989

I lost my vision, but I kept running. I was bumping into trees and stumbling over branches. I heard the snapping of twigs and knew the Evil ones were close up behind me, circling in on me from both sides.

One of them grabbed my hair and I jerked back hitting the ground hard. I fought blindly, flailing my arms, but they soon had me pinned down. Using all my core strength I kicked my legs up over my head, trying to kick them off me. Strong hands gripped my legs and flipped me onto my stomach.

They were yelling at each other, but the pain ringing in my ears was so loud that their voices sounded muffled. They dragged me by the legs for a short distance. My stomach scratched along the floor of the woods. I dug my nails into the ground but I couldn't gain any traction against their pull. My right hand found a small tree trunk and latched on, clinging to it with both hands. Suddenly a heel slammed down hard on my hands and I felt bones break in the right hand. Pain starburst out my fingers, down to my elbow and up to my shoulder. My entire arm drug limply out in front of me.

There was more shouting and then they stopped dragging me and let go. I reacted immediately, jumping onto my knees. No hands grabbed me to pull me down. For a second, I thought I could escape. I lifted my chin, willing my eyes to make out some shapes or forms that might guide me. Nothing but black.

A thwack across my left shoulder sent me face into the dirt. My left arm was flaccid at my side. Another hit across my lower back deadened all feeling from the waist down.

I think that's when they took turns with me, but I was fading in and out of consciousness and I couldn't feel anything. Finally, I stopped fighting and let myself be swept away into some incognizant state.

A part of my brain awakened after sometime. I was not sure how long. And I sensed an eerie stillness. When I opened my eyes, my sight line was still black. I moaned a little as the sensation of pain returned. I lifted my head and heard a single voice. Still inaudible. But I sensed I was the target.

Using my left arm and all my strength, I reached up to my neck and gripped my pearl necklace as a sharp instrument met with the back of my skull.

And that was it.

I never suffered any more pain after that moment.

My ears opened and my eyes started to see white. Like if you were in the middle of a cloud in an airplane. At least that's what I imagine from the pictures I've seen. I've never actually been in an airplane before.

Then color. Comforting blues and greens wrapping themselves around me. They had warmth and peace. My body felt lighter and lighter and I could breathe! Deep, deep breaths of the cleanest air. It smelled like fresh laundry the moment you open the dryer and press a clean shirt to your face.

I realized I was traveling somewhere. Nothing was recognizable. But I didn't seem concerned about that. Or about being lost. Or where or when or how I was getting there. Or what I would find there. Or even what I would do once I got there. It was complete contentment. The kind I had never experienced before. Not even with Adam. Or Tucker. I wasn't worried about getting home to make my Dad breakfast. Or being out past curfew. Or my crappy relationship with my Mom. Or getting that job I so desperately wanted. None of that mattered.

My memory was dulled of anything bad. Nothing pulled my thoughts down.

I was certain in that moment of one thing… I was finally safe.

Chapter 8

RILEY ST. JAMES

Nina Laramie's body is being exhumed this morning. When she was laid to rest she was already skeletonized. Only a few flaps of flesh clinging to the back of her rib cage. This I read from the medical examiner's report. I can't imagine what they expect to find twenty years later. The local police department is acting on a call from a Facebook tipster who contacted the Derby police and revealed that someone had left a confession note in her coffin.

The initiation of Nina's cold case investigation was announced in the paper a month ago. So was the tip about the note in Nina's grave. Feels coincidental to me. But I would have ordered the exhumation just the same. Better safe than sorry. Over the past twenty years the Derby County police have received 2,637 tips on the Laramie case. The last one, before this one, was in 1994.

"Detective Kevin Grable. Derby County Police. Nice to finally meet in person," says a man stepping into the tent set up over the gravesite. He extends his hand to me.

"Detective Riley St. James," I say.

"I expected someone more, I dunno, rough around the edges. Meatier."

Did he just say meatier? I'm a petite 5'3" who keeps my fiery red hair in a bun or ponytail.

"You've never met a female cop before?" I throw back at him.

"No. Of course, I have. It's just your voice over the phone. Sounded gruffer than you look."

I think that's a compliment. I have a pretty bland sense of style when I'm outside my uniform. Jeans. T-shirts. Simple stud earrings. I do like my heels though. You can dress up anything with heels. Even the past.

"You look exactly like your fly fishing pictures on Facebook," I tell him. I don't believe anything good can come from a Facebook page. It's not safe.

"You ever try fly fishing?" asks Grable.

"I have not."

"I can take you sometime. If you like."

"We'll see." It sounds like the kind of activity one resorts to in a cultureless town.

"At any rate, welcome to Derby. Your trip up go smooth? You all settled in?" he says.

"Mostly." He shifts in the light and I get a better look at Detective Kevin Grable. He's trim with muscular arms. Probably all the fly fishing. Angular face. Smooth forehead and deep set hazel eyes that take everything in. A protector-type. Not bad to look at.

But I'm not looking at the moment.

"I'm your point of contact for the Laramie case. We're all extremely pleased the state is putting resources behind this. Finally. Too bad it took this long."

"Nina and her family deserve justice. And I'm ready to jump in. What and who do I need to know here today?" I ask.

"The Commander Hinkle, Scott Hinkle, is under the tent standing at the head of the grave. Next to him is the medical examiner, Berlyn Hardenberg. He's been with the Laramie case since the body was found."

"How about the Commander?"

"He came to the Derby department six years ago. After Ray Polland retired. He hasn't ordered anything be done with the case because we just don't have any new tips. Or resources. Until now." Grable smiles wide at me.

"Polland was the original detective, right?" I ask.

"That's right. Polland took the initial missing person's report. Outside the tent, we've got a few reporters. And a handful of Nina's friends and family members, including Nina's dad, Jim. Laramie."

"The smaller fellow with the grey jacket?"

Grable nods.

Jim is easy to spot. Deep, deep worry lines etched into his forehead and long crow's feet spanning from the corners of each eye.

"That's his ex-wife on his left. Ogin."

"How long have they been separated?"

"Long time. Since Nina was eight, I think," says Grable.

"Is someone recording this?" I ask, glancing around.

Grable points to a camera person standing to the side of the tent.

"He looks like a kid."

"He practically is. Nineteen. Justin Harper. He's the newspaper editor's son. Photo journalist in training. We hire him sometimes to document things for us."

Very hometowny. "You can trust him?"

"Hell, yeah. I've known him since he was a kid. I know his Dad."

"And he can handle what he's about to see?"

"Ain't no worse than dressing a deer. Hey, step on up. They're lowering the flaps for privacy. Let's get in there." He takes me by the elbow and presses me toward Nina's grave.

I shake his small town chivalry off my arm and step ahead to introduce myself to the rest of the team.

Chapter 9

RILEY ST. JAMES

The few of the local law enforcement, the medical examiner, the prosecutor, and I are gathered around Nina's casket. The press, Jim, Ogin. They are not allowed inside the tent. It takes the mortician some effort to open the casket. It's not an elegant process with a crowbar. I watch as he jimmies it open, cracking off one of the handles. His gloved hands are joined by the grave diggers and Grable's to lift the top. It creaks and cracks as they shimmy the box top open.

Inside, the white satin lining is yellowed and Nina's body, just bones wrapped in some sort of faded satin material. It has all shifted to one side. Nina was just over five feet tall, but her disintegrated bones look to be like a child's. Justin has his 35mm digital camera pointed into the coffin. He wears a go-Pro on his forehead. This is a big job for him; probably his first murder case.

The smell of rotting wood and mildew hits our nasal passages. It's actually tolerable. Much more so than fresh decomp. Grable shines a flashlight into the box.

"Anyone see anything that resembles a note?" Grable says.

Everyone leans in to look. Berlyn Hardenberg carefully removes the bones and places them on a waiting gurney.

"Where are those going?" I ask, concerned about chain of custody.

"To the hospital morgue. While we have her above ground we want to do another autopsy," Hardenberg says. "See if there's any more DNA they can lift. There's a lot of new DNA technology today than there was thirty years ago."

"My eyes tell me the box is empty," says Hinkle. "Anyone else see anything?"

I scan the box. No note.

"I think we should check under the lining," says Hinkle. He looks to the mortician who nods. The grave digger grabs a box cutter from his pocket and the mortician slices away at the edges of the casket lining.

I look over at Justin again. He's doing great. Holding it all together. Getting everything recorded. Outside I hear the murmur of hushed voices. They're speculating about what we're seeing. This is how rumors start.

The mortician and Grable peel away the lining, feeling around the interior of the box for the tipster's note. They find nothing but a few crunchy bug carcasses caught in spider webs.

They close the casket and the mortician and his assistant roll the empty casket out of the tent and toward their waiting hearse.

Inside the tent, Hardenberg zips up the body bag. Grable rolls up the tent flap on one side and two EMT's appear. He puts the tent flap down again. The EMT's grab onto either side of the body bag. Grable raises the tent flap again, allowing them to emerge from the tent with Hardenberg and whisk Nina's body into the back of an ambulance. I can hear the press cameras clicking like mating crickets.

I wait with Grable under the tent until both vehicles have exited the cemetery. Then, I follow Grable over to Jim. Jim pulls away from the small crowd of family and friends who have gathered to support him. We step aside.

"I'm sorry, Jim. Nothing's in there," Grable tells him.

Blunt, mid-western manners. Jim nods. There's a flint in his eyes. He's used to lack of hope.

"Well, we all knew it was a long shot," Jim says.

"Mr. Laramie, I'm Detective Riley St. James. I'm a member of the cold case team assigned to your daughter's investigation."

Jim extends a hand and I shake it. Bones and loose skin. "Sounds like you won't be needed here much longer," he says.

"My stay here is not predicated on today's findings." Jim looks to Grable. "I'm staying as long as it takes to find the person who killed Nina."

I see a flicker of revolt in his eyes. "You mean persons."

I give him a blank stare that conveys there's nothing I can reveal in a moment like this. "I'll be in touch if there's anything you can help with," I say.

There is no inflection in his grey tone. "I appreciate that."

"How are you doing with all this?" asks Grable.

As I glance over my shoulder I see Nina's gravestone with a fresh bouquet of flowers. Jim shakes his head and looks away.

"It's unrestful. Her spirit can't take much more. Least that's what her mother says. I feel it too," says Jim.

I must have a confused expression on my face because Grable cuts in, "Nina was half Chippewa."

"Oh, interesting...I didn't... it wasn't in the reports."

"Everyone around here just knows it," says Jim. "Her ma and I split up when she was eight. Ogin moved back up to the UP to live in the Cherokee nation."

Jim points to three women standing near the edge of the empty grave. The middle one waves burning sage over the hole in the ground.

"That's Ogin. She came down with two tribe members to make sure Nina's body and resting place are not desecrated."

So, Nina didn't live with her mom. I nod at the spiritual ceremony they perform. "And when you two divorced, who was granted custody of Nina?"

"I was."

"That's pretty unusual for back then. May I ask how you were able to arrange that?"

Jim looks over at Nina's gravesite again and hushes his voice. "Ogin means Wild Rose in Cherokee. She lived up to her name. Beautiful. But full of thorns."

I give him my full attention.

"I had to petition for her and the court finally saw it my way."

"Was it hard for Nina when her mom left?"

"She didn't understand at first. She really missed her Mom. But as time went on, the crying spells stopped. She didn't ask about her very often. We went up to see her during the summer and on holidays. Nina was always happy to come back home when visits were over. Last two years, before she died, she hardly ever saw her mother."

"Sounds like you and Nina were close."

Jim's expression hollows. He's somewhere far in his mind. I allow the silence to settle between us. The smell of the burning sage reaches my nose. Earthy, dank. Like frankincense. It brings me right back to the sacristy of my childhood church, St. Mark's Cathedral. Back then, I was more open to believe things like faith and forgiveness were possible.

"We had those father daughter moments. Teenagers. You know. But overall we got along just fine." Jim pulls a photograph from his wallet and shows me.

"She's beautiful." I tell him. Striking. Authentically Cherokee. Gorgeous black hair. Dark brown eyes. Full of light.

"I was so mad at her when she cut and permed her hair when she was sixteen," says Jim.

"That was the style back then, I guess," I say.

"She did it because she was embarrassed by her long, dark Indian hair."

"Sounds like something I would have done as a teenager." I give Jim a warm smile and hand the picture back to him.

"I see that now. Just wish I wouldn't a hollered at her." Regrets. They prick at you like burrs through your socks that barb into your ankles when you step through a thicket. He tucks the photo safely behind the plastic window flap in the front of his wallet.

"It's not over, Mr. Laramie. I'll see to it that her spirit is put to rest very soon."

Jim touches my arm lightly and walks toward Ogin.

I glance for Grable. He's at his squad car chatting it up with Hinkle. From the looks of their arms flinging about, they're practicing some fly fishing move.

I turn back to Nina's grave. Ogin is motionless over the hole. The last of the sage smolders and burns out. She drops the stub into the ground as her lips whisper a prayer.

Chapter 10

NINA, 1989

I 'm worried I may have "crossed over", as they say in Ojibwa. I am half Chippewa Indian. From my Mom's side. I don't like to talk about that side of my family. I haven't seen them much in the past couple years.

The Chippewa say the deceased are supposed to journey westward for four days to some afterlife in the sky. I've been walking. A lot. Way more than four days' worth. But my feet don't hurt. And I'm concerned because there doesn't seem to be anyone else here.

I keep thinking that those guys dropped me off in some other state or maybe Canada. It kinda looks like Canada. Back woods Canada. Canada's actually the only other place I've been outside of Derby County and the UP.

What's weird is that I'm not hungry or tired or cold. I feel pretty good except that I'm just really lonely. I'd love someone to talk to. I miss Dad. And Tucker. And, of course, Adam. I'd just really like to go home.

My Grandma on my Mom's side tried to teach me about Ojibwa. I liked hearing the stories when I was a little girl, but later it just seemed like fairytales to me. I'm not overly superstitious, I guess.

Dad is the furthest thing from superstitious. And he's not particularly religious. Unless you consider hard work a belief system. Some of his favorite sayings are: "God helps those who help themselves. Pull yourself up by your bootstraps. The early bird gets the worm."

Dad is practical. Resourceful. No non-sense. None of this dream-catcher mumbo jumbo. I can see why he and Mom clashed. At home I had to "toe the line." His words. I had my list of chores – meals, grocery shopping, laundry, cleaning. And my curfew. 10:30 p.m. That sucked. Parties didn't even get started until 11 or mid-night. Only time I could stay out til mid-night was if I was with Adam. Dad trusted Adam.

A couple weeks before the Hole in the Woods, I actually ran away to my Mom's house. I was pissed at my Dad because he went through my things and found my birth control pills. So, I hitch hiked it and caught a ride eight hours up the interstate with this couple who was going to the UP to camp. They were probably in college. Really friendly. And kind. They gave me a sandwich and a Coke. I slept most of the way.

When I got to my Mom's house she wasn't there. Big surprise. Probably off drinking at the bar. It was the only place that had cable.

Grandma was home. Grandma never touched a drop of firewater (as she called it). She was respected in the tribe. She said she knew I was coming because the Master Spirit had told her. I just nodded and sat down on the couch. She was watching Wheel of Fortune on one of only two TV channels they got up there in the trailer park. I fell asleep on the couch and woke up when Mom got home. She curled right up next to me with a big hug. Her breath smelled like alcohol and her eyes were glassy. She is actually a very sweet drunk. She held me there for a long time and I let her. It felt good. She never even asked me why I was there or how I got there. She rocked me and sang an old Ojibwa song.

I stayed with my Mom for about a week until my Dad found out where I was and had the police bring me home 'cause I am... or... I was... only seventeen at the time and under his custody.

Truth? I was ready to head back to Derby. Mom was always gone during the day drinking. Grandma creeped me out with her potions and herbs. But I didn't tell Dad any of that.

Just a few days ago, before Hole in the Woods, Mom called me. She never calls me. She wanted to know if I was okay? If Dad was okay? If everyone in the family down here in Derby was okay? We were. She sounded a little anxious. I asked if she was okay?

"I saw Wendigo last night."

"What's Wineko?"

"No, daughter. Wendigo. The Spirit of Lonely Places."

"That's a bad thing?" Grandma had told me the story of Wendigo a long time ago. But honestly, I had forgotten it. They all kinda blended together in my memory.

"I was walking in the forest and..."

"Were you drunk?" I asked.

"No. No drink. I was just walking. Thinking about you."

"You were?" I was surprised to learn that I was a thought on my mother's mind.

"He came out of the wind. Glowing orange. Pulsing. There was his star on his forehead. I knew it was Wendigo."

"Wow. That sounds scary. What did he do?" I wanted to believe she wasn't drinking, but this sounded like another one of her drunken dreamscapes.

"I could see right through to his heart. There was ice around it, but it was beating fast. And his fangs dripped with the blood of his last victim."

Maybe she had been smoking something?

"I felt his hissing hot breath on my face," she went on and I could picture her large, dark eyes, full black moons. "I knew what he wanted."

"What?" I was getting kinda mesmerized now.

"To feed on me."

"He wanted to eat you?" I said.

"Yes. The Wendigo is a cannibal."

"So, he's human?"

"He was human. At one time."

"Okay, I see." I didn't see. This was really confusing and I was 99.9 percent sure she was on the sauce right now.

"He chased me with his bloody feet," my mother hissed over the phone line.

"Did he hurt you?"

"No, no, I got away. I ran out of the forest."

"That's good. I'm glad you're okay."

"No, it's not good, Nina. Wendigo appears to those right before a death in their family."

"Oh. Okay." Yeah, she was loopy. "Well, we're all fine down here."

"Please, be careful. This is a very bad omen."

"I will. We will."

"Don't do anything stupid."

Like she should talk.

"Don't tempt Evil. Don't walk in its path," she said.

I had no idea what she meant. "I won't, Mama."

"I am seeking guardian spirits to protect you, Nina."

"Okay. Thanks. How's Grandma?"

"She is well. She is also praying for protection. I have to go. The Midewiwin is here to perform the guardian ceremony. Pray with us, Nina."

"Okay, Mom." Midewiwin was the medicine society of her tribe. That I did know. The service would go on for the rest of the day and into the night.

"Call me if you need anything." She hung up.

I probably won't. Call or pray.

Chapter 11

RILEY ST. JAMES

A couple days after the exhumation, I meet with Dr. Berlyn Hardenberg M.D. acting Medical Examiner at his home where he hosts the county M.E. office. Hardenberg stands at 6'4" with little to no body fat and a graying mane of thick, wiry, salt and pepper hair. He's in his early sixties and looks like someone who runs long distance races. The thought no more than passes through my mind when I glance up to notice his race medals hanging in a display case above his desk. Marathons. All over the country. The world.

He explains to me that Derby County never provided him with an M.E. office so he decided to set one up at his home, which suits him just fine because this way he can keep an eye on the paperwork, files, documents, and other biological evidence the M.E. office must keep track of. I am curious to know exactly where those tissue and blood samples are kept, but I don't even have to ask.

"I keep the pathology slides and blood vials in an extra fridge in the basement and all the case files are stored in those file cabinets," he says pointing to one wall of his immense office that looks like it used to be an attached garage.

I feel very comfortable in his office. Hardenberg's definitely had an interior designer in here because it's a far cry from the dingy white-wall, fluorescent lit boxes you usually find in county buildings. The whole room is an expansive remodel with twelve foot ceilings and French doors that lead out onto a side patio deck. Two of the walls are floor to ceiling bookshelves. Tall windows draped in sheer curtains face the back yard and bring in daylight to illumine the space. Hardenberg's desk spans the fourth wall but is mostly hidden in stacks of paperwork, slides, and a very impressive microscope. Hardenberg makes sure to inform me of his credentials. He's a forensic pathologist with thirty-six years of experience. He had been acting M.E. for twelve years when Nina's case came across his path.

Hardenberg has Nina's file setting out on his desk and he hands me a copy and invites me to sit in an oversized, puffy leather chair. I sink in, wishing I could curl up there for an afternoon with an afghan, cup of coffee, and my Kindle.

He starts with bad news right out of the gate. "I discovered no new evidence on the Laramie remains during the recent autopsy. I guess I had hoped we'd see something today that we couldn't detect with early 1990's technology, but I'm afraid there's just nothing left to examine."

"I see." I'm not completely surprised, but had hoped for more.

"I wish this second autopsy could have pointed you in a new direction," he says.

"It's a hurdle, but certainly not a stop sign." I am very good at remaining undaunted in the face of bad news. I get enough of it every day. "I was wondering if you could tell me more about what you discovered during that first investigation."

"I'd be happy to and I expected you would be interested in a copy of Nina's autopsy report. So you can refer to it later if you need to." I've already seen the autopsy report, but he hands me a manila folder of my own copy. "Are you ready?"

"Yes, please. I'm all ears." I tilt my head slightly to the right to show him that I have his full attention.

"When I came to the scene, I observed that Nina's body was in very advanced stages of decomposition. We call this mummification. She was positioned prone and there was a little bit of flesh still attached to her skeleton and ribs. But none elsewhere."

"Her skeleton was intact?" I ask.

"Mostly. Her skull was a few feet from the rest of her skeleton. And her left hand was missing. We never found it. I suspect an animal ran off with it. There was a pair of panties around her right ankle and a blue shirt scrunched up around the vertebrae of her neck. In her right hand she was clutching a necklace."

"A necklace? What did it look like?"

"Simple gold chain with three pearls. I learned later it was a gift from her mother."

I try not to let my mind wander to Nina's last minutes, holding on helplessly to this piece of her mother as her life was sucked from her.

"What can you tell me about her injuries?" I inquire.

"Open the file."

I do. There's a series of autopsy photos.

"She was struck in the ribs and the right shoulder blade. She also sustained three blunt force strikes to the base of her skull. Based on the depth of the cracks and the strike patterns, I ruled that the force of impact resulted in brain hemorrhaging."

"And that's ultimately how she died?"

"Correct. It wasn't a pleasant death. Painful and not quick."

I imagine the fear racing through Nina, stronger than the pain, and a nauseating knot twists my belly.

"But there's more to it," he continues. "Take a look at the close up of the picture of her pelvic bone."

I turn the photograph right side up. "I'm not sure what I'm looking for," I say.

"Cut marks. From a knife. All around the pelvis bone," he explains.

"I don't understand." I examine the picture closer and see the uneven, jagged indentations. "What happened there?"

"The killer cut out the flesh around her vaginal region. The cuts are so deep they penetrated down to the pelvic bone."

My stomach wrenches again. Brutal sadomasochism. I force my mind to rocket away from a dark place in my memory. "What's your theory on this?"

"My best guess is that the killer took that region as a prize or to somehow destroy evidence of sexual assault."

I know that in 1989, semen detection analysis was possible, but very rare. And there was no widespread DNA testing available, or a national database to link a criminal to a crime or a missing person to a victim.

"This is a lot more brutal than I was originally led to believe," I say. But of course, I know violence of this extreme exists in every corner of the world. There are no safe places.

"Yes. One of the most disturbing cases I've ever worked on." I detect the frustration in Hardenberg's voice.

"What instrument do you believe caused these injuries?" I ask, pointing to the images of her ribs and skull.

"I have a strong theory about his." He turns his computer screen toward me and clicks onto a file. Several images pop up which, to me, look like bluish purple blobs. "Unfortunately, you'll be hard pressed to find a murder weapon. Especially since we haven't been able to iden-tify the tool that was used. Let me walk you through this."

Hardenberg takes a pencil from a cup on his desk and uses the tip to point at the screen. "These are two images of some of that left over skin that was on Nina's ribs and backside. See these four dark spots all lined up in a row." He draws my attention to them on each pho-tograph. "These indicate bruising under the skin. I took these under ultraviolet light. Notice anything about the spots?"

"Well, they seem to be the same pattern and the second spot on each pattern is slightly larger," I note.

"Exactly. They are made from the same instrument. I've been studying these images for years trying to figure out what sort of instrument caused this injury."

"Any luck?"

"If I had, you wouldn't be sitting in my office today."

I immediately regret my dumb question.

"Do you think this tool is still around somewhere?"

"Who's to say?" He shakes his head. "I just wanted you to know all the facts the autopsy revealed. For obvious reasons, this hasn't been released to the public. Even her own father doesn't know about the pelvic cuts or the tool used. You understand the sensitivity in this matter."

"Of course. I won't breach confidence here," I say.

I am somewhat encouraged because this kind of information could become a potential lead in making an arrest.

"Any other questions, just reach out." He hands me a business card. I notice his running shoes off to the side of the couch.

"Who do you think killed Nina Laramie?" I ask him as I prop myself from the depths of the leather lounger.

"My theories don't matter. Right now, you have the greatest gift in this investigation."

"And what is that?" I ask.

"Fresh eyes."

I nod. "Thank you for your time. And great care in your work."

I am impressed. His was no hack job as I had seen from medical examiners in Detroit.

Dr. Hardenburg sees me to my car. And as I am opening the driver's door he reaches into his pants pocket and pulls out a pocket knife. He flips it open. The small, thin blade snaps into place. He holds it there. I stare at it, wondering what he's planning to do next.

"It takes a strong person to carve up another human with nothing more than this," he says.

"Yes." It comes out in a whisper. My eyes won't let go of the blade. A sharp pain singes through my gut.

Dr. Hardenburg snaps the blade back down and slides the knife back into his pocket.

I give him a quick nod and duck into the driver's seat. I drive off. I can't get the images from the autopsy photos out of my mind.

This monster… or monsters… if Derby urban legend proves true… have been free. For three decades. Living. Dating. Marrying. Maybe procreating. Going to ball games and eating hot dogs and apple pie and singing the American anthem. Just like any other normal person. Just like Nina or her kids or her grandkids… will never do.

Chapter 12

RILEY ST. JAMES

G rable shows me to my office. It's an eight by eight room painted sometime last century in dingy eggshell white. The laminated desk shows signs of wear at the corners and has a deep scratch along the right side. There's a single unit bookcase stacked with paper file boxes. Two mismatched guest chairs face the desk. Under my feet, worn, Berber gray carpet with two stains by the door.

Coffee? Blood?

There's no window. The life sucking fluorescent lights buzz overhead. I'm already plotting how to transform it into something palatable.

"Don't go changing the paint color. I have a feeling you won't be needing it too long," says Grable standing at the door.

"You've given up before I've started." I reply with a testy tone. "Thanks for the vote of confidence."

I set my bag down on top of the desk. The computer monitor is at least ten years old and I don't see a hard drive stack under the desk. Clearly, no one has given any thought to my arrival. Good thing I brought my laptop.

"I wouldn't say given up. But it's a stuck case. After Ray Polland retired, Hinkle and a few of us went through those boxes, thinking there was something he missed."

"You didn't trust him?"

"No, it's not that. It was a different time back then. You gotta remember that we don't get but a couple homicides a year. Domestic violence. Accidental shootings. Farm accidents. Ray was the only detective in the county. He ran this case with little outside help. The county didn't have the resources. He single handedly interviewed 465 people on this case."

"That's incredible." And now I see why it was entirely possible that he overlooked something. "How could one man do all that?"

"Polland's a rare bird. Investigates like a sloth. Drove a lot of us nuts. But he was meticulous and thorough especially after..." Grable notices the computer has no drive. "I'll have Gayle up front get you set up with a computer and get you linked in. You can use it for emails and internet. But warning, nothing from this case is in the electronic files."

I nod.

"After what?" I say.

"Huh?"

"You said Polland was thorough after—and then you stopped."

"Oh. Ah… nothing." Grable's gaze shifts to the door. "Of course what little physical evidence we do have is secured in the lockers. Not those boxes."

"Why'd you tell Mr. Laramie we were at ground zero?" I press.

"Because we are. And I don't bullshit a man who's been relentless about finding his daughter's killer for three decades. There's nothing more in those case files to point us anywhere."

It dawns on me in this moment that Grable doesn't have an ego. Not a shred. Not an ounce. He's just a genuinely nice guy. A straight shooter. That's what's grating on me. I'm used to keeping my guard up. Detroit PD is full of egos.

 "I don't agree. I think a fresh pair of eyes is likely to spot something new or overlooked."

"I guess that's what the state's paying you for." Grable lets out an exaggerated sigh.

I feel the exhaustion as my eyes travel to the ten file boxes stacked on the shelves. "Can you walk me through the time line. What am I looking for? What are your theories?"

"How 'bout some lunch first. I'm starving," says Grable.

Men. Why is everything predicated on them filling their stomachs.

"What about a guy named Solomon Newton? What do you know about him? He's mentioned in the original report."

Grable shrugs and slouches into one of the chairs. It creaks under his frame.

"He and his twin brother, Silas, were with Nina that night and supposedly the last two people to see Nina alive."

"I met Solomon last night. At Pub Griffin. Award winning personality," I tell him.

"You didn't tell him who you are?" Grable says.

"No, of course not. But it's not going to take him long to figure it out."

"They were never arrested because there was absolutely nothing tying them to the crime. Evidence wise. You can read their statements." I will. Most definitely. "Can we please grab a bite?" Grable's stomach growls audibly.

"I want to get settled in and start reading." I hang my jacket on the back of my chair.

Grable stands and stretches into a semi-back bend. "My back is killing me. Spent two hours on the river early this morning."

"Catch anything?"

"Couple blue gill. One salmon. You eat fish?"

"I tend to stick to land animals." I take out my laptop and plug it in. I pull a few items from my bag and set them on my new desk. "Can you please tell me the box you think I should start with first?"

"So, do you have a plan in mind?" Grable passes over a box labeled: LARAMIE, N. BOX #1. I let out a little laugh. "Guess it wouldn't have been too hard to figure out."

The masking tape sealing it has yellowed and begun to peel off.

"I do have a plan. I want to retest all the physical evidence. DNA has come a long way in thirty years. And while that's happening, I plan to read through every scrap in these boxes. I want to know everything about Nina that day. Who she saw, talked to, where she went, what she ate, who she hung out with."

"We already did that."

"Then we'll do it again." I know what I saw in Solomon's eyes.

"What about the person who gave you the coffin tip."

"Misty Beckett. She lives for gossip. Check out her Facebook page. Three thousand friends. Most of them here in Derby."

"Is there any kernel of truth to what she says?" I ask.

"Not usually. But you're welcome to go over there and get your ear talked off."

I smile and make my second realization about Grable. Not only is he overly-friendly; he's too close to the case and everyone involved.

"I'll talk to everyone on this list again if I have to."

"Be my guest."

"Look, I was told you were going to be teaming up with me. What role do you see yourself playing in all this?"

"Teaming up? Oh, no. You have your job. I have mine. My man hours are going into this community's current crime activity." He strokes his hand over his growling belly. "That said, if you have any questions or wanna run something by me, I'm here."

"I do have a question. What do you think happened? You said there was a suspect list. Who else is on it?"

At this Grable reaches toward the ceiling and I hear his back crack twice. "Nina was hanging out with a small group of friends that night. Not the cream of the crop if you get me. There were four guys and another gal and Nina." He slaps his hand atop a stack of boxes near my desk. "Read. Read. It's all in there. And, hey, if you're gonna keep quizzing me, can we please at least order a pizza in?"

"Go. Eat. I'll circle back around after I've had a chance to dig into this more." I send him off with a look and I can tell Grable's relieved to be off the hook.

"Can I bring you anything?" he asks, one foot already out of the door.

I shake my head.

"You have to eat. I'm bringing you a chicken salad. You seem like the kind of girl who eats salads for lunch."

"Patty melt, extra cheese and onions, and a side of fries with ketchup and mayo. And they better be crispy and hot when you get here." I glance up at him.

"Where are you gonna put all that?" he laughs.

I give him a quick smile. Even though I'm petite, I am not at all concerned about my fat intake. I burn it off in mega-units of stress. Grable starts to leave. I pull him back in with a final question that's more of a test. "Grable, one more question. Do you think I can find the person, or persons, who killed Nina Laramie?"

Grable stops and pauses. He turns to look back at me. "This cloud has been hanging over this town my whole adult life. Nina and I grew up here together. We went to the same school."

I suspect Grable's burnt out, apathetic, or just plain lazy. Maybe a combo of all of those. What he isn't, is driven. But maybe it is because he is caught in their code of silence?

"You've heard things that aren't in these reports, haven't you?" I pry.

"Derby's a small county. You can't believe everything you hear. And most of the time it's not admissible," he shrugs. "You want a Coke?"

"No."

And he's out the door.

Small towns. Close alliances. Kept secrets. Grable's got liability creased in his forehead. I hate to sound so cynical, but I stopped trusting people years ago. There is a code of silence in Derby. And Grable will not stand in my way to crack it.

Chapter 13

RILEY ST. JAMES

My eyes hurt and my brain is fried. I've been reading for nine days straight. I had this giant white board mounted in my office a few days ago so I can start piecing together a timeline for the last forty-eight hours of Nina's life on earth, Monday, August 7.

It's a bit sketchy, but here's what I have so far:

1) Nina had breakfast and then headed down to the river near her house late morning to meet a friend and go swimming. Apparently, Nina left her shirt on a picnic table by the river after she left, and her friend Melanie took it home so she could return it later to Nina's house. Melanie confirms all this in a statement on September 28. I find it odd that the interviews start on this date. Almost two months after Nina has disappeared. But then I learn that her body wouldn't be discovered until late October. Detective Polland thought at first that

Nina was a run away. He only started interviewing her social circle after Jim pushed him to.

I wonder how Jim was holding up these two months and what he was doing to find his daughter on his own? He must have been super frustrated with the lackluster police efforts.

2) After the river, Nina came back home and picked up some laundry. She headed up the street to the Laundromat and did a couple loads. We know this because she saw a family friend there who later confirmed she had seen Nina and shared some of her fabric softener with Nina.

3) By now, late afternoon, Nina is on her way home from the Laundromat. I note here that she's walking. Nina did not have a car or a driver's license. I also note that Derby is a small town and Nina lived just a couple blocks from downtown where the laundromat is still locally owned and operated. She stops at a friend's second story apartment downtown. Seems there are two other people there who Nina doesn't really like so she doesn't stay long. She stays just long enough to buy some marijuana. Ah, interesting.

4) Statements from her Dad say that Nina came home around dinner time and made dinner for them. Jim was just getting up for the day. He worked nights driving a delivery truck. He and Nina always had dinner together. He didn't notice anything unusual about her behavior. He states that he razzed her a bit about getting a job. At dinner, Nina got a call from her boyfriend, Adam. Jim states that he liked Adam and he talked to him, as well. After dinner, Jim states that Nina was getting ready to go out for the night. He told her "nothing good

happens after mid-night." But she was eighteen now and he couldn't legally keep her in for a curfew. He kissed his daughter goodbye, and headed off to his third shift job shortly after 10:00 p.m.

5) About thirty minutes here are unaccounted for until the next account from her friends states that Nina appears at the Argo gas station a few blocks away to meet up with some friends. Alyson Peters. Bradley Hollinga. Richard Wright. And the twin, Silas and Solomon Newton.

6) Nina seems to know Alyson, Brad, and Rich from high school. Silas and Solomon are Rich's cousins visiting from Brantwood, the town twenty miles to the south of Derby. She gets introduced to them and the six of them hang out for about a half an hour in the parking lot of the Argo gas station. Drinking. Smoking. The twins are doing hard drugs. The report doesn't say what kind. Then there's a verbal scuffle between two of the guys over Alyson and pretty soon they all take off in separate cars. Alyson, Rich, and Brad in Brad's car; Nina in the Newton's car.

7) From here there's some time discrepancy. But the gist of everyone's statement seems to conclude that they drove around the county for about an hour before they ended up at the parking lot of a Green Acres market in a blip of a town just south of Derby about ten miles. They got out. Alyson went inside for a pack of gum and while she was gone Rich and Brad had a verbal argument over who was going to take Alyson home. Rich was about to punch Brad when Alyson came out and broke it up. This whole time no one really talked about what Nina was doing. But from what I can gather she never left Silas and Solomon's car. Rich, Alyson, and Brad got back in their car and sped

off, leaving Nina with the Newton twins. This was the last time they saw Nina alive.

8) From here, Silas and Solomon gave an account that they dropped Nina back at home around 12:30 a.m. and then took off for Rich's house. This is confirmed by Rich who says he met up with them on the dirt road in front of his house and they knocked over his mailbox. Rich says it was sometime after 2:00 a.m.

I am vibrating with questions.

Why did Detective Polland think Nina had run away? To where? To see whom?

Where were Silas and Solomon between 12:30 and 2:00 a.m.?

Did anyone else see her after she was dropped at home? Did anyone see the Newtons during this time? Andhow did Nina get transported from her house to the Hole in the Woods? Did someone else come by and pick her up?

In every report I read, no one seems to address any motive for killing Nina. She didn't seem to have any enemies. She wasn't on anyone's bad side. She hadn't stolen anyone's boyfriend or shredded anyone's reputation. She wasn't caught up in selling drugs. Just occasionally buying them. And taking them. She was a good friend. A good daughter. Who wanted Nina dead?

Sometimes just being in the wrong place at the wrong time is motive enough for a predator to seek a ripe opportunity to snare his victim. So, I'm not going to focus my search too hard on motive just now. It's the timeline that's bugging me.

And what exactly does Grable know? What has he heard over the years that didn't make it into police reports? Why is he holding back? Again, the code of silence.

What makes this case particularly difficult is that with the exception of Jim, no one really searched for her for months after she was killed. This left ample opportunity for the killer, or killers, to erase any traces of evidence. Anything on the car. Any weapon. Clothes.

And plenty of time to come up with a believable alibi.

I stand up and stretch my arms to the ceiling bringing them down to my sides and all the way to my toes. Blood rushes to my brain. I feel lightheaded.

This case and this dirty eggshell white office are getting to me. I need some fresh air. And answers.

Grable picks up after the fourth ring. He must be out fishing, I surmise.

"I'm surprised I even get reception out here!" Grable yells into the phone. I hear rushing water like static in the background. "Say again?"

I raise the receiver to my lips and shout, "Can you take me to the site?"

Chapter 14

RILEY ST. JAMES

G rable drives me out to the Hole in the Woods. I want to get a mental picture of things. Nina's last moments. Where she was found. What her last sights, sounds, and smells may have been. He parks on the north side of a large fielded area with a bog covering the southwest quadrant. A thick grove of pines and oaks surround the spot and quickly I see why it's called Hole in the Woods. An aerial map view shows the hole is the shape of a square clearing.

I notice a campfire area and a few red Solo cups littering the ground.

"It's still a party spot after all these years. The kids come out here to drink and smoke and make teenage mistakes," Grable tells me.

"I bet you never came out here to party when you were in high school? Goody two shoes Grable," I joke.

"Actually, I did. A lot."

"I didn't peg you as a hellion."

Grable nods with a sheepish grin. "I was a very different person back then. Not proud of it."

"What was your poison? Wine coolers and clove smokes?" I joke.

"LSD and whiskey."

"Wow. Okay." I never touched drugs or hard liquor. Beer and wine are always enough to blur the technicolor images of my haunted history.

"Experimentation turned into addiction. I spent half my senior year in rehab after I crashed my Dad's truck coming home from here completely shit-faced."

"Tough love."

"Rehab proved pivotal, but not a cure. I stopped drinking and doing drugs. And I met a girl there."

"Nice. Did you marry?"

"No. But I got her pregnant."

"Your kid must be in high school by now? Or college?"

"Heaven, actually."

"Oh. I'm sorry."

"Not half as sorry as I am."

"May I ask...how?"

"We terminated the pregnancy," he says.

I twitch at the word terminate. I manage another polite 'I'm sorry'.

"Never quite lets go of you. You know?"

I close this chapter.

"What made you become a cop?" New chapter.

"Seemed like the best path to redemption. It was either that or the priesthood, but I'm not Catholic."

He laughs and so do I. Tension liquifying.

"Three years into the force, I started getting really depressed. The drinking, the drugs didn't stop. I finally marched myself into a twelve-step program. It was either that or my job."

"Looks like you made a good pivot," I add.

"Everything misaligned in my life all stemmed back to that abortion."

I quiver at that caustic word.

"Sometimes I talk to him," he goes on.

"He? How do you know it's a he?"

"Saw it in a dream."

I nod. I don't discredit dreams. Or nightmares. But I don't trust them to provide anything fruitful that will shed hope or alleviate the suffering in my life.

"I'm grateful every day for my bad choices because God used them for my good."

"Oh, so is that why bad things happen to good people." The snark sneaks up on me.

"I chose a bad thing. It's different. The law of cause and effect. You play, you pay."

"You must take great pleasure in coming out here to save these young heathens from a life of sin."

Grable gives me a grave look. "Riley, I don't take pleasure in catching people doing bad things."

"It's kind of your job, isn't it?"

"I don't look at it that way. Love sometimes requires tough consequences to get people back on track."

"What do you do? Send them all to AA?"

"Arrest them."

"Give them a good scare, then?" I smile.

"I'd rather do that than scrape one of their carcasses off the side of the road after a crash. Or worse, deal with them after they've survived a crash where they've killed a family of five."

"What about Nina. She didn't ask to be raped and killed." I ask. "She didn't make a bad choice."

"Debatable," he says. "She got into that car with those guys."

"You're saying it's her fault?" My voice went up a register.

"No. That's not what I meant."

"It sounds like you're assigning her part of the blame."

"I'm saying we live in a world where evil exists. And I think the Newtons are evil. And unfortunately, Nina walked into their path."

Grable starts walking into the woods and I follow. There's no path. Grable's counting under his breath as we traipse over fallen logs and push through overgrown branches.

"Here. It's right here." Grable stops and points to a spot between two trees.

"You're sure?"

"Positive."

It looks no different than any other area to my left, right, front, or back. "Seriously? You just automatically know."

"I've been out here quite a few times. I've studied the survey maps and compared them to the pictures of the scene. Then, I pace it out from where we parked. It's a bit overgrown now compared to back then, but I know this is the spot. Her remains were right there. And they found her shoe about fifty yards to the east."

"Okay, I believe you. It's just it seems so close to the campfire. No one smelled her body?"

"I think about all the weeks after her death that we'd be out here. Dozens of us. And she was just right over here. Us guys would walk into the woods to piss. It's incredible none of us found her."

I walk closer to the exact spot and do a 360 and try to imagine. It would have been dark. The landscape is all the same. And other than the drive that we took to get into the hole, there's really no other outlet or road. Just acres and acres of woods. And being August, the brush would have been overgrown. I can see how it would be easy for a victim to get lost and easy for a killer to hide a body.

Grable turns and starts to head back.

"Stay as long as you like. It weirds me out," he says.

"Hey, wait. Will you walk with me? I wanna check out the area."

Grable shrugs and wanders back to me. I start carving a path east through the woods.

"One thing I don't get is, why Nina? What was she like?" I ask after we've been walking for a few minutes.

"Nina was friendly. I mean, like, she made friends really easily. She liked to party. But she was…"

I keep the pace, ducking under low branches and weaving around brush. Grable doesn't miss a step behind me. "Was what?"

"Let's just say that what I knew about Nina was based on her reputation."

"What did people say about her?"

"That she got what was coming to her," says Grable.

It takes every ounce of my will power not to explode. "Explain." Grable sees my twisted look and throws his hands up.

"Hey, I don't think that. I'm just repeating what's been said. She had a good boyfriend. So what was she doing running around the county with a bunch of guys she just met two days after Adam left town for his new job? That's what people were wondering."

Here we are again. "Are you saying the victim participated in her own crime?"

"She was a flirt. She liked attention."

"So, you're saying she deserved to be murdered?"

"No. But she raised her risk factor when she got into that car with those guys."

"How so?"

"She didn't know them," says Grable.

"They were friends of friends, right?" I defend.

"She knew them enough to know they had bad reputations."

"She liked bad boys," I respond.

"When you walk with the devil…" says Grable and then goes silent. He knows so much more than he's saying.

"All I'm asking is what you, Kevin Grable, resident of Derby county and classmate of Nina Laramie, know that is not in those files?"

He doesn't answer at first, cracking small twigs with his heavy-footed steps.

Then with a big sigh he stops and turns to me and says, "Any hearsay I repeat won't amount to a hill of beans."

I let it lie there waiting to see how he'll turn the conversation. We're almost to the edge of the woods. I can see where it comes out onto a dirt two track. Grable keeps quiet again.

"Okay. If it's not the Newtons, who else?"

Grable shrugs. "Her other friends all had alibis. They were sleeping, working, with their families, or out of town on summer vacation. To continue down that line of reasoning, we'd have to make up a pretty exhaustive explanation to create a completely new suspect."

"What are you so scared of? You admit it was them."

"I don't want to go around accusing people without proper proof."

"People like Silas and Solomon are not your friends. They are a threat to society," I say, calling him out. "And isn't that what you're called to protect?"

"I don't get why the state is spending all this time and money on sending you up here when there's a shortage of cops in Detroit. We don't have a rash of crime in Derby. We'd all be better served if you were back there catching the real bad guys."

"That's exactly what I'm doing."

"It's a fool's errand," he says.

It'll take more time to unpack him. No use blasting my chances now.

We are at the edge of the forest and I stop, a little out of breath. "How far do you think that was? A couple acres?"

"Maybe three at most." Grable brushes small leaves out of his hair. I notice that heading north down the dirt road about twenty-five feet away is a driveway leading to a one story home set back into the woods.

"Did you know there was a house this close?"

Grable shakes his head. "Literally never saw it before."

"Maybe because you never went this way?" I dig at him a little. Familiarity can breed blindness.

We walk toward the drive. The home, probably built around the 1950s, comes into plain view. The white paint is peeling and the shingles are curling up on the corners. There's a rust bucket minivan sitting up on blocks in the front yard. A wheelchair ramp leads into the front door. The mailbox leans to the left on a spindly post with worn plastic lettering reads –HE TA--L--RS. Which I'm guessing is supposed to be THE TAYLORS. Judging by the aged look of the place, The Taylors have been here a long, sorry time.

"You ready to head back?" says Grable.

I try not to let his question rile me. No drive. No curiosity. I'm gonna have to turn over every stone myself.

"Not yet," I say.

Fresh eyes.

Chapter 15

NINA

I know now that time doesn't feel the same in death as it does in life. One day is like a thousand years and a thousand years is like one day. I think that's from the Bible. My grandma took me to Sunday school a couple times when I was a kid. If I try to think in calendar terms, it's been at least thirty years now since I went to the Hole in the Woods.

I can't stay in one place for long. I get restless. I can sense the place I'm meant to be, but I can never get there. Sometimes I even get a glimpse. It looks like a crack in the heavens. Or a fading in the atmosphere. Clouds parting and then just as quickly thickening the sky and shutting me out.

I try not to lose hope that someday I'll be settled. At peace. At rest. There's really no sleep here so I'm always very tired and yet very awake at the same time. And still very lonely.

I've seen everyone I ever loved move on. Adam married and now has a couple kids. One of them is already in college. My friends are all married. Some divorced and on their second marriage. I see how they spend their days. Kids, jobs, cooking, eating, sleeping. What I wouldn't give to have such an unremarkable life.

Mom's still single. And she still drinks, a little less now than when she was younger. Even Grandma's still alive, old as dirt, doing her medicine woman thing. I don't wish her dead or anything, but I do think that if she died she would come here and help me. She always told me that once we died we were given a spirit guide to walk with us in the afterlife. Well, grandma, guess what? That was just a load of crap your ancestors told you to make your people feel better. Where's my spirit guide? I'm getting tired of dwelling in limbo... purgatory... whatever this is.

I worry about Dad cause he just sort of shuffles through life. He had a few girlfriends, but never remarried. I know he talks about me a lot. And I know he's never given up on me. I can see that his health is declining. I worry he will die before he gets his wish for justice. I've tried a billion times, but there's no way for me to get the message through. I can't seem to touch the earthly world any more than I can see what's beyond the existence I've been wandering since my murder.

I check in on my gravesite from time to time. I went by the other day, on a prompting from the Great Spirit. You can imagine how shocked I was to find myself unearthed. My casket opened. My skeletal remains being picked over by a team of detectives and doctors. I laughed out loud. There's nothing to find in there. The elements of nature have stripped it all away.

My spirit caught the sensation of someone new. I sensed it was a female spirit and all the feral emotion collected within her. Tenderness. Pain. Urgency. Drive. Compassion. Hurt. Anxiety. Eagerness. Determination. All these I sensed radiating from her.

Our spirits immediately called to each other and then collided in an awkward dance and shuffled away from one another. I searched for the person inhabiting these sensations. My eyes found a short woman with a police badge poking out from under her jacket collar. She emanated a spunky spirit and I liked her fiery red hair smoothed into a tight twist that pulled the sides of her cheeks taut.

It surprised me when her gaze moved up, over the trees, landing in my direction, as if trying to locate a bird's call in the branches. I felt her soften as her soul met mine. Our spirits stopped and stared at one another for a moment. Recognizing something kindred.

In that moment, I didn't feel so alone. And I realized, it was the first time since my death, I had been able to reach into the temporal world.

Chapter 16

RILEY ST. JAMES

B etty Taylor looks twenty years older than her sixty-three years. She tells me how she's lived in this house since February 1989. I ask if she knows about Nina Laramie. She doesn't know the girl or the name. I tell her she was killed three acres from here on August 7, 1989. She says she was living in this house then. With three very young kids.

But she does remember something bone chilling from that early August. Betty hoods her eyes and sets a kettle of water on the burner. A watched pot never boils. Still, she stands over it until her stare forces the spout to hiss.

"It was hot that night. Humid. You know, the kind of night you can't sleep. You jest sit in the kitchen with the lights out and ice cubes on your forehead."

I nod. I know those nights. In Detroit. Working third shift patrol with windows down so we could detect the direction of gun shots.

"The kids were asleep, thank God," she says.

"And your husband?" Grable asks. "Where was he?"

"We separated the previous fall."

"So he wasn't in the house at all?" I ask because separation means different things to different people. She shakes her head. He had taken off with a waitress.

"I had heard teens out there all summer long. Blasting their music. Revving their engines. Yelling. Hollering. Til three, four in the morning."

"You ever call the police to complain?" Grable asks.

"Nah. I didn't have a land line."

I find this peculiar. "No phone at all?" I ask.

"No. I didn't want my husband bothering us. You register a phone number and your address goes into the phone book."

"I understand." I shoot Grable a look and I know he won't press the matter, although I can tell from his face he finds it just as strange as I do that a woman with three little children would have no phone.

Betty runs her hand over the worn wooden handle of the tea kettle. "All the windows were wide open and it was still as glass. Not a tree rustling or a bird chirping. And I heard a scream that went right up my spine. I dropped my ice cube and I actually jumped a little in my chair," she says.

"Did it sound like a male or a female?" I ask.

"Oh, it was a girl's scream," she confirms. "Then I heard some voices. Male."

"Some voices?" Grable asks.

"Yes. Two shoutin' back and forth at each other."

"What did they say? Do you remember?" I ask.

Betty shakes her head and pours steaming water into a teacup. Her hand quivers and water splashes over the rim onto the saucer. "I couldn't make out words. Just sounded… you know, troublesome."

"Like they were in trouble?" I say.

"They were yelling. Like… well… like my husband yelled at me. You know?"

I nod, empathetic eyes trained on Betty Taylor, victim of domestic abuse. Hidden with her little chicklings, safely away in the woods.

"I got up and went to the window so I could try and hear better. And then another scream. Just put a sick feeling in my stomach. And another one right after that. I didn't know what to do. I just stood there. I thought surely the kids would have heard it and I expected them to come find me. But then, just silence again. And since I didn't hear it again, I wondered if I had really heard it or if it was just my mind playing tricks."

"How long did you stand there?" I ask.

"Well, I don't know exactly. I checked the clock after the last scream and it was almost 1 a.m. My sister lived just down the road at the time and I told myself that if I heard it again, I'd run down to her place and use her phone."

"To call the police?" Grable clarifies.

She nods.

"Did you hear anything else?" I ask.

"Nothing. But I couldn't sleep the rest of the night."

"And the next day?" Grable says. "Did you report it to the police?"

"I didn't tell anyone." Betty shakes her head and tells us the next morning the sun had dawned large and hot, pulsing the ground with August heat and melting away the night's demons, making everything sluggish and ugly and tiresome. Betty only had so much energy. And this particular morning that energy had to be directed to hungry kids.

Chapter 17

RILEY ST. JAMES

I leave Betty Taylor's home and walk back through the woods with Grable. I imagine Nina's screams pealing through the woods and into Betty's kitchen window. Three bloodcurdling screams so vivid she recalled them with clarity thirty years later.

Betty's description manifests and I hear them piercing past tree limbs. Their high-pitched vibrations turn my skin cold and I cup my palms over my ears. But I still hear them. They multiply in my ear drums and nauseate my stomach. I stop walking and double over, leaning up against a tree trunk for support. When I try to look up, the woods are spinning and my lungs are closing. I find the pressure point in the inside of my wrist and apply firm pressure with my thumb to suppress the nausea. The screams are now throbbing with the rhythm of my pulse.

Over the screams, I hear Grable calling out to me. *Can I breathe?* I manage a small nod just as my body slides to the ground. The nausea waves over me and I vomit.

I have been through this before. But every time I'm entirely afraid of what my body and mind are doing to me. I've been told that from the outside it looks like a heart attack. It must be very scary to the observer.

I look up and see Grable kneeling next to me. I feel his dry, scratchy hand against my neck as he holds my hair back. He commands me steadily, "Breathe, Riley, breathe…. Breathe!"

I'm trying. I'm just hyperventilating and there's nothing Grable can do about it. I'm now right side down on the forest floor, curled up in the fetal position. I know it looks like I'm going to die. But I will not. I wish I could convey this to Grable who is totally panicking.

"Oh my God, help us!" Grable cries out.

Each word marches into my ear drums shutting down Nina's screams. And I hear the familiar prayer begin in a ticker tape across my brain. *"Lord, have mercy. Lord, have mercy. Christ, have mercy."* The words come gurgling up from the depth of my St. Mark's memories even though I haven't uttered them my entire adult life.

My peripheral vision is tunneling to black. I struggle to let the light in, but it's gone in three… two…

The next thing I see is a dark moving image and I realize I'm in my own dream, or rather some sort of memory flash. I'm walking swiftly through the wooded setting that lays between my college and the small downtown area where I worked on weekends. It's night. Late night. I've got my work clothes on. Faded, ripped jeans, a black t-shirt, thrift store jean jacket, and tennis shoes coated in kitchen grease. I was a prep cook for four years in an upscale restaurant. The path is well traveled by all the college kids who worked here and used it as a short cut to campus. It shaves off a good ten minutes than going by street sidewalks. I almost always took the street. It's well lit, safer, and I don't mind the extra walk. It is a good way for me to clear my mind and wind down after long shifts.

Tonight is one of those dark nights where the moon is covered by thick clouds creating an opaque blanket of blackness. I can't even see shadows. I've got my headphones cranked and I'm pouring all my moody, grungy, emo angst into *The Cure*. I don't know it yet, but I'm making the first and biggest mistake victims make -- I shut out aware-ness to my surroundings. I walk into Evil's path unknowingly.

I check the time and I have only fifteen minutes before curfew. It's going to take me at least thirty if I use the sidewalk. My small college has a midnight curfew and they lock the dorm doors and you aren't allowed in after that. It's a dumb rule because people are getting locked out all the time and then having to crash at off-campus apartments or in their cars. Not very prudent of the administration. But rules are rules.

Since I don't have time for the street walk. And I don't have a car or a friend who lives off campus. I make split decision to take the woods. Even then, I'll have to keep a fast jog to make it on time.

I'm naturally a fast runner on pavement, but here, on uneven gravel path, I have to slow my pace and take cautious footing in the dark. There's a spot along the path where it dips down to a small hill. The woods here are darkest and I have to slow my pace again to a fast walk because there are exposed roots I could trip on. I make it down the slope and start to climb the hill on the other side of the dip, when I feel an arm pull me back and wrap around my neck. My first thought is that I ran into a low hanging tree branch. But another hand pulls a winter hat over my head, completely blinding me.

I try to lift my arms, but human force has them pinned to my body. It hits me with a hot woozy wave of panic.

I am being attacked.

A deadening kick behind the knees drops me to the ground. I want to scream, but my voice dies out as a hand covers my mouth and I smell something garlicky on the palm and wince away. The grip tightens and I can't help but try to suck in a gasp of lifesaving air. Soon, I lose feeling of my body and let go of all struggle to keep conscious as my face slides down the canvas jacket of my attacker.

Wait. I can breathe again. I can breathe.

And then, nothing.

Chapter 18

RILEY ST. JAMES

I pull and tear at my face as I jolt from the terror of my dream to a semi-awakened state. I realize my bed sheet is over my face and suffocating me. I untwist myself and throw the covers back.

Where am I?

I jolt straight up. Look around. The objects in the room start to form a familiar connection in my brain.

I'm in my bedroom. In my bed. In my rented house in Derby.

I look down at my body.

I'm fully clothed. And I'm okay.

I swing my quivering legs off the bed. Shaking off the grogginess and see a full glass of water and plate of uneaten saltine crackers on my nightstand. I don't remember putting those there. My stomach growls and I reach for a cracker, letting the salt tip my tongue. Nibbling off a bite, I see the corner of a folded note tucked under the plate.

It's from Grable. "I brought you home and put you in bed. I'm here if you need me."

My legs are a still little shaky as I rise from bed. I need to find my phone. The wood floor creaks as I cross to an overstuffed yellow chair by the window where my coat is draped over the arm. I find my phone in my coat pocket where I left it and text Grable.

Me: Thanks for getting me home. I'm good now. See you at the office.

I take a seat on the chair to rest for a second and see if Grable responds.

How long have I been out?

I check the time on my phone. It's nearly twenty-thirty. Military time. Wasn't it late afternoon when I saw Betty Taylor? This was a longer spell than usual.

A text comes back.

Grable: You need anything?

Me: I'm good. Thanks.

Grable: Are you coming down?

Coming down?

Grable: Should I come in?

What? No. Where is he?

Grable: You should see a doctor.

I have. I'm fine. It's my memories that are sick. And please, Grable, for god's sake, don't try to be the romantic hero. Others have come before you thinking they can save poor Riley.

You just need a good, long spa vacation, Riley. Spoil yourself for once. I know a really good behavior therapist, Riley. Here's his number. Give him a call. Have you tried cannabis, Riley? Takes the edge off. I've got a shaman who can take you on a trip inside yourself, Riley. Frees you from all this crap right here, in the heart chakra.

Grable: You okay?

Me: Where are you?

Grable: Look outside.

I toss the phone onto the bed and rush to the window. Grable's truck is below and I can see him in the driver's seat. He waves up to me. I assure him I'm okay with a two finger wave and pull back from the window.

Outside I hear the truck rev down the driveway. I crawl back into bed. Even though I know sleep will never come.

I turn over a few times trying to settle into a comfortable position before deciding my best strategy is to read. I flip on the bedside lamp and open the nightstand drawer where I keep my novels of guilty pleasure. Young adult fiction. I reach for the book on top that I've read a couple times already. After a few paragraphs, I glance into the drawer to check on my back up pistol. It's not in view. I lean over to get a better look and lift the stack of books to one side. Maybe it's hiding underneath. It's not. Panic flutters in my gut.

I scoot to the edge of the bed and toss everything from the draw. No pistol. I check the other night stand thinking I misplaced it. I haven't. I search under the bed, between the mattress, my dresser drawers, the closet, the bathroom. I spend a good hour scouring the house. And another half hour tearing my truck apart. I can't find it.

My head is starting to pound. If I don't lie down soon, I'll pass out again. I dart back to the house, texting Grable to ask if he took it. It's the only plausible explanation right now.

I get inside and set the alarm. His answer comes through as I'm climbing the stairs to my bedroom.

Grable: Yes. Sorry. Forgot to mention.

Me: Bring it back. Now.

Grable: Get it at the office tomorrow.

Me: No. I'm fine.

Grable: You're not fine.

Me: I'm not suicidal.

Grable: Tomorrow.

Me: Now. Come on.

I pace in my bedroom.

No reply. No reply. No reply.

I call him. No pick up.

It's not a good idea for me to get into my truck and drive over. After an hour, I crawl into bed with a cup of coffee and a couple books. I'm going to force myself to stay awake all night. If I sleep, I may end up back in the woods. And I don't want to go there again.

Chapter 19

RILEY ST. JAMES

I walk the expansive back yard of a lakeside house belonging to Former Derby Detective Ray Polland who I see is dressed in a bee suit and tending to one of his dozen bee hives near the lakeshore. He motions for me to come closer, but I hang back and wait, enjoying the view and the breeze that cools my warm cheeks. Plus, I'm fearful of getting stung. Not allergic or anything. Just don't like the pain. I clear my throat and sense a little scratch at the back of my throat that makes me wonder if I'm coming down with a cold. It's probably just exhaustion, I tell myself because there's absolutely no time to be sick right now.

After a few minutes, Ray approaches cradling two large jars of honey.

"Hi. Detective Poland? I'm Detective Riley St. James," I say.

"I know who you are. And I wondered when you'd be coming around. Here. It's good for what ails you," he says handing me a jar. "And you look like you could use a little boost."

"How could you tell?"

"I'm trained to observe," he says with a smile. "It's unpasteurized and raw. Full of antioxidants."

I take the jar, its contents still warm from the hive. "I just need more sleep."

"Take a couple spoonfuls a day. Wards off bacteria. Sooths the throat."

"A spoonful of sugar," I say wistfully recalling my days as a kid watching Mary Poppins with my Mom who was nostalgic for old Disney flicks.

"Except this stuff's a super food," he says.

Ray takes his hood and gloves off. "How are they treating you at the station?"

"It was a warm welcome at first. Now, I think they're tolerating me."

He laughs. "Come. Take a seat on the patio. You don't mind sitting outside, do you?"

"I'd love a little fresh air. It's a beautiful place you have here," I say.

"My sanctuary." Ray shows me to a large patio table on the back deck of the house. The view from here is even more stunning than from the yard and I can't seem to take my eyes off the peaceful waters lapping the shore.

"Well, I'd say you've earned this life," I tell him, more than slightly envious of the view.

"How's the investigation going?" he asks.

"I'm catching up. I think I found something interesting yesterday. Do you know a Betty Taylor?" I can't help but unscrew my honey jar and dip my finger into the gooey sweetness. It's cut with a taste of something I recognize, but can't pinpoint. Woodsy... barky... piney. My taste buds take to the savory flavors. *What is that exactly?* I have another lick and Ray reads my mind.

"Rosemary. The hive is near a large rosemary bush," he says.

"It's like nothing I've ever tasted before," I say.

Ray doesn't know Betty Taylor. He peels off his bee suit and lays it across one of the patio chairs and I tell him about my conversation with her and Ray goes quiet, his eyes drifting into the middle of the lake.

"Interesting," he says with a sad shake of his head.

"Do you think she really heard Nina's scream?"

"She remembered it all these years. That counts for something," he says.

"Yes. It seemed very personal and disturbing to her," I add. "I think it still haunts her."

"I suppose it does."

"I'm just having a hard time believing she never heard about Nina's disappearance and put two and two together?"

"People have their reasons. And most don't want to go borrowing trouble. This is a small community, you know."

I think about the abusive Mr. Taylor as I follow Ray's gaze to a fishing boat trolling the shore around the lake. The two fishermen drop drag lines and wait for a catch. The water ripples concentrically from their boat bottom across the still lake.

"I met Solomon Newton the first night I was here. He didn't know who I was," I say. "I saw it, Detective Polland. I saw the evil in his eyes."

Ray nods again. "Here's something you won't find in those files. Did you know five years after Nina's death, Solomon served six years in Jackson for assault and rape."

My eyes widen. "And after that?"

"He was freed. Living here. A few years ago, before I retired, I pulled him over for speeding and found duct tape, rope, and lubricating jelly in his trunk. I had to let him go."

"What? Why!"

"It's not illegal to own those items. And there was nothing else on which I could arrest him at the time," says Ray.

"He had a rape kit in his trunk!"

Ray nods sadly. "I put out an alert with the Michigan police. I got some hits back from a detective in upper Michigan about some unsolved murder cases that have striking resemblances to Nina's. But again, not enough evidence."

"That's infuriating."

"I know. Even more so since he's been the model citizen. At least in the public eye."

"Town rumors may tell otherwise," I say. "Code of silence."

"Yes. I know. I've been aware, but not privy," Ray says. "Be very careful, Riley St. James. You are dealing with the devil." His serious look warns me like a grandfather instructing a grandchild not to cross a strong stream. It looks manageable on the surface, but underneath, a deadly current will trap and hold you to the bottom.

"What is Grable hiding?" I ask after a moment.

"I honestly don't know. But you can subpoena his statement if you like."

"If you were me and you could do it all over again, where would you start?"

Ray is quiet for a moment as something brooding finds its way through him and then disappears. He looks up at me.

"Are you familiar with the issue of legend?" he asks.

"Is this some local folklore I'm missing?"

"No, the issue of legend is a forensic analysis term that has to do with the testimony given to the first investigators compared with the testimony you will get today. Thirty years later."

"I'm not sure I understand." I cock my ear towards Polland.

"You have a record from the first investigators of the case. Mine included. This is what they said they saw and experienced the night of Nina's disappearance."

"Yes, but how does that factor into moving the case forward today?" I ask.

"You need to re-interview them. See what they recall today. See how much things match up."

"Memories can fade. They become more unreliable," I argue.

"Usually. But sometimes earlier recollections can become cleaner with time and space. Sometimes there's a detail or two that comes out later. Sometimes a helpful memory suddenly becomes dislodged from the brain due to some trigger we can't always explain or understand."

"Are you saying there are things that couldn't be said then that can be said now?" I ask.

"That's part of it. Have you ever held a memory so strong for years and years? You remember it one way. And then one day, something happens, you may not even be thinking about that memory. And an image or bit of conversation pops into your brain that is associated with that memory. It's like a lost puzzle piece. And when you fit it into the puzzle of that memory, the memory changes. Maybe it rounds out or becomes more complete or answers a question you had about that event."

I nod. Yes, I know that feeling.

"That's what I mean. Revisit the past with the people who lived it and see if there are any missing puzzle pieces."

"Do you think I should talk to Silas and Solomon?" I ask.

"Not right away. You don't want to trigger any ripples in the community. Besides, they already know why you're here. It would do you no good to question them. They will stick to their story. It will not change. Leave them alone until you have a solid case against them and can make the arrest. Start with the friends who were with Nina that last night."

"Alyson Peters, Bradley Hollinga, and Richard Wright."

"And Kevin Grable," he says.

"What? Why? He's not listed in the reports."

"No. But he was with Nina and her friends that night."

"Why didn't he tell me that?"

"He asked to have his name expunged from the records once he decided to become a police officer."

"He can do that?"

"He can because he was never a suspect."

"What do you think he's hiding?"

"It's his story to tell," says Ray.

"But do you think he is withholding something that could solve this case?" I ask.

"I interviewed Kevin back then when he was 17. There was nothing in his statement that led me to believe he was involved in her murder."

"And since then?"

"I think he's heard and seen things, but my guess is that it's nothing that could be used to build an arrest or he would have done so."

"Would he?"

Ray pauses. "I trust Kevin."

"He isn't exactly chomping at the bit to get this case solved."

"Keep pressing," Ray says.

"Detective Polland, be honest with me. Am I on a fool's errand here?"

"No. It was your good instincts that already unearthed the Taylor tip. Seems to me like you've already made a little crack in the code of silence."

"Betty? I feel like we just kinda stumbled on that one," I sigh. "Besides, hearing a girl's scream and indistinct male voices doesn't exactly point the finger to Nina or the Newton twins."

"Everything comes together at the perfect time for perfect reason for the good of all. Including you. You're here for a reason," he says.

Ray smiles at me and rises from his seat.

"The smoker should have released all the bees by now. Time to gather more honey," he says.

Ray dons his bee suit and heads back to his bees and I travel to my truck thinking, how on earth can Ray Polland remain so altruistic after the depths of human grime he's mucked through?

I feel my shoulder muscles constrict and realize the source of this tension is my anxiety about Grable. I'm angry that he camped out in my driveway. Angry he took my gun. Angry that he thought I needed rescuing. Angry he won't step up to guide me to more sources. Angry that he's holding back local legends. Angry that he withheld himself from that report. And angry there's not a darn thing I can do to force him.

Chapter 20

GRABLE

There is no way Grable is going to diffuse the red wave rising from the base of Riley's neck as he slides Riley's "lost" pistol across her desk when she comes in later that day.

"Here. I even got you some extra ammo," he says.

Riley's face sours at him as she grabs her gun and checks the chamber, then the magazine. He would have done exactly the same.

Grable passes her a paper bag. She unfolds the crease, her eyes counting the bullets inside.

She slips everything into the handbag by her feet, her steady eyes never leaving his.

"I could arrest you," she says without an ounce of anger. He had expected this threat. Or at least a good yelling at.

"I was worried about you. You were... you took the gun out and you were waving it..."

"Was I?"

"It's happened before then," Grable responds in a calm, interviewy voice that sends Riley into an eye roll.

"I wasn't going to do anything," she says.

"This is a classic sign of depression stemming from a post-traumatic stress disorder."

"You read my file." She is point blank with a furious hiss.

Grable takes a couple steps back, slouching into a chair. As soon as he left her house, he called up the state police records office and requested it as a matter of background checking. Her file read that Riley had been diagnosed during her physical when she went through the academy fifteen years earlier: "St. James suffers post-traumatic symptoms and refuses to divulge details of any event or incident causing such trauma, as is within her right. She has been assigned to a department psychologist for treatment."

"You don't know me like you think you do," she says.

"You freaked me out, St. James. Your sergeant is listed as your emergency contact. So I called him."

She glares at me. "Mind your own business."

Grable notices sweat forming along her brow.

"I know what I saw. And you're not right yet. You need to see someone," he says.

"I successfully completed my required therapy fourteen years ago."

"What if you had been alone out there?"

"I'm fine. My blood sugar gets a little low sometimes. It passes," she says.

"Bull shit. You're in my department. Therefore, I'm responsible for you."

"I'm hired by the State. That's who I'm responsible to."

"You need more help," Grable says.

"Who doesn't?" She throws up her hands. "Ninety-nine percent of us have some form of PTSD. So what? You suck it up and you get back out there."

"What triggered that out there in the woods?" he asks with a gentler tone.

Riley takes a deep breath. And this point, Grable knows there's no use flaming this fire if he wants to get her to trust him.

"Let it go, Grable. We both know some secrets about each other now. So leave it." She spears him with an annoyed look. "Speaking of. I paid a visit to Ray Polland today. I know you were there that night."

"I want to put the Newton brothers behind bars as much as you do," he says not lifting his gaze from her.

"If we don't make inroads now, the state will set this file on the back burner. And that's where it will stay. Forever."

"I understand that you may be the only hope left for this case," Grable says.

"Then let's talk about our next steps," she says curtly. "What do you think about re-interviewing Nina's friends? See if we can unearth anything new in their stories."

"I'll let you in on a little local secret, the decent folks of Derby county don't want anyone bulldozing around their private and past lives," he tells her.

"You afraid that'll hurt our case? Or that you'll have to give your statement again?" she says.

Grable doesn't answer. How stable is she, he wonders? What demons is she holding onto? Is there anything he can do to help free her?

"Look, I'm sorry that I took your gun. It was wrong of me," he says. "And I should have returned it when you asked."

The prickly shell retracts as Riley's shoulders drop into a less defensive position.

"Apology accepted."

Grable weighs the moment. He firmly believes that every thing and every person that crosses his path has purpose. What was his purpose with Riley? What did she need from him outside of investigative assistance?

"You ever wish you could go back to some moments in life and just... choose differently?" he says, drifting to a melancholy tone. Grable glances up to gauge her reaction. Riley's face has lost its ruddy hew. "That if you had, in that moment, done just one thing differently, that your whole world... and someone else's whole world... would have turned out differently?"

She nods. "Of course. Who doesn't have those moments?" She crosses her arms and leans slightly forward onto her desk. Grable feels immediately vulnerable in her presence. Her skin around the corner of her eyes smooths out. The pools of green reflect a deeper pain, but with no judgment focused on him. He feels he can tell her anything right now. Where to start? What to reveal? Sentences won't form.

"What would you have done differently that night?" Riley asks in a slow voice.

"Listen." His answer slips out automatically.

"Listen to what?"

"That voice… you know that voice?" he asks her. "The one that warns us that something bad is about to happen… and that we need to pay attention and protect ourselves… and those around us."

"I know the voice," she says.

Grable feels his voice crack as he opens his mouth. "Yes— I could have…. I could have made an excuse to get her into the store… or I could have jumped in the car with her… I could have made sure she actually got… home… I could have."

He sits in silence for a long time, his guilt releasing in deep exhales. Riley's gaze never waivers from him. Never accuses. There is comfort in Riley's eyes and he doesn't want to stop looking at them. This case is going to test this woman to her limits.

"You know it was them, don't you?" she says, breaking him out of his trance.

Grable nods.

"Why didn't you listen?" she says.

His instant answer: "Fear."

"And what is that voice telling you now?" she asks.

"That there's nothing left to fear."

"Except failure," she says with remarkable confidence.

"Then, we're on the same page," Grable responds, thinking, this is going to test us both.

Chapter 21

RILEY ST. JAMES

G rable is wrong. Most decent folk in Derby do want justice for Nina. They're tired of secrets and silence. They want the black cloud of her murder removed. After thinking about it, however, I realize Polland is right about one thing, re-interviewing suspects and friends will stir up a firestorm of gossip in Derby. I have to proceed with discretion.

I start by re-testing the physical evidence. I have the evidence sent down to the state crime lab, and I request that Maria Jimenez examine the samples, because we've been friends since

I started on the Detroit PD. I trust her to go the extra mile. She's also great at breaking down the science to me, which really helps when I have to testify in court and explain things to juries.

Maria meets me in the lobby of the state crime lab on the university campus and greets me with a quick hug.

"Interesting new assignment," she says indicating Nina's thick file in her hands. "How are things up there in woods? You miss the city?"

"I do. It's too quiet," I say. "But I'm starting to adjust."

"Any good looking lumberjacks?" says Maria lobbing a grin my way.

"If I find any, I'll give them your number."

"Please. You know I'm not picky," she teases and motions for me to follow her into the elevator. "How about that detective up there? Grable?"

"He's not bad to look at. You want me to give him your number?" I joke back.

Maria laughs. "Maybe so. Maybe so."

When we reach her lab she pulls up an image on her computer screen. "I kind of hate that you had to make the long trip down because I don't have a lot of great news for you," she says.

My heart sinks. I had hoped that after thirty-plus years of advances in DNA science, she'd be able to offer more clarity to the case. "At least it's a nice chance to see you. How have you been?" I ask.

"Working a lot of overtime. Trying to get through the sexual assault kit backlog."

"You're a modern day hero, Maria."

"Just doing my job. More funding would help. As would more staff."

In the past Maria has shared abysmal stats with me about the state of rape convictions in the U.S. Four hundred thousand rape kits sit in two hundred forensic labs all across the United States. I know it takes years, even decades, to process a kit and in most cases, DNA only helps solve about .2 percent of sexual assault crimes. Sadly, only a third of women ever report their rape and of those, only a third actually go through with a sexual assault exam to collect DNA. And only one percent of rape kits will actually result in a conviction. Under those stats, it would be tempting to give into despair, but Maria is bright light of change and hope, relentless in her work as an advocate for sexual assault victims. She even volunteers at the local emergency room to assist the under-staffed nursing pool process the testing for rape victims.

"So, what did you find?" I ask.

Maria is sensitive to my disappointment as she walks me through the results in her clinical manner.

"You gave me four samples. Hair from the necklace. Hair from the victim's blouse. Hair from a bracelet. Hair from the victim's right hand. We also tested skin samples from the victim and eight of the suspects, friends, and family members. Every one of them is inclusive. There's just not enough DNA to make an accurate interpretation," she explains.

"There's no new technology you can apply? I thought you could get reads off partial touch DNA samples now?"

"There's a lot of new technology but you need viable DNA samples, even if minute. The samples taken from the victim's body were exposed to the heat of the summer and damp of the fall for three months. These samples were also greatly degraded by sunlight, bacteria, and humidity. There just wasn't enough there for me to develop an accurate sequence. I'm sorry."

The Newton brothers had not been included in the original DNA sampling as they were not suspects at the time primarily because there was no physical evidence to place them at the scene of Nina's murder. But now it didn't matter. Even if they had been part of the study, none of the DNA was readable. None of it could be matched back to anyone... even Nina's own hair samples.

Maria interrupts my thoughts.

"I guess you're gonna have to detect this the old-fashioned way," she says.

I nod and give her a small smile as I try to boost my own confidence. I know better than to put my eggs in the physical evidence basket. Truth and proof are never black and white. Cases are tried and decided solely on circumstantial evidence every day. And so would this one.

"You can ferret this thing out. I know you, Riley St. James. This is going to be a big break for you. Don't give up. Got it?" Maria pats my arm.

"Never ever," I say and give her a quick hug. "You either."

"Call me anytime," says Maria as she hands me Nina's file. "And keep me posted on this."

I wanted to treat Maria to lunch, but she couldn't fit me in. I see myself out and am crossing the parking lot when the sky unleashes a soaking shower. I tuck Nina's files in between my jacket to protect them and dash to my vehicle.

I am in no hurry to make the two-hour drive back to Derby. I bide the speed limit allowing the swish of the wind shield wipers to lure me into a meditative frame of mind as I keep my eyes glued to the white line on the right of the two lane highway that snakes through the woods, clearing now and then for small towns that consist of only a gas station, liquor store, and home-grown café.

I am about ten miles south of Derby nearing the Green Acres Market where Nina had last been seen by her friends. I pull in to fill my tank and take a look around. From the pictures I have studied in her case file, I note that nothing significant has changed about the place in thirty years. The building is still in desperate need of a paint job just like the old photos show. The asphalt is cracked and potholed. The windows are sooted in black grime from weather and constant exhaust fumes. Either the landlord lives out of town or doesn't care or has no funds for a clean-up job.

I fill my tank and go inside to pay. The clerk tells me their credit card machine isn't connecting to the internet. *Do I have cash?* I dig into my purse.

"What if I don't have it?" I ask out of curiosity.

"Then, I guess, you don't," he says with eyes glancing to the video on his mobile screen.

I pay him. I do have cash.

"You have a bathroom here?" I ask.

"Behind the building. You need a key." He hands me a fly swatter with the bathroom key attached to the handle. I can make out the frayed wings of several insect victims on the head of the swatter. Gross.

"Thanks," I say under my breath. He doesn't even glance up as I exit.

I don't actually have to go to the bathroom. I just want an excuse to look around. I'm not even sure what I'm looking for. Stalling for time before I have to go back to that vacant house with my vacant evidence results.

I wander around to the back of the building and find a narrow door with the words "Shitter" stenciled across the middle. Classy.

I turn my footsteps to the gravel lot behind Green Acres which houses a dumpster and several pieces of lawn equipment rusting alongside a shed. Leaning against the shed are warped, weathered plywood boards. I wander over. The largest one, probably ten by twelve feet, faces out. It's painted in solid black paint, now faded and pealing at the edges. Across the center white lettering has been chipped away by time and elements. However, it's unnerving message remains legible: "Who killed Nina Laramie? Someone knows."

Jim Laramie reports in his daughter's case files that he had set out on his own investigative journey when the cops wouldn't. He posted signs like this one all around the county. He was convinced that Nina's circle of friends knew who had killed her and weren't saying.

Who killed Nina Laramie?

Yes, someone still knows.

Chapter 22

NINA, 1989

I was folding the clothes at the kitchen table while watching our small, 19 inch color TV. Dad was too cheap to spring for a 24 inch. He wouldn't even get cable, which is why I spent so much time at my friend Laura's house. She has a 32 inch with all the cable channels. Even MTV.

I had the phone pressed to my ear and was talking to Alyson Peters. She wanted me to go out later and to meet at the Argo gas station after my Dad left for work.

I had two more towels to fold when I heard Dad get up and go into the bathroom. I handed him a towel through the door and asked him what he wanted to eat for supper. Spaghetti.

I started a pot of water boiling on the stove and while I was waiting for that to heat up, I quickly washed my hair in the kitchen sink. It was dirty from my swim in the river earlier that day. I wrapped it in a fresh towel and sat at the table to finish watching a game show.

Dad came into the kitchen and tripped over Tucker who was lying half under the table. Tucker yelped and scurried all the way under the table.

"Dad, be careful," I yelled.

"Nina! Watch the stove!" he yelled back.

I looked up. The pot was boiling over, water sizzling in the grates and creating a plume of scalding steam. I grabbed a hot mitt and took it off the burner.

"That dog made a mess in the hallway again. Nearly stepped in it. You gonna clean that up?" he demanded.

"Yeah, Dad, I'll get it."

"Right now."

He was so cranky when he got up.

"I will. I will."

"You need to take care of that dog better. Can't just sit around watching TV and expect him to take himself out."

"I got it, Dad." I opened a jar of tomato sauce and poured it into a small pan. Then I tossed a package of generic brand spaghetti noodles into the hot water and turned down the burner.

"Who was that on the phone?" he asked.

"No one."

"When I was getting in the shower. You were on the phone. I heard you."

"Oh. Just Alyson."

"I don't want you going out tonight," he barked.

"Why not?"

"Those friends ain't the best crowd."

"I've known them since fifth grade," I said.

"Doesn't make what they do right."

"We're just gonna hang at the gas station. Maybe head to the park," I told him.

"You need to be in by midnight so you can get up early and look for a job."

It was the same old argument. I slipped into the hallway to clean up Tucker's mess. It was a doozy, too. I had to scrub the carpet with laundry detergent to get the smell out. Meanwhile, Dad finished up dinner in the kitchen and had it on the table when I returned.

We were three bites in when the phone rang.

"I got it," I said leaping up.

"Leave it."

Too late. The receiver was already in my hand.

"Hello?"

"We're eating, Nina. Tell whoever it is you'll call them back."

"Hey, Adam... just eating."

"Tell him you'll call him back."

"My Dad says hi." I headed back to the table stretching the long baby blue phone cord with me across the room.

"Ask him how his new job is," said dad, whose plate was almost empty. He was a notoriously fast eater.

"How's your job going?" I ask Adam.

Dad twirled the last few strands of noodle onto his fork and inhaled it down.

"He says it's good. Tiring."

"Then it's honest labor. When's he coming back up here?" said Dad.

"Dad. Why don't you just talk to him." I handed Dad the phone and cleared our plates from the table. I wasn't hungry anymore.

Dad really liked Adam. Talked to him like he would an adult. Before Adam left for Ohio, Dad gave Adam his blessing to marry me. I'm not supposed to know this, but I overheard them talking one day on the back porch before Adam left for his new job. Dad wanted to see me settle down as soon as possible so I stayed out of trouble. He thought it would teach me more responsibility. Help me grow up. I loved Adam. I really did. And I wanted to marry him. Some day. But not now. I had just turned eighteen a couple months ago.

I rinsed the plates and fed Tucker while Dad told Adam to work hard and take care. He handed the phone back to me.

"Hang on a sec, Adam. Dad's leaving for work." I cupped the mouthpiece to my stomach. "Dad, don't forget your lunch in the fridge."

"Clean up this kitchen. And lock that dog up if you're going out. I don't want him roaming around making more messes."

"I will."

"I wish you wouldn't go out."

"Just hanging with some friends."

"You can do that here."

"Dad--- don't worry."

"I'll see you in the morning." He gave me a quick kiss. There was worry in a fine crease above his brow. "Love you."

"You, too," I said pressing the receiver back to my ear.

He grabbed his thermos, keys, and coat and was out the door.

That was the last time he saw me.

Chapter 23

RILEY ST. JAMES

I spend the next couple weeks of the Laramie case interviewing former key witnesses, friends, family, and suspects. Twenty-seven, to be exact. None of the stories had changed in nature. The issue of legend was not breaking. Sure, memories had faded some. Names and dates got a little squishy. But nothing to raise a red flag. Nothing to point us in a new direction to Nina's killer.

I have just three left. Two are out of towners. Laura Wriggens in Illinois. The best friend. And Adam Larkin in Ohio. The boyfriend. Both have solid, proven alibis, but I will speak with them. What do they remember? What do they leave out? What has stuck with them? What are their theories? What have they heard since then?

And then there's Jim. Nina's father. I have a dinner meeting scheduled with him at six. There was a brief second back in November of 1989 when Ray Polland interviewed him as a potential suspect. It fell apart quickly, but I want to hear his version of what happened. I want to give him a space to talk about it. I want to get to know Nina from his point of view.

I glance at the clock hanging above my door. Five thirty-four. Too early to walk the three blocks to The Happy Hunter pub. I decide to review Laura Wriggen's statement from November 12 of 1989 for the third time.

I got off work around ten.... That's ten at night... oh, I worked at The Merry Market... and I went home to shower and change my clothes... it was a humid day and I kinda smelled bad. A friend came over about ten-thirty and we made a quick dinner. We liked to cook... and I had this hamburger meat that they gave me from the meat counter... you know, like, it was going to expire that day and they would have to throw it out... but I told them I would take it.... so we made spaghetti and meatballs. Then, as we were eating I remembered.... I told my friends that I... well, I remembered that I had to go tell Nina about the job. Yeah, the job at Merry Market. Nina had applied a couple weeks before that... but there were no positions available. And then that day, my manager said if Nina could get to the Market by nine the next morning, she could have a two-week cashier trial. What was the question?... Oh... Why didn't I just call her? I... I dunno... she lived just down the road and I guess... well, we always just went to each other's houses... like, it was just easier that way. Ya know? I just remember that I went to her house and... what? Oh, what time? Um... I guess it was about eleven-thirty? Yeah... that's right. Eleven-thirty. The house was all dark inside. Like, no lights on inside or outside. Which I thought was kinda weird because Nina hated being home alone at night and she lit that place up like a Christmas tree. Her Dad was always telling her to turn off the lights cause the electric bill, ya know? And I went up to the door and knocked and her dog, Tucker, went nutso barking and scratching at the door. Which was also weird because she was supposed to lock him away when she left the house to go somewhere. So, I figured she must be home if he was out. I knocked again and no answer. I tried to open the door, and it was unlocked. I stuck my head in and yelled for her. No. She wasn't there. I left. Yeah, at that point we took off. Where? Where did we go? Um... yeah... we just went to get some ice cream. The Brown Cow, well, you know, it's open til midnight .... in the summer, you know... Lots of tourists... so we just sat by the river and had our ice cream. Went home? No, we didn't go home after that. We went back to Nina's house. Um... time.. yeah, now it was like an hour later. So, twelve-thirty? Probably. And still no lights, barking dog, no one around. I banged on the front door. I banged on the windows. I threw a couple stones up at her bedroom window... yeah... on the second floor... yeah, her bedroom faced the street. I don't know, I think we were there about ten minutes. Maybe fifteen. I went back to my car and I wrote her a note that said to call me as soon as she got home. I stuck it in the door in the crack between the door and the door frame. And then we took off. We went back to my house because I had to get up early for work the next day... yeah, I started my shift at seven. So... you know... that's it.... The next day?... I was surprised I didn't hear from Nina because she wanted that job bad. Really bad. After work I drove right over to her house and her Dad was getting up and was starting to wonder where she was... her dad always liked me. I stayed and we talked for a bit. He was mad 'cause Nina hadn't left a note and Tucker had made messes all over the house. I said if I saw her I'd tell her to get her heinie home. He was not very pleased."

It was a clean testimony. Except for one chink. The Newton broth-ers claim they returned Nina at 12:30 a.m. And their cousin Richard Wright claimed he was with them at his house at two a.m. If this were true, Nina must have left the house again after 12:30 a.m. But with whom? All her friends and family had solid alibis. No one else had come forward or claimed to have seen her. Who else would she have been with? Still, in thirty years, the Newton twins claim could not be disproven. I feel like the whole case hangs on what really happened between 12:30 and 2:00a.m.? And no one seems to know.

I check the time. 6:07 p.m. I am late for my meeting with Jim.

Chapter 24

RILEY ST. JAMES

The Happy Hunter is Derby's "other" local hang out, down a block and across the street from Pub Griffin. The black carpet and dark wood paneling haven't been changed since it opened in 1972. Taxidermy animals line the walls, glass eyes glaring around a dining room of a dozen flat tops. I find Jim Laramie at the bar, already into his first can of beer. I sit next to him and he offers a polite hello and wonders if I've found anything. I can't talk about it. He understands. After a few more swigs on his can, Jim begins to open up to me.

"Detective Polland thought she had runaway at first. Thought she was hiding from me," Jim starts. "Because she had done it before.

"When she ran to her mom's. Right?"

He nods.

"That must have been frustrating," I say. He nods again. "What did you do then?"

"I kept showing up at the police station. Two or three times that first week. I knew something was off. I didn't think she ran. I thought maybe she was staying at a friend's. I taped her bedroom door shut with scotch tape to catch her if she came home. But the tape was never broken."

The bartender asks if I want anything. I order a club soda. With lime.

"Police didn't do a whole lot for me after I put in that missing person's report."

"But you searched for her?" I say.

"Hell yeah. Every day. Friends. Family. We just didn't know where to look, you know? I was even out near the Hole in the Woods a couple times. Probably was close to her at some point."

"The case report states you made fliers and delivered them all over this side of the state," I say.

"Yup. Every gas station, police post, grocery store." Jim's eyes drift to the bottles behind the bar and then back to his wrinkled, veiny hand wrapped around his Miller Light can.

"What came of all that canvassing?" I ask.

"Nothing. I heard nothing. Cops heard nothing. One month went by. Two. I started working a few extra shifts just cause I didn't want to be in that empty house. Didn't want to walk past her room."

"Why would she be staying at friend's and not call you?" I say.

At this he pauses and chugs down the rest of his beer.

"I loved my daughter, but I was frustrated with her at the time. And I let her know it," says Jim.

"You fought?"

"We had words all the time. She was running with a bad crowd. Got caught shoplifting. Was taking from her savings. She had completed high school on a GED. I was after her. But for her own good."

I nod. "That's what a good father does."

Jim doesn't respond. I see the tears start to well up and I excuse myself to the ladies room for a moment so he can regain composure. When I return Jim is shucking peanuts from a beer bucket and tossing the shells to the floor. A fresh club soda is at my spot.

"I found a sign about Nina out back of the Merry Market in Derby," I say in an effort to direct the conversation.

"After they found her body, I bought space to put up some billboards around the county. I put ads in the paper. I made bumper stickers. But the cops had already lost three months investigation time. Three months those killers had to hide all the evidence."

"Killers? Plural?" I ask, wondering what Jim's theory is.

"I know there's no evidence to tie the Newton twins to Nina's death, but I know it was them," he says.

"How? How do you know that?" I glance around to see if anyone is listening to us. The bartender's in the kitchen and the only other patron is seated at a four top in the corner, staring at a football game on TV.

"They didn't drop Nina home that night like they said they did," he says.

"How do you know?"

"Cause of Tucker. He had messed in the dining room, the living room and by the back door. If those Newtons had really dropped her off at home, then Tucker wouldn't have messed all over the house."

"How can you be sure of that?" I press.

"We fought about it before I left for work. I nearly stepped in his shit in the hallway. I threatened to give the dog away and she begged me not to. Said she would take better care."

"But what if she forgot?" I push hard, playing the devil's advocate.

"No. See, Adam had given her that dog as a graduation gift a month earlier. I think she may have loved that dog more than she loved him. She would have never wanted me to take Tucker away." Jim smiles and it makes me smile. But as quickly as it comes, it disappears. The lines on his forehead crevice with despair and he speaks darkly. "They took her. They took my only child and flayed her open like some prey they caught in the woods," his voice rises and cracks. He takes an inhale and I hear a slight rattle in his smoker's lungs, "And they've been living full, free lives for thirty years. Silas has got kids. Solomon, too. Nina and Adam should've married. I should have grandkids coming to visit me." He stops and sweeps a peanut shell off the bar top to the floor. "They took everything from me."

"Not everything," I manage in a whisper. "You will have justice."

Jim turns to look me in the eyes for the first time since I sat down. Immediately I wish I hadn't said that. It's over confident.

"Do you know her mother never even came to her funeral?" he says picking up another peanut and cracking the shell between his thumb and forefinger.

"I did not know that," I say.

"We did a public funeral—empty casket-- in October. Police released her body four months later. We did her burial on Valentine's Day, 1990. She was wrapped in pink satin," he says. "She loved pink. Ever since she was my little girl."

Chapter 25
GRABLE

Misty Beckett's 2006 Ford Focus squeals into the police station parking lot around 10:38 p.m. just as Detective Grable is heading out on patrol. Grable recognizes it out of the corner of his eye and picks up his pace to his squad car, hoping she won't see him.

But no such luck. She pulls her car up along-side him and rolls down the window. "Kevin. Hey Kevin! I just came from Pub Griffins. Silas and Solomon were there talking about Nina's murder."

Grable stops and looks inside the car. "Are you driving under the influence Ms. Beckett?"

"Cut the crap, Kev. I'm trying to tell you that you should go arrest those sons of bitches right now!"

"Officer Grable," he sighs. "You need to address me as Officer when I'm in uniform."

Her eyes are glossy; her face flushed. She giggles. "Okay, Ossifer."

"Park your car, Misty."

Misty parks the car, angling her Focus next to him.

"Terrible park job," he mutters.

"There's no one else here. What's the big deal?"

"Don't get out of the car." He instructs and goes to his squad and takes the breathalyzer from the glove box. When he returns she's out of the car and leaning against the back passenger side.

"Kev... Kev... you have to listen to meeeee... I heard them with my own two ears talking about the murder weapon and how no one was gonna be able to pin the murder on them because they got rid of it a long time ago."

"Oh, you heard that huh?"

"They melted it in the foundry. 'Member how Solomon worked there one summer? He took it into work and tossed it into the furnace."

"Well, what difference does it make now if they melted it in the foundry?" says Grable.

"He JUST admitted it. Me and Joyce heard him talking about it to a couple guys. This is big, Kev." Misty wobbles on her four-inch patented leather, cherry red stilettos. Grable reaches out to steady her.

"Misty, you're drunk," says Grable.

"They're still at the Griffin. Go! Go!" She waves her pointer finger towards the bar downtown.

"Your hearsay is not enough to make an arrest. Breathe into this thing."

"I'mmma not gonna do that."

"Breathe into this," he commands.

"That's stupid. I only had three vodka tonics."

"Misty, I can't let you get into that car unless you do this."

"You're crazy." She takes a few steps back to her vehicle. "I'm telling you Silas just admitted he killed Nina and you're talking about arresting me?"

"You just admitted to drinking three cocktails. You can't stand up straight. And you're slurring."

"Whh--at? No, I'm not," she says, blending the "m" and the "n" together.

"Don't make me arrest you. I've got better things to do." Grable waves the breathalyzer towards Misty's mouth.

"You're a coward, Kevin Grable. You're protecting them. You always have."

"I have not," he says, his jaw clenching.

"Doesn't it eat you up?" she says.

"Misty, you wanna spend the night in there?" Grable points to the station where they have two small holding cells.

"You were with them that night. You know it was them."

"Misty, please." He holds up the breathalyzer to her face.

Misty leans back onto her car and stares at Grable. "You told me you had a funny feeling at the gas station that night."

"I get a funny feeling when I eat something bad, too," he says sarcastically.

"You said you should have gotten Nina to leave with you in your-rrrr carrrrr," drawls Misty.

Grable's throat quivers as he starts to say something in defense. Misty's eyes land on his. He clears his throat, "Misty, breathe into the mouthpiece. Now."

Misty stamps her heel onto the pavement. "I'm not taking that breathalyzer."

"I will arrest you," Grable insists.

"Fine. Do it," Misty dares.

Grable shakes his head. It's stupid, small town crap like this that wears on his sanity. "I'm calling you an Uber."

"In Derby? Gimme a break," she laughs. "You gonna call Duber?" That was what Darryl Jenkins called his ride service.

"Anyway, he's on a fishing trip." Misty reaches for her door handle.

"Don't do that or I'll have to cuff you."

"Can't you just drive me home?" whines Misty.

"I can call someone to take you home. Who do you want me to call?" Grable reaches for his cell.

"You were on your way out to patrol. Can't you just drop me? I'm only a few blocks away."

"No. Why don't you just walk?"

"In these?" She flings her leg up, placing the point of her stiletto on his car door.

"You're gonna scratch my paintjob!"

The attempt at some sort of sexy move backfires as Misty's foot slips and sends her wobbling backwards. Grable reaches out to keep her from biting the asphalt.

"Hey, Misty. Pull it together."

"Kev, come on. You could've had me home already."

Grable gives up and opens his back door for her. "Get in."

Misty grabs her purse from her passenger seat and locks the car. She squats awkwardly to fit her well-rounded backside into the seat. Grable turns away as her skirt rides up to the point of embarrassment. After a moment, he sees that she's settled in and he starts to close the door. She stops him with her stiletto and looks up at him.

"You're afraid to arrest them, Kev. Just admit it."

He stares at her. "Watch your foot, I'm closing the door now."

Misty tucks herself into the car and curls away from the door. "Okay. Go ahead. It's safe. All arms and legs are inside the vehicle now."

Grable shuts the patrol car door and gets into the driver's seat. He should ask for a raise for having to deal with this kinda chauffer crap. He gets into the car and puts the key into the ignition when Misty pipes up from the back.

"Don't you even want to know what it was?" she says.

"What-what was?" Grable puts it into reverse.

"The murder weapon."

"No."

He doesn't want to have this piece of information added to the mental visualization of the crime that loops itself in his mind when he can't sleep.

But she blurts it out anyway.

Chapter 26

RILEY ST. JAMES

T he next morning I drive to Chicago to see Laura Wriggens, Nina's best friend from high school. The building landscape of the Chicago skyline comes into view as I crest the I90 Skyway overpass that snakes along the grey, grimy industrial shore from Gary into the Windy City. It feels good to be in a big city again. I like how the city looks restful and full of possibility from this distance. I only hope it yields some clue about the night Nina disappeared.

I had spent my entire four-hour drive from Derby to Chicago in silence, thinking about Laura Wriggens. Her name hadn't drawn out any significance the first couple times I saw it. Laura had kinda slipped off the police radar fast. She wasn't with Nina that night. She was never connected to anyone suspected of Nina's death. It wasn't until I put myself in Laura's shoes that I realized how devastating Nina's death would have been to her. Laura was Nina's best friend from childhood.

They had met at church Sunday school and stayed friends through grade school, junior high, and high school. They couldn't have been more opposite. Laura came from a stable, two-parent family of six, upper middle income. She was the happy-go-lucky, blonde, blue-eyed cheerleader type.

A quick Google search and brief phone call had revealed that Laura and her husband live in the Loop, both working as financial investors. I contacted her through her personal email. Yes, Laura thinks about Nina. A lot. Yes. She will answer some questions. Did they have any new leads?

Working on it. I can come to Chicago and meet you in person to speak about it.

Of course, was her instant reply.

The trek into the Loop from the I90 Skyline during the morning rush hour takes me almost two hours. I find the address to the high rise and pull up to the valet.

"Are you here for a guest?" asks a graying, genteel African American valet.

"I am. Laura Wriggens." She hadn't changed her name after she married. For professional reasons, I assume.

"Your name, Miss?"

"Riley St. James."

The valet checks his iPad and finds my name on the register. "Welcome, Ms. St. James. Ms. Wriggens is on the fourteenth floor. Apartment 1407."

I start to turn off the car.

"Keep it running and I'll park it for you."

"Thank you." I'm a touch embarrassed by my lack of gold coast protocol. But hey, it's not every day that I use valet services. I don't run in those circles in Detroit.

The valet hands me a receipt and I wonder if I'm supposed to tip him? He answers my thought with a smile and points me in the direction of the front entrance where a doorman opens the golden gilded front door. Fancy. And to think that Laura's journey took her from the Merry Market in Derby to Michigan Avenue, Chicago. Not a bad climb for a small town gal.

As the elevator doors close, I feel underdressed in my jeans, jacket, and running shoes. I'm soon engaged in an awkward silence with a velvet-suited lift operator who hovers by the buttons so I can't press them myself.

"Which floor, ma'am?" he asks.

"Oh, yeah, fourteenth, please."

Missed protocol again.

I exit the elevator into a sound-proofed hallway and check the placard on the wall that points me left to suites 1400-1410. My fist is about to rap on the door of suite 1407 when Laura opens it with a friendly smile.

The Windy City hasn't stolen Laura's small town charm and she and her husband, Richard, make me feel right at home. I shed my shoes at the door and they hand me a pair of fuzzy slippers that massage my drive-tired feet.

"Can I get you something to drink? Beer? Wine? Gin and tonic?" Richard says showing me into the living room. It's just after lunchtime. Little early for a cocktail, I muse.

"Water, please," I manage to say as my attention is engulfed in the expansive view of the city and lake Michigan spread out across floor to ceiling windows of their open concept condo.

"Sparkling or still?" says Richard.

"Um, sparkling is fine." Richard heads to the kitchen fortress of black marble and stainless steel. It's so spotless and well-stocked. Le Creuset cookware hangs from a wire rack above a butcher block island. I bet they're one of those couples who don't even cook.

"Thank you for driving all the way down here. You know, I would have been happy just to answer your questions over the phone." Laura is wearing the same fuzzy slippers with her pencil skirt and silk blouse.

"I know. But I think talking face to face is more personal. Especially about such a sensitive topic. And let me tell you, this view is worth the drive." I want to make her feel comfortable with me.

"Thank you. We love it. Bought it six years ago. Got tired of commuting from the suburbs."

Richard returns with two glasses of water topped with slices of lemon. And a goblet of red wine for himself. They take a seat on the white leather sofa and I take a seat in the oversized chair with the fur pillows opposite them.

"I'm sorry I have to drag you through all of this again," I start.

"It's okay. My Mom says the whole town is talking about you and how you're going to break this case and finally put those Newton twins behind bars."

"I'm trying my best," I say.

"That's all I've ever wanted for Nina, so I'm happy to help."

I take a sip of the cool, lemony water. It's silky and refreshing. Geez, even their water has expensive taste.

"Do you have some new evidence? I mean, there have been a lot of advances in DNA since 1989. Did something new show up?"

"Unfortunately, not. I… we… are trying to just go over the statements again. Fresh eyes."

"Doesn't sound like a lot to go on," Richard says.

"If you don't mind, I'll just dive right in. I've read through your statement. Several times," I say.

"Yes, and I reread what you sent me. My statement that is. I sound like such an idiot."

"You were seventeen. I'm sure it was kind of scary."

"I was scared shitless," she takes a sip of her drink.

"How does the statement look to you? Is it how you recalled the events of that night?" I ask her.

"Yes. I'd say everything is exactly how I remembered it. Except… I got to thinking more about that night…"

"Oh?"

"I don't know. Maybe I didn't say it? Or maybe they didn't write it down? I don't know why it's not there. But the thing is, I remember I went to Nina's house a third time that night."

"You did?" Immediately I think of Ray and the issue of legend.

"Yes, I did."

"After the twelve-thirty visit?"

"Yes. I dropped off my friend at her house and then I went home. But I couldn't sleep. I wanted Nina to get that job so badly. So, I got up and drove back to her house to leave her a note to come to the market at nine the next morning."

"Okay. Do you remember what time that was?"

"Yes. I left my house just before two am. I remember looking at my alarm clock and thinking I only had a few hours before I had to be up and at work at eight."

I nod. "And what did you find when you got to Nina's house?"

"Same things. Dark. Dog barking. Door unlocked. But no signs of Nina."

"She wasn't home. You're sure?"

"I'm sure because I was shouting for her and pounding on the door and the neighbor lady stuck her head out the window and told me to shut up."

That's odd. In all the statements given from Silas and Solomon, they claim they dropped Nina at her home around 12:30 a.m. If that were true, she should have been home. She would have heard her best friend knocking and shouting, Tucker barking, and a neighbor lady yelling.

"So, the third time you went to Nina's house was two a.m.?" I clarify.

"Yes."

"And she wasn't there."

"No. I'm positive."

"She wasn't sleeping?"

"I finally went inside and up to her room. She wasn't there."

"She wasn't sleeping on the living room couch? Or--"

"No! Those monsters had her out there in the woods. I know they did."

Laura chokes up on her words and rises from the couch. She crosses to the window, taking small sips of her lemon water as she composes herself. Richard rises from the couch and takes her glass to the kitchen to top it off.

"So, you went to Nina's three times that night." I have to be 100 percent certain I am understanding Laura's statement. This will definitely be questioned in court.

Laura nods.

"Any idea why you only thought of that recently?" I ask with a touch of scrutiny.

"I don't know. I didn't mean to. I did my best to remember when the cops questioned me. I don't know... I was seventeen... I guess I just didn't remember. And I was... sad.... And scared."

Sad I understand. "Scared. What of?"

"Maybe that... that I would be next," she says.

"Were you afraid they would go after you?"

"They knew I was friends with Nina. Solomon had even asked me out once."

"He did?"

"I said no," Laura snaps.

"And you're sure you're remembering the timeline correctly now?"

"I am positive. I remember because the third time I went alone. And that lady yelled at me."

"Are you willing to testify to this?"

Laura nods.

Those monsters had concocted an alibi. A shared story. And they had stuck to it solid and steadfast. For thirty years. No one had been able to challenge it. But this... this small detail was significant. The issue of a legend was proving fruitful. A crack in the code of silence.

"I wish I could've done something to help her," Laura says turning to me and looking more like the sorry seventeen year-old Merry Market cashier of Derby, than the forty-seven year old financial princess of Michigan Avenue.

"You just did," I tell her.

You just did.

Chapter 27

JACOB

Later that evening outside of Derby on a dirt paved country road, Jacob Zachary was sitting on his front porch of his weathered country cottage drinking canned beer when Silas's black Ford 150 pulled up. Being an old, frail, half-crippled Vietnam veteran, Jacob felt no compulsion to stand and greet the twins as they got out. He waited until they met him on his porch and he offered them a seat.

"How ya holding up, Uncle Jacob?" Solomon said.

"Good days, bad days." Jacob squinted his eyes from behind his thick glasses and their forms came into focus.

"How's today?" asked Solomon.

"Somewhere in between. Leg's bothering me," he said.

"Maybe you need a little something to relax it," said Silas.

Behind them the screen door, half off its hinges, creaked open and Genny Zachery, Jacob's wife, stood there with a sour, wrinkled look. She was their aunt by second marriage.

"Boys. Haven't seen you for a while," she said, drying a ceramic bowl with a tattered dish towel.

"Hi, Aunt Gen," said Solomon.

"You two doing okay? You drive all the way out here for something specific?" asked Genny with a wry eye scanning them up and down.

Solomon looked to Silas. Silas shook his head. "Just wanted to catch up," said Silas.

"You in trouble?" Genny pressed.

"No, no, Aunt Gen. We ain't in no trouble. Can't two nephews come visit their aunt and uncle?"

"How late ya stayin'?" She didn't pull her focus off them for a second.

"It don't matter. Stay as long as you want," said Jacob. "Genny, let 'em alone and grab two more beers, will ya, hon?"

"Grab 'em yourself, boys. I ain't no one's slave around here." She stepped back inside, letting the screen door slap the frame.

"Well, you heard her. Go on, help yourselves," said Jacob.

"Nah, it's okay," said Silas reaching into his shirt pocket for a large joint. He lit the butt, took a long drag to feed it, and passed it to his uncle.

"Been a while since I did this," Jacob said.

"It's medicinal quality. Take the pains out of those old limbs," Silas said. Jacob drew in a long sip of the sweet plant. Solomon went next. They lay silent, passing the blunt back and forth. There was no one to spot them down Jacob's long driveway out of view from any roads or neighbors. Then he remembered, it didn't matter now. The state had legalized the drug last year.

The spring evening capped a slight chill as a breeze blew up across the pond and caused Jacob to shiver. He had less flesh on his bones now and his diabetes always interfered with the way his body regulated temperature.

"So, how's your ma doing these days?" said Jacob.

"She's okay. She misses the old man," said Solomon about their deceased father.

Jacob nodded, his leg feeling the first relief it had in over a month. "Where'd you say you got this stuff?"

"Didn't," said Silas. "Is it working?"

"Like a lube on a tire chain," said Jacob.

"We can bring you more," said Solomon.

"Maybe it's not a bad idea," said Jacob.

"You will not," Aunt Gen hollered out the door.

"If you want to be part of the conversation, we can pull up a chair." Jacob smiled at the shadowed figure behind the screen.

"You're stinking up my house with that skunk smoke," she said.

"Shut the door then," Jacob called out.

"You boys don't stay too long now," Genny added.

Her clunky footsteps made their way to the back of the house before Jacob spoke again. "What else is new? You boys working?"

"We're good. We got work here and there," said Solomon.

"How are the kids, Si?"

"I got one in college and one ready to go to college, if you can believe that," said Silas.

"Must be his mother's genes," Jacob said with a chuckle.

"Got that right. I told him I wouldn't pay a dime for that waste of an education when he could get a good job and start earning his keep. My daughter's in high school. Don't see too much of her though. She's just busy. Into everything, drama, Spanish club, sports. Shit like that."

"Keeps her off the streets, huh?" said Jacob. "You ever see your son, Solomon?"

"When Wendy's in a good mood," said Solomon. "Which ain't often."

"How old's he now?" asked Jacob.

"Eleven. I think. Maybe gonna be. I dunno. She reminds me when it's his birthday," said Solomon.

Jacob was not surprised by this. His nephews did not fall far from the tree. His sister had married beneath her and spawned three children with their father's malfeasant genes. Over the years he tried to help them in whatever ways he was able. He didn't have much but when they needed something, they could always come to Uncle Jacob. Jacob wondered what they needed tonight and why they needed to get him stoned to ask for it?

Three decades of drug use had built up his tolerance. This must be some fine weed. His body and mind were pleasantly relaxed and his thoughts swirled around until they landed on something he had heard when he was getting groceries in town a few weeks ago. Before he could stop his honeyed tongue from oozing out the words, he said, "You boys hear about that detective they brought up from Detroit to help find the guy who killed Nina Laramie?"

Jacob saw Solomon shoot a stiff glance at Silas.

"No, I don't think we heard anything about that," said Silas, refusing to return his twins' look.

"It's a girl detective, I heard," said Jacob.

"Yeah, I heard about it. Some woman. Thinks she's hot shit," said Solomon, rubbing his hands along the top of his thighs as Silas continued to launch a glare at him.

"You think they'll find the guy?" said Jacob.

"It's been a long time ago," said Silas.

Solomon answered under his brother's guided eye, "I don't think they got anything on the ones that did it."

"The ones?" said Jacob.

"The guy," said Solomon.

"Was that detective bothering you for something?" said Silas.

"No." Jacob realized it was a mistake to bring it up.

"Did she come around here?" asked Solomon.

"Now, why would she do that?" interrupted Silas.

With his sixth drag on the sweet bud, Jacob could feel the stone being rolled away from the tomb of his ancient memories. "Maybe 'cause you was with that girl the night she was killed," the words stopped like a boulder at the twins' feet.

"We were never bothered about all that," said Silas.

"Why you bringing this up?" said Solomon.

"No reason."

"Musta been a reason or you wouldn't've brought it up," said Silas.

"I just remember you talking about that girl. I know one of you boys liked her."

"You do any fishing yet since that pond thawed?" said Silas, changing the subject.

"We barely knew her," said Solomon.

"You said you thought she was pretty," said Jacob, remembering the two of them sitting around his kitchen table as young lads, drunk and high.

"We didn't say that," said Silas.

"You did. Right there in my kitchen." He was in it thick now and the words flowed from thoughts he hadn't seen in thirty years.

"I think you remember wrong," said Silas, his voice taking an edge.

"When did we say that?" said Solomon.

"It was right after those cops found her body. You came over to do some huntin' on my property and afterwards you sat in my kitchen half the night drinking and you was acting all nervous and I asked you were ya high or something and you said, Silas, you said you didn't wanna talk none about it."

"You got us mixed up with someone else," said Silas. "Or maybe it was the weed?"

"I know my memory ain't perfect, but it was you two. I came into the kitchen and asked y'all if there was anything you needed to unload and you said, Solomon-- you said, 'I think we're in the clear. They don't got nothing on us.'"

"Because we weren't involved," said Silas.

"Yeah, I mean, I remember being here, but you were in the other room watching TV," said Solomon, oblivious to the daggered look propelled his way.

"The more you drank, the louder you got," said Jacob.

Silas's voice rose. "What's your point here? We just came over to smoke a joint with you. Why you razzin' us?"

"I just... I've always been bothered by something you said that night. And now with all this coming back around..." Jacob's voice drifted and he pursed his lips tight.

"What is it? What did we do that night?" Silas leaned forward and bore a dark look into his Uncle's eyes that frightened Jacob. "You were stoned, old man. You don't remember shit."

Jacob glanced out over his greening property. The two-track driveway was slick with mud from the thawing ground. He hadn't had his old clunker running for a week and the sphere of oil under the engine was widening. Jacob knew he wasn't quick or agile. His nephews were big and strong and young. And it was never far from his mind that Silas had been arrested and served a six-year sentence for rape.

It wasn't worth the fight, he thought and smiled at his nephews.

"Perhaps you're right," said Jacob. "The doctor at the veteran's clinic tells me I got a thirty percent memory loss."

"And the disability checks to prove it," said Genny, from behind the screen. "It's gettin' late, boys. Make sure you get home safely now."

Jacob was grateful for her eavesdropping at that moment. "Aunt Genny's right. I gotta be getting inside now."

Genny stepped out onto the porch next to her husband and the boys took their cue to say goodnight. They slapped old Jacob on the shoulder and Silas bent over him and whispered in his good ear, "You keep to yourself now, old man."

They took off down the stoop and Jacob watched them get into their truck and pull out. His eyes never left their trail until the red and white taillights from their Ford went out of view. Taking a seat next to her husband of forty-one years, on the wooden rocker love seat, Genny's short legs didn't touch the porch floor as Jacob gently rocked them. Coral sky faded into dark, forest green.

Jacob turned to Genny. "I know what I heard. Silas said, 'she shoulda given us what we wanted and we wouldn't of hit her so hard.'"

"You remembered it correctly," Genny said, pointing to the first twinkle in the dark sky above them. "And you took it to Detective

Polland, but he wouldn't believe you 'cause you had alcohol on your breath."

Jacob nodded. "What difference would it have made? The cops had already cleared them at that point."

"There's no physical evidence to connect them to that girl's death," said Genny. "Let's leave it alone."

"It bothers me, Genny. All these years... no amount of pot can scrub that conversation from my memory."

"You want to go stirring things up in this family?" asked Genny. Jacob gave his answer as he reached for her chapped hand and squeezed. He didn't mean to stir anything up. It's just that their Heidi had been ripped from them by a drunk driver when she was nineteen. And he understood a piece of Jim Laramie's suffering.

"Nothing you say can or will bring that girl back," said Genny placing her other hand atop Jacob's as she rested her thin, white-haired head on his shoulder.

Jacob didn't know if she was talking about Nina or Heidi.

Chapter 28

GRABLE

G rable is at his desk the next morning trolling Misty Beckett's Facebook feed when Riley phones to tell him about her conversation with Laura Wriggens. He adds the note to her file. He admits it's an interesting addendum, but there's not much they can do with it at the moment. Alone, it's not enough to make an arrest or build a whole case on. He can hear Riley's frustration over the phone. But there's no way he's going to bring those twins in based on revised statements by Laura. And yes, he has located the woman who lived across the street. She died years ago. She gave no statement at the time.

He hangs up and scans a conversation at Pub Griffin overheard during the weekend that Misty had posted on her "Who Killed Nina Laramie?" Facebook page: *Silas admits he had murder weapon! When will Grable and that sassy red headed detective get a clue and arrest these assholes? Justice for Nina!!*

There are a few clapbacks posted:

How do you know they were telling the truth? They lie all the time. Don't be so gullible.

Silas jerks off to the attention. It's like Viagra for him.

Derby legend. S&S are innocent! Get a new hobby!

There is one that makes Grable pause.

Reina K.: Sounds kinda like that time at our bonfire party.

What time at what bonfire party? Grable dials up Reina King at the farm house. She has just gotten the kids off to school and is catching up on paperwork. Sure, he can come over. She'll put a fresh pot of coffee on.

Grable pulls up to Reina's 200 acre five-generation family farm. She and her husband are doing well for themselves with their asparagus crops, small dairy, and chickens. They have hired a farm hand and small staff. They run a farm stand where Reina makes fresh baked breads and pastries and on the weekends in the summer, they host the largest farmer's market in the county on their expansive, several acre, front lawn.

Reina wears a long bob and a touch of coral lip gloss. She has a fresh loaf of sourdough waiting for him. They sit at the kitchen table making small talk of local gossip while the coffee finishes brewing. She places a locally handcrafted ceramic mug in front of him and fills it. Grable smooths soft churned butter onto a piece of warm sourdough.

"Heard you've got some state girl cop over there now working on Nina's case. What's she like?"

"Hard worker. Kinda private." The bread melts in Grable's mouth.

"She find anything interesting yet?" says Reina.

"Too early to say," Grable mumbles with bread melting in his mouth. Fresh bread was love. Pure love.

"Seems like that well's kinda dry, isn't it?"

"She's a fresh pair of eyes."

"Why now?" says Reina.

The coffee gurgles its last drops. Reina pulls the pot from the burner and pours Grable a mug.

"I think it all started with the exhuming." Grable reaches for another slice of bread.

"Awful to get Jim's hopes up again," says Reina.

Grable nods. "I was on Misty's page and your comment had me wondering."

"The one about the bonfire?"

"Yeah. I don't remember that bonfire," says Grable.

"You wouldn't. You weren't there."

"When was it?"

"Couple summer's ago. Three maybe. At our annual pig roast," says Reina.

"I usually get an invite."

"You did. You were out of town on some fishing trip."

He remembered the fishing trip, not the invitation.

She pushes the butter dish to him so he can slice off a slab. It melts as he spreads it over a third slice of warm bread.

"I didn't know you and Dale were friends with the twins?" he says, referring to her husband.

"We're not. They crashed the party. Drunk. Stoned. Big surprise. I was inside taking the youngest to the bathroom when I looked up through that kitchen window. There they were standing out by the fire pit with about half a dozen of our friends. Not a good scene. They were antagonizing Misty and her friends. I looked around for Dale but didn't see him in the yard."

"That doesn't sound good," says Grable, disappointment sweeping his face as he pops the last bit of bread into his mouth.

"I ran out to try to simmer things down and ask them to leave. Misty and a couple other girls had also stepped in to try to coax them to leave. The twins were being really belligerent and they started pushing Misty around. I yelled for Dale and the guys. And they came running from the barn to break it up."

"Did they hurt Misty?"

"I think they would have if Dale and the guys hadn't showed up when they did." Reina rises from the table.

"What started it?" says Grable.

"Misty verbally attacked Silas."

Autumn Flame Misty starting fires. "What did she say?" Grable washes down the bread with swig of coffee.

"I don't know for sure. I wasn't close enough to hear. But later someone told me that Misty got upset because Silas was bragging to some of the guys about what they did to Nina."

"What was that?" says Grable.

"That he and Solomon took her out to the woods and when she tried to get away they chased her with the car and knocked her down. Then they took turns having sex with her."

"You sure?" His gut twists.

"Don't be so clueless, Kev," she tops off his mug. "You've heard the rumors over the years."

"Didn't anyone report this to the police?" He raises his voice, not meaning to. He's just so frustrated with the secrecy.

"What would you or anyone in your department have done?" she challenges.

"At least file a report. Add it to the record," he pleads.

"Only to stir up the hornet's nest. No, thank you."

Grable looks at Reina and she stared back unwavering. "Most of us have children and we don't trust the Newtons. You get what I'm saying?"

"Are you and Dale afraid of them?"

"No... I don't know. We just... none of us want to have to put ourselves in a position where we would have to take... action."

"Action? Reina?" Grable pins her with a look. "What do you mean?"

But she dismisses him by getting up from the table and opening a kitchen drawer for some parchment paper. She begins to wrap the bread. Grable had no idea the code of silence extended this deeply, this seriously. Even amongst his own friends. Or who he thought were his friends anyhow.

"You'd all rather let two killers run loose than do the right thing?" says Grable.

"Who are you to talk?" she digs.

"Reina, don't put that on me. I already paid for all that when I promised to stick around to serve and protect this place the rest of my life."

"No one asked you for your cheap heroism."

It was a low blow and Grable had to bite back bitter words. "I have always done exactly what I can under the law."

"Under the excuse of the law," she murmurs shaking her head with a wry smile.

"What do you want from me? What do any of you want? I'm not the enemy."

"Please don't drag us into this re-investigation, Kev. Don't rock our boat. Business is going well. Our family's doing good. We're happy right now," says Reina handing him a long look and the rest of the loaf wrapped in parchment paper. "I'll make sure you get invited to the next pig roast. You're always welcome at our home for social purposes."

Grable took the bread, still warm in his palms. And now he knew what they all really thought of him. A coward.

Chapter 29

NINA, 1989

W hen Dad took the night shift at work, I told him that I didn't like being home alone at night and that I wanted a dog. I begged him for a full year and a half. Dad never budged. Then, after my high school graduation, Adam gave me Tucker. He got him from the shelter. Tucker was six months old when he came to live with us. What could Dad say? He came around to the idea that maybe having a dog would teach me responsibility he thought I needed.

Dad made me promise to do all the feeding, cleaning, and house breaking and in exchange he would buy the dog food and let Tucker stay in the house instead of a pen in the back yard. Neither of us had ever owned a dog before and we didn't know the first thing about how to train Tucker. My cousin gave us a lot of tips. She had three dogs.

At first, Dad barely tolerated Tucker and cursed at him when Tucker was under foot. Tucker loved to curl up in Dad's favorite chair. Dad would shoo him out, sit down, grab the remote control and find Tucker bouncing up on his lap insistent on taking a nap with him. It wasn't long before Tucker's silky golden fur and puppy breath won him over. Sometimes I would even find Dad and Tucker napping in the chair together.

My last day on earth I took Tucker for a walk around the neighborhood. He wasn't very good on the leash, but I was trying to train him like my cousin taught me. Making him stop at my side, walk on my left, and keep his attention focused away from chasing the squirrels.

Later that night when I was getting ready to go out, Tucker kept running circles around my legs. I nearly tripped over him a couple times. He took a pee on the floor in the hallway and when Dad got up to shower, he nearly stepped in the puddle. I cleaned up the mess while Dad bellyached about getting me the dog in the first place and why wasn't I training him better, and maybe he should bring him back to the shelter or send him to live with Adam. Empty threats. Dad was always cranky when he woke up.

After Dad left for work, Tucker kept acting restless and agitated. He raced around the house. Barked to be let out. Raced around the yard and demanded to come back in. He was stuck to my side wherever I went in the house.

I remembered something Mom told me about the animal kingdom having highly perceptive spirits flowing through them. They have premonitions about things that we can't see or feel. Like if there's going to be a storm or a natural disaster. They know way before we do. I check the weather forecast. Was there supposed to be a thunderstorm?

No. Dry as a bone for the next week. Which is odd for summer in Michigan. We usually get rain at least once a week. But what does the weatherman know? Michigan's weather turns on a dime. Maybe Tucker's radar was better.

Before I left, I tried to lock Tucker into the laundry room, but kept whining and whimpering. Finally, I let him out and put fresh blankets on his bed in the living room and tried to get him to lay down. I assured Tucker I would be home later that night before the storm started (if there even was one). As I knelt down to settle him in, he put both paws on my shoulders like he was hugging me and sent his tongue across my whole face. I pushed him off, but he did it again. And again. Finally, I just gave into it and hugged him back, letting him lick my ears and my neck until it was wet and I had to use a towel to dry off. He followed me to the front door when I left. I could hear him scratching and whining to get out, to come find me. As I dashed down the sidewalk, I yelled over my shoulder, "Stop it, Tucker! Go to your bed."

But I could hear him barking three blocks away as I walked to Argo.

There was no storm that night. Or for the next two weeks. We were in a mid-summer drought, as it turned out.

Tucker was trying to warn me not to go out. Trying to get me to stay home with him. Where I would be safe. I think, maybe he knew if I left, I wouldn't be back... or maybe he was trying to say goodbye.

Chapter 30

TAMMY

Misty Beckett didn't have to knock on Tammy Tyler's back door. She just went in. They had a standing coffee date every Thursday morning. Tammy and Misty had been friends since junior high, went separate ways in high school, and then reconnected in their late twenties when Misty moved back to Derby. Misty had never married. It was more fun to play the field. Though the fields were sparse pickings these days. Tammy was recently divorced with two kids in high school.

"Did you see the posts today?" said Misty setting a bag of donuts on Tammy's coffee table.

"You know I don't go on Facebook," said Tammy, the introvert of the pair who hated social media and barely checked her email.

"There's been a lot of activity now that that new detective is on the case. You should check it out. Besides, I heard she went to the Hole in the Woods to scout the murder scene and fainted!"

"How'd you hear that?" said Tammy.

"I've got my eyes around town. Besides, Grable was at her house. I think they're sleeping together," said Misty.

"Good for them. Grable probably could use it." Tammy opened the bag of donuts and selected one with sprinkles. "Why did they go to the Hole in the Woods?"

Misty gave Tammy an astonished look. "Cause that's where it happened. Hello!?"

"No, it didn't."

"Tammy, it did. What are you talking about?"

"No. They found that girl in the Oconee National Forest. That's like two hours north of here." Tammy polished off her donut and peeked into the bag, breaking a chocolate covered cake donut in half.

Misty shook her head. Was she talking to a deaf and dumb person? "Where have you been? Seriously, I've only been talking about this literally forever. The Hole in the Woods is in the Oconee National Forest."

"What? No, it's not."

"Yes, it is. The forest extends from the north, near the tip of the mitten, all the way down state through parts of Derby and south past Brantwood. It's a huge mass of land. Hundreds of miles." Misty selected a cinnamon twist and dipped it into her coffee mug.

"Okay. Geez. So, I'm not as smart as you. I didn't know the national forest land came down to Derby." Tammy passed the other half of the chocolate donut to Misty.

"How could you not know? I mean… you've lived here all your life and you didn't know our woods were part of the larger chain of the Oconee National Forest?"

Tammy shrugged as a pain pinched the pit of her stomach. "I'm bad with geography."

"Okay, whatever, the point is, we're actually making real progress on Nina's case," said Misty.

"We?"

"I'm helping the police. Well, trying to. I told Grable what I heard about the murder weapon. But he couldn't have given two shits. So typical. I'm gonna need to talk to that lady detective instead."

"What's her name?" said Tammy.

"Riley St. James. She's from Detroit. And she's really cute. I can see why Grable wants to doink her."

"Yeah. Maybe talk to her," said Tammy feeling a rumble in her gut.

Misty took a second donut and looked at Tammy who had a pained look growing on her.

"You okay?" said Misty.

Tammy shook her head. "Stomachache. Maybe it's this stuff." Tammy smelled the coffee creamer container. "Disgusting. Does this smell to you?"

"How could it go bad? They put so many chemicals in it," Misty said.

"Shouldn't be. I just bought this." Tammy rubbed her belly hoping it would calm down.

"I'm not smelling it." Misty put her hand up.

Tammy smelled it. It smelled okay. She poured a little more into her coffee.

"I still don't understand you, Tammy Tyler. How could you not know that was Nina's murder site when you used to go up in the Hole in the Woods all the time two-tracking that summer. With that guy—"

"My neighbor."

"Yeah. Isn't it strange how you, like, never saw anything, you know? Or smelled the body."

"Can we talk about something else?" A sharp pain jabbed Tammy in the ribs.

Misty stayed another half hour polishing off the donuts and jabbering on about her kids, her lame boss, her overly-curious neighbor who installed cameras pointed at Misty's driveway, and her disappointment that she couldn't get some stupid guy at Pub Griffin to take her home last night. Meanwhile, Tammy grew grey in the face and her stomach felt like a washing machine wringer.

"It probably was that creamer," said Misty. "You shouldn't have added more."

"I'll just take an Alka-Seltzer and lie down," said Tammy.

But instead, Tammy paced the kitchen until Misty had driven away. Then, she reached for an old county map stuffed in a junk drawer. She scanned it until she found the green shaded area of the Oconee National Forest. The Hole in the Woods was dropped smack dab in the center of forested area. Her stomach curdled and churned.

She reached her phone and scrolled through her contacts, stopping at: NORTHERN MICHIGAN CORRECTIONAL FACILITY. She pressed send and waited to be connected to an inmate there.

After a ten minute wait, a gruff voice said "Who's this?" into the receiver.

"Wallace? Hey, it's Tammy Tyler."

The other end of the line is silent.

"You there?" she asked.

"Yeah. What do you want?" said Wallace.

Tammy realized this was a bad idea.

"I know it's been a while... sorry, I've been... how are you?"

"Living the dream." He was all snark. Just like he was at nineteen.

Tammy felt the strength drain from her legs as she melted into her armchair in the living room.

"Did you know Oconee forest is down here, in Derby?" she said.

"You called me for a geography lesson?"

"No... no... it's just I always thought Oconee was just up north. By where you are. I didn't realize it was so big? Do you know what I mean?"

"It's a big fucking forest. So what?" he said.

She drew in a shallow breath and the pain pinged her gut.

"Remember that time we went there?" she asked him, hushing her voice, although she didn't know why because she was alone.

"I went there a lot. Look, Tam, I'm not sure why you called or what you're getting at, but you've only got five seconds left before I'm gonna hang up."

"No, but I mean, that one time… that night when…"

More silence on the other end.

"I gotta go," he said.

She heard the line click.

A flood of disturbing memories fought their way into Tammy's mind. She pushed them away. Maybe she should tell Misty. Misty would know what to do. Tammy tried to dial Misty's number, but her hands were shaking so much that she dropped the phone. No, she couldn't tell Misty. Misty was a blabbermouth. It would end up all over Facebook. What was she thinking? She was alone in this. Alone with Wallace who said he would kill her if she ever mentioned it.

Tammy rushed to the kitchen sink. Coffee and donuts were on their way back up.

Chapter 31

RILEY ST. JAMES

After the visit with Laura, I take a day in Chicago to sight see but Nina's case has me distracted the whole time. I wake up early the next morning to avoid rush hour traffic out of the city and drive to Canton, Ohio, to speak with Adam Larkin, Nina's boyfriend at the time of her death. He's not a suspect, but I want to know his understanding of the sequence of events surrounding Nina's death. And if he knew the Newtons.

When I arrive around 2:30 a.m., Adam's wife has already left for work. His youngest daughter, a high school sophomore, is getting picked up for school as I park in front of their home situated in a cul-de-sac.

Adam, now a building contractor, has done nicely for himself. A Wife. Two story home. Two daughters, one in college, one in high school. And a four-car garage. His life blends in perfectly with his

Midwest setting. No one will ever guess the hell he has been through before he exchanged it for this calmer chapter of his life.

He welcomes me with a fresh pot of coffee and a coffee mug crafted cleverly in the shape of one of those red paving bricks.

"When my oldest, Katy, turned eighteen, I thought about Nina a lot. As hard as I tried not to, I couldn't imagine what she must have gone through in those final hours," his eyes draw inward and he gets locked in that place for a moment. I know that place. And I leave him in that place, waiting for his return when he's ready. After some silence, he says, "If that ever happened to Katy... I don't know that I could survive it. I'd probably die of a heart attack. Or kill the bastard who did it and end up in prison for the rest of my life."

I know he wouldn't really. It's just something we all say. We dream revenge dreams.

I point out that he has already survived it.

"Just barely," Adam says retreating again into the dark recesses of his thoughts.

"I'm sure it was difficult being so far away when it happened."

"I felt immensely helpless."

"How did you get through it?" I ask.

"My boss gave me a month off at my new job to help Jim search. Every day. Every single day... I think I knew after a week that she wasn't coming home," says Adam.

"You did? What told you that?" I ask.

"If she had run away, she would have called me. She would have let me know where she was. We were close. We talked a couple times a day."

I nod. There is nothing I can say, even thirty years later, to ease that type of suffering.

"Why do you think she got in the car with Silas and Solomon?" I say.

He winces at their names.

"Nina had a small town view of the world. Nina could be naive. She trusted everyone."

"What do you mean?" I am thinking about Grable's comment that Nina walked into the path of evil.

"I don't think she realized what she was doing hopping in that car with them. They were Rich's cousins. She had known Rich since grade school."

"She trusted them."

"Because she trusted Rich," he says.

"Do you think they forced her?" I ask.

"Not at first. I think she went willingly."

"Do you think she flirted with them?"

He shrugs. "Maybe. I don't know. Nina was friendly. They may have misinterpreted that."

In the end Adam doesn't really have much to offer, investigation-wise. Maybe it's cathartic to talk about it after all these years? Maybe it just stirs everything up again in him? It's hard to tell by the calm way he answers my questions and talks about Nina. His first love. The girl he was going to marry.

"I'm sorry to have to bring this all up again," I tell him as he sees me out to my truck. "I appreciate your time and if anything else comes to mind, please let me know." I hand him my business card.

"Can I ask you something?" Adam says.

"Of course."

"Is there any hope of connecting those brothers to her murder?"

I am still not sure. Laura's new testimony was helpful. But nothing to hang a case on. I try to offer Adam an encouraging smile. He sees right through it.

"It's okay. I know you're trying," he says with a lilt in his tone. "You're the first person since Polland gave up who is trying. Good luck. Drive safely."

I erase the smile from my face as Adam turns around and heads up his driveway. He disappears into the house with shoulders slumped. The door closes quietly behind him.

Don't get me wrong. I'm sure his wife is lovely. I'm sure they are in love and fully committed to one another. But I wonder how many times over the last two decades has it passed his mind that this is the life he and Nina should have shared.

Chapter 32

NINA, 1989

I walked three blocks from my house to the Argo gas station. This girl Alyson from school was already there and high. She offered me a joint. I had already smoked earlier that afternoon with Laura before she went into work and didn't feel like it. Alyson said she wanted to get something to eat. The munchies were kicking in. I had spaghetti with dad, but snacks sounded good. We went inside the quickie mart. I bought a large bag of chips and a package of Chips Ahoy. When we came out Brad and Rich were there. Kevin Grable was just pulling up in his Chevette that shot out a plume of black exhaust from his rusted-out muffler. I waved the gas fumes from my face.

"What's he doing here?" asked Alyson.

I wondered the same thing. Grable didn't usually hang around our crowd. A lot of kids from school, including his regular friends, were out of town on vacation.

"He wanted to come," said Brad. Brad and I had been friends since pre-school.

"You're a dork," said Alyson. "He doesn't belong here."

Grable got out of his car and sauntered up. He started to say hello when a deafening engine roar mounted our conversation. A green Mustang pulled up and Rich ran over.

The rest of us followed curiously. "Guys, these are my cousins, Silas and Solomon. They live in Greendale," said Rich.

"Where's that?" I asked eyeing the driver, Silas.

"About an hour south of here," said Solomon from the passenger seat.

"You don't get out much, do you?" said Silas.

I didn't. And I didn't like that I had showed it or that they had pointed it out. I glared at them noticing how much they look alike.

"You guys twins?" Alyson stole the question from my lips.

"Yeah. Two for the price of one." Silas laughed and revved the engine. So cocky. I'm naturally attracted to cocky bad boys. Except Adam. Well, not completely true. He was cocky until I got to know him. Some people still think he's cocky. They just don't know him. Besides, most people just judge you by what they hear and never give you another chance.

"What's going on?" asked Silas looking at Rich.

"Just hanging," said Rich.

"And eating Chips Ahoy?" Solomon joked when he saw me clutching my cookies. I smiled a little. He was kinda cute.

"Why don't you guys park it and join us?" said Grable in his nerdy way.

"Looks lame," said Silas. "Let's get out of here and have some fun."

Alyson reached for Brad's hand. They had been dating off and on since graduation. "Thanks. We're good here."

"Come on, Alyson. I didn't drive all the way up here for my health. You know why I'm here," said Silas.

"What the hell are you talking about?" Brad snapped his head in Alyson's direction. "How the hell does he know your name?"

"I met him once at Rich's house."

"Once when?" Brad demanded and let go of her hand. I could feel the heat in the group go up about a hundred degrees. Brad had a temper and a full load of testosterone.

"Couple weeks ago, wasn't it?" said Silas.

"Yeah, couple weeks ago," Solomon added.

"Why didn't you tell me?" said Brad. He took a step towards the Mustang and Grable went in between them. "Nothing happened," said Rich. "I was there."

"That's right. Nothing happened, Brad," said Solomon. "That you need to know about."

Silas grinned at Alyson. "You look good. I like that top." Alyson jerked back towards me, almost knocking me down. The bag of chips went flying to the ground, and as I was trying to regain my balance I crushed them. Pop. Crunch. Ruined.

"Alyson!" I wasn't on her side right now. "You owe me a new bag of chips."

Brad was getting ready to lay into Silas right through the driver's side window when Grable intercepted and shoved him out of the way. Silas revved his engine and squealed across the parking lot.

"Come on. Let's go," called Solomon. "You. Chips Ahoy girl. We got room."

Before I could answer Grable butted in and said I was riding with them.

Rich was walking Brad and Alyson to his Pontiac LeMans.

"There's no room. We can't fit five in there," I said.

Grable tried again. "We'll take mine."

I didn't want to go with him. Bo-ring! But Brad, Rich and Alyson were already pulling out of the Argo. I shrugged and walked over to his rusted out Chevette and got into the passenger seat. Grable put his key in the ignition.

"Crap," he said.

"What?" I ask impatiently.

"It's on E."

Stupid Grable!

"We're at a gas station. Hurry up."

"I don't have any cash." His face flushes.

"Well, I just spent my last five on snacks. So, I guess we're riding with the twins."

I got out of the Chevette and walked to the Newton's Mustang. Silas opened the door and smiled at me.

"Nina. Hey, you have beautiful eyes. You know that?" He had been paying attention and knew my name.

"You can squeeze in here," said Solomon as he pried the front seat forward to let me into the back. They smell like cologne and my stomach flutters.

They were both so cute.

Chapter 33

GRABLE

G rable sits at his desk reviewing paperwork when St. James arrives at the station. He mumbles a hello and she doesn't respond. After a minute, he follows her into her office.

Grable notices the circles under her eyes are a shade darker than when she left Derby three days ago. It's getting to her and she doesn't seem like the kind of person who has a good outlet for the pressure. Does she have friends? Hobbies? Does she work out? Drink? A pet might help.

"You need some fresh air," he says.

"I need sleep," she answers.

"So go home. Get some," he says.

"Can't sleep."

"You got anything going on the rest of the day?"

She shakes her head. "Just spinning theories."

"Let's go."

"Huh? Where?"

"Just grab your jacket." He stands up and waits for her to gather her things. "I'll drive."

She leaves her office and Grable follows, holding the door for her as they exit the police station.

"Is this a burger trip?" she asks.

"No. Unless you're hungry."

"Are we going to a scene?"

"Nope."

"You have a lead on something?"

"I wish."

She heads to the parking towards his truck. "This way first," he guides her.

"You're taking me fishing, aren't you?"

"That okay?"

"I'm too tired to argue."

"It'll help clear your mind."

Grable leads them three blocks to the bait shop and selects a few new lures. He glances to St. James and sees her looming over the beef jerky counter.

"Made here in Derby County," he notes proudly.

"Yeah? How does the bison one taste?"

Grable gets the clerk's attention. "Half a pound of bison. Half pound sweet BBQ. And half pound turkey. Please."

He pays for everything and they head to his truck. He opens the passenger door for her and she slides in. He hands her the bag of jerky and closes the door. She takes a bison stick, gnawing off one end of it.

Seventeen miles later they are at the Grand Gorge River, which comes into the northern most part of Derby County and cuts a large gorge diagonally through the hilly terrain, eventually arriving thirty miles down-river into the big lake. Lake Michigan. Grable's been fishing here all his life. He knows these woods and he knows the flow patterns of the river. It's been a rainy year and the river is running fast and strong. Get caught in the undercurrent and you're a gonner.

After they park, he walks them up river along the bank about a hundred yards to a small inlet where the current isn't as severe. He unpacks their gear and hands her a pair of waders.

"You'll want to put these on," he says.

She slips into them and he helps her tighten the straps to fit her small frame. They are still too bulky, but it will keep her dry enough. Grable hands her a fishing rod. One of his old ones. It's good luck. He's caught a lot fish with it. She looks a bit confused.

"I have no idea what I'm doing," she says gripping the rod like it's a shotgun. He moves her hands into position.

"Now, stay like that. Hang on a minute and I'll show you how to cast the line." He assembles his rod and slips a lure on each pole.

"You don't use worms?"

"Not for fly fishing," he says extending his hand to her. "Grab my hand and I'll take us out."

"I think I can manage walking into a river," she says rejecting his hand as she takes a lumbering step forward and nearly tips over from the rushing under-current.

"Here." He tries again with the hand. "Just till you get used to the current and the feel of the waders."

She grabs his hand and he moves them slowly into the dark waters against the current's pressure that claims them, wanting to send them down stream. Grable fights it and soon has them in steady position closer to shore. He then shows St. James how to cast her line and isn't surprised when she's such a quick study. Once she's confident to cast on her own, Grable moves a couple yards upriver from her to give them space.

"This is fun," she says after a while. "But it isn't clearing my head."

"It will. You have to lose yourself in it."

"How?"

"It's not a formula," Grable says.

St. James tosses out the line a few more times before reeling it back in. Grable sees she's made a tangled mess of it. He gets out his pocket knife and wades over to trim her line.

"So, are you ever going to tell me exactly what happened to you that night," she says.

He really doesn't want to bring the case to the river. This is his sacred space to unwind and detox from humanity's ugly flaws. "Let's just fish."

"I want to hear it from you. Come on," she presses. "You're the only person I haven't re-interviewed."

She's not going to let it go. Grable sloshes away from St. James hoping she'll drop it.

"Why did you have your statement retracted?" she asks.

"I'd really like to keep today off-record?"

"I thought we both wanted the same thing." He can hear the relentlessness in her voice.

Grable casts his line.

Out of the corner of his eye Grable sees St. James fling her pole back too far and too fast so that her line ends up in a tangle around her head. Grable goes over and unties her and again snips the line, pulling out fresh line from the reel. "No higher than forty-five. Steady your torso and let your arms flow with the pole. You want a figure eight in the air."

She tries again and the line sails out over the water, landing perfectly. Grable enjoys the smile spreading across her face. "That's it. Nice job."

If she could drop Nina's case for one second and just enjoy the river, it would relax her. And definitely him. He casts his line upstream about twenty feet from hers. Nothing is biting this late in the day. But the exercise and fresh air are worth the trip. After a moment, he turns to find St. James standing a few feet from him.

"How did you end up at the Argo that night? Doesn't seem like your kind of friends," she asks.

Man she's a digger. "Won't quit til you're satisfied, huh?"

St. James grins. "Don't make it so difficult."

"I wasn't popular back in high school. Still am not really," he says. "I was looking to hang out with someone that night so I didn't have to sit home alone."

"I thought you were a partier?"

"Oh. Yeah. I was. Always trying to fit in. But never quite making the cut, you know?"

"So, Nina's crowd… they didn't really want you there?"

"Let's just say I wasn't their first choice."

"What really happened at the Argo?" she asks.

"Nina was always nice to me. She was always an includer type. At one point, she was in my car. But then… my car was out of gas. Nina hopped out and jumped in with the Newtons. I was devastated. I knew the second I looked at those twins there wasn't anything good there."

A lump in Grable's throat swells and he stays quiet until he can swallow it away.

"And that's it? You went home?"

"No, I cobbled together some spare change and put gas in my car and followed them.

"How did that night end for you?" asks St. James.

"I went home after we made the second stop."

"And the next day?"

"Didn't talk to any of them. Went to work. I wasn't a part of their inner circle. Why would they bother with me?"

"Because you were with them the night Nina disappeared. Who told you about Nina?"

Grable suddenly becomes aware that St. James has locked her gaze on him and is paying no attention to her line which is growing longer and longer downstream. The end of her pole bends at a ninety-degree angle.

"Hey, I think you caught something!"

Grable reaches over and takes control of her pole and reels in the line. A healthy salmon struggles from the end of it. He swoops it up with his net. "Nicely done."

"Beginner's luck," she smiles, admiring her catch. "Do we keep it?"

"Anything over twelve inches." He measures the flopping fish. Fourteen. "It's a keeper."

Grable readjusts her lure and St. James is ready to cast it out again.

"You know, I didn't know for about five days that Nina had never returned home that night," he says. That was not in the report. This is the part that cut so deeply. Rich, Brad, Alyson… they cared so little about him… thought so little of him that no one had even bothered to let him know about Nina's disappearance.

"Why not?" asks St. James.

"When I questioned Rich about it, he said, 'sorry man, we kinda forgot you were with us that night.'"

"That must have stung," she says.

"I kinda deserved it. They knew I was only hanging with them because I had no one else."

"I don't think you deserved to be ignored," she says.

"Thanks. I mean, I did fail. I failed at being a friend to Nina when she really could have used someone to watch her back."

"She used her own free will to get into that car with those guys," says St. James.

"And I used mine when I chose not to go with her."

"Did you search for her?" says St. James.

"Every chance I got. I even stalked the Newtons down in Brantwood. 'Til they saw me one time and came after me."

"And you never reported that either." She smiled softly at him. No judgment.

"I was embarrassed. And I was afraid of them," Grable chuckles. "I knew by the way they came at me…I knew they had done it. And I knew they would do it again."

"You must wanna nail them, bad?" says St. James.

Grable clenches his jaw. There was not a day that went by he didn't fantasize about arresting the Newton twins.

"I know it doesn't seem like it to you. You probably think I'm lazy or too involved emotionally," says Grable. "But it's not like that. It's on my mind all the time. All the regrets, the secrets, the silences. A lot of my friends moved out of Derby. And the ones that are still here. They moved on in other ways. Married. Kids. I'm not blaming them. I made my choices, too. But I'm still an outsider here. And it can be kinda lonely."

"Except for Misty. She still talks to you," St. James says with a grin. "What does Jim think about all this?" she asks. "You ever talk to him?"

"He's never been privy to the files and the interviews. But he knows my personal story."

"And?"

"He doesn't hold anything against me," Grable cast his line out. "He actually kinda saved my life."

"What do you mean?"

"Before I was sober. Before I became a cop, I was coming outta the Argo quickie mart with a bottle of Vodka one day. Jim was coming in. He stopped me. Pulled me aside. Asked me what I was doing? Where I was going. I couldn't look him in the eye. And he knew I was going nowhere I should be going. He told me that I should stop hating myself."

"Did you… hate yourself?"

"Hence, the drinking. He sat me down and got me to admit what I hadn't been able to tell anyone."

"And what was that?" her voice landed softly on him.

"That I didn't know where was I supposed go where she wouldn't be."

Grable pulls his line in and glances up at St. James. For a split second, her green eyes envelop him, full of a deep, deep resonance. No one has ever looked at him that way before. It wasn't romantic. More like she was searching for something she had lost, and then realized that she had found it in him.

"What did Jim say to that?" she asks with a steady voice.

"He started to tear up. And he said, you need to know that you are loved."

Grable knows she's locked into her forensic analysis mode, her brain picking apart every tidbit of information he's feeding her to see how it stacks up with the hundreds of other conversations she's read or heard about Nina. He's never opened up this much to anyone but his AA sponsor and maybe, Jim. Here he is, blabbing about the details of his redemption story in his favorite spot on earth with Riley St. James, a woman he's only known a few weeks. He notices the way she cocks her head to look at him allows the warm breeze to clear away the red curls around her face. It's intimate. Attentive. Seeking. So much seeking it almost devours him and he has to look away.

"What did you take from that conversation with Jim?" she says.

Grable shakes himself back to the present. "That I should get sober."

"What?" St. James laughs a little. "Sorry. It's not funny. I just… didn't expect that answer."

"I know. It surprised me, too. But I was at rock bottom. Felt like maybe I owed that much to Nina. And myself. So, I did my twelve steps. And the rest is history."

"I see," says St. James. "Congratulations."

Her gaze turns to her pole as she casts out her line. Grable watches as she lets it drift with the current, then yanks back hard. She swishes the line out over the rippling water. Then again. And again.

"Have you forgiven yourself for your attack?" he says, knowing the consequences it might bring.

She doesn't respond. Grable sees her upper body tense as she tries to fling her line out again. It tangles in a branch hanging over the river. Grable wades over and unsnags it. He clips off another several knotted feet and places it in St. James' hands.

"Flow with the pole," he coaches.

St. James jerks in her line and plods a few steps towards shore before needing to stop for a rest.

"Look, Grable, I've been going over everything in my mind. Aside from a few new pieces of legend, there's nothing moving the needle to arrest the Newtons. I don't think there's anything more I can do here. I'm going to write up my report to the Commander and see what he wants me to do next. But I think I may be done in Derby soon."

She trudges out of the river and steps out of her waders. Fishing trip over. He knows she hates him for that last question. She is hemmed in by fear; the strongest demon on earth. Just as he had been.

"Don't let those bastards dictate how you live your life," Jim Laramie had told him. "Love wins. That's how you beat this."

It was incredible advice from a wrinkled, hardened truck driver on whom so much suffering had been inflicted. Grable held on and held on and held on to that advice, until love finally did win.

Once he has the poles and equipment packed away, Grable plucks the fishing net from the bank. He expertly whacks the head of the salmon on a nearby rock, killing it instantly. He lays his kill on the bed of ice he has prepared inside his small beverage cooler. He will give it to Riley.

Love wins. Grable aches to tell Riley St. James as he heads to the truck with his fish.

Chapter 34

SILAS & SOLOMON

Silas stepped out of the john at the back of Pub Griffin to see Solomon at the bar cajoling Joyce to serve him a sixth beer and shot of whiskey. But she wouldn't budge. The bitch.

Retaliating, Solomon slid his beer glass off the end of the bar and shattered it to the floor. Joyce didn't flinch and didn't move a single inch to clean it up. She just stared at him. Then at Silas.

"I'm adding that to your tab," she said folding her arm across her chest directing her comment at Solomon. "And you boys are through here for the night."

Silas nodded to Joyce and leaned over to Solomon.

"Hey, I just got a text that Megan's home," Silas said.

"Why's she texting you?" asked Solomon. "I thought you were through?"

Megan was Silas's off again-on again hook up. His wife didn't know about her and he didn't like to drive his truck to Megan's house. It was better if Solomon drove.

"She wants to see me. Let's get outta here," says Silas.

"All right. Fine."

"Gimme the keys. I'm not letting you behind the wheel."

Solomon dug for his keys and tossed them to his brother. He headed out first and Silas lay a ten dollar tip on the bar for Joyce. Silas could feel her eyes follow them all the way out the door. They got into Solomon's pickup truck. He pulled out of the parking lot and turned left to head up the hill.

"This ain't the way to Megan's," said Solomon.

"No shit. We ain't going to Megan's," said Silas.

"Why not?"

Silas didn't answer as he turned into the Argo.

"Shit. She didn't text, did she? You fucking liar." Solomon plugged his phone into the car charger. Silas didn't say a word. He knew that his brother was about to cause a row back at Pub Griffin and he knew how to diffuse the situation. Most times it worked. But he had to be more creative these days. Solomon was drinking a lot.

"I wasn't gonna start anything back there," said Solomon.

"Yes, you were," said Silas.

"Did Megan really text you?"

"Yes, she did," said Silas. "But I wanna get a snack first. Pringles. Sour cream and onion."

"And you want me to get it? I ain't your slave."

Silas handed Solomon a twenty. "Fuck you. Get it yourself," Solomon cranked up the stereo.

Silas sighed and got out of the truck. He glanced back at his twin, head banging to the radio. His brother's keeper. Silas had always been the more level-headed of the two.

Inside, Silas was reaching for two cans of Pringles when he noticed a long wavy ponytail of red hair bobbing down the candy aisle. His eyes followed the female figure to the cashier. She was good-looking, even from behind. Beautiful hair and skin. Those green eyes. Great body. Petite. He liked small women. They were easier to handle. He watched as she paid for a cheap bottle of wine, loaf of wheat bread, and a candy bar. As she turned to go, she glanced up and caught him staring at her. He quickly snapped his gaze to the chip display he was standing in front of. Once he heard the bell on the door ding, he glanced back. She was out and heading towards her truck.

Silas gathered his snacks, paid, and made his way back to his truck. He had to knock on the door because Solomon had locked it. Jerk. When Silas got into the driver's side, he handed Solomon his Pringles and a Coke and noticed Solomon's gaze tracking the good-looking red head getting into her truck.

"You know who that is, don't ya?" said Solomon.

"She was just in the store," said Silas unscrewing the cap on his soft drink.

"That's that detective. She skeezes me out," said Solomon as he fumbled with his Pringles can. "Let's give her a little scare."

"Why?"

Silas revved the truck's engine and they skirted through the parking lot to the main street.

"Cause she's a bitch," said Solomon.

"We just let sleeping dogs lie."

"She's been talking to everyone about Nina," said Solomon. "What's that about?"

"It's nothing," said Silas shoving three Pringles into his mouth.

"I don't trust her. We gotta get on top of this thing."

"What exactly do you want to do to her?" asked Silas. He noticed he was white knuckling the steering wheel and speeding through the back city streets.

"She's up in that house all alone," said Solomon. "Just drive by."

"What house? Where?"

"Jason's old place," Solomon said. He and Silas and Jason had been friends in elementary school. They had spent a lot of afternoons in that old house before Jason's family had left the state and kept the house as a rental property.

"Yup. There's a door off the kitchen that goes down to the cellar." Silas felt Solomon had a plan in his voice.

"Yeah. So, what are you saying, Sol?"

He didn't answer as he bit down on a chip and clenched down on his cheek flesh instead. "Ouch! Damn it. I bit my cheek," said Solomon.

Silas didn't know how it happened, but they were in front of Jason's old house. He pulled down the street and shut off the engine.

"I just want her to know that she shouldn't mess with us," said Solomon.

"She hasn't messed with us. Don't send up any red flags now," said Silas.

"Yeah, well, it won't be long and she'll be hunting us down."

"That's ridiculous. You don't know that."

"Oh, she's coming," said Solomon.

"You're talking like a fool," said Silas. "Calm the fuck down."

"We need a plan!"

"We have a plan. And we tell her what we told all of 'em back then," said Silas laying three more Pringles together into one bite.

"You ain't the one who went to prison. No way I'm going back to no prison." Solomon unlocked his door, jumped out, and adjusted the pistol he was carrying in the back of his pants.

"Hey, what're you doing? Come on back here!" hissed Silas.

But Solomon was weaving down the middle of the road towards Jason's house.

"Shit. Shit!" Silas scrambled to undo his seatbelt as he grabbed the spare pistol from Solomon's glove box.

Chapter 35

TAMMY

The ball of Tammy's foot bounced on the tile floor in a quick staccato as she sat in the visiting room of the Northern Michigan Correctional Facility. She had driven the three and a half hours north to face Wallace unannounced and talk about *that* night. The summer night when she was fourteen and snuck out of her friend's house to go party with her nineteen year old neighbor, Wallace, already twice in trouble with the law. He had been drinking whiskey and was high on coke. When she showed up at his house after midnight, he said he wanted to look for a party spot and see if Wendy was there. Wendy was his cool, older girlfriend. Tammy didn't care. She just wanted to sneak out and do something fun and dangerous. With Wallace.

Wallace felt nothing romantic for Tammy. But Tammy had a crush on him, even though he had always treated her like a little sister. Tammy loved how easy it was to be with him. She felt no pressure to be anyone but herself. After what happened that night, Wallace took a job an hour south and never contacted her. A month later he was arrested for armed robbery the same day Tammy started high school. They had not spoken since her phone call.

Tammy didn't like the disgusted way Wallace looked at her when he sat down at their table.

"Hi. Surprise," she said with a lift in her voice.

Wallace sat down and stared at her.

"What are you doing here?"

"Thought you could use some company. You get many visitors?" she said keeping her tone up.

"No."

"Why not?"

"It's a long drive," he said.

"How's your family?"

"Ma died five years ago. My brother lives in Florida. Dad's still around."

Wallace folded his hands on the table and gazed around the room with a bored look.

"Your dad doesn't visit?" asked Tammy.

"No."

Tammy pressed her hand on her leg to stop her foot from tapping and massaged her thigh.

"What do you want?" Wallace said returning his stoic gaze to hers.

"You hung up so quickly when I called..." she said.

"We had an agreement. Remember?" he said.

She shook her head. There was no agreement. "You threatened to kill me if I talked to you."

Wallace lowered his voice, "Tam, there's nothing to discuss."

Tam. She hadn't heard him call her that since he dropped her off that night at the cemetery.

"I wanna talk about it," she said. "And I'm not afraid." Although the waiver in her voice betrayed her.

Tammy shifted her gaze to a guard standing by the window. He was watching a squirrel run rings around a tree outside.

"You still married?" he said.

"We divorced seven years ago."

"You dating?"

"No."

"How's your sons?" he asked.

"Good."

"They play any sports?"

"Baseball."

She wanted to find a way back to the Oconee National Forest that night.

"It's nice to see you again. You look good. You've really taken care of yourself," he said easing back in his chair.

"I'm not fourteen anymore. I'm not scared of you." She was. A lot. Even though he was behind bars, he could still get to her. She knew that.

"I hope not. I'm still your friend. Right?" He sounded like the old Wallace from her childhood.

"Yes. Still friends."

"Good. Good to hear," he laughed.

She always liked his laugh. It was big. Full. Welcoming. It enveloped everything and everyone around. Made you feel you were a part of the special Wallace club.

"How's the food here?" she forced a smile.

"Five star chefs. Filet mignons on Fridays." He cracked a sarcastic smile.

A laugh slipped out of Tammy. The guard snapped a glance their way.

"You were always full of shit," she said, glad that the ice was finally broken.

"Five more years before I can get my hands on some prime rib," he said. "In the meantime, I would kill for your chocolate chip cookies," said Wallace.

"You remember those?"

"Yeah, I remember you bringing 'em over to my mom's house when you had made an extra batch."

"Well, I can arrange that. If I remember, you liked the batter better."

"Got sick on it. Bring some of that, too," he reached for her hands, but she slid them onto her lap.

"No touching," she whispered. "What makes you think I'm coming back?"

"Because you didn't get what you were after."

She saw he still carried a shrewd and unrelenting judge of character. She decided to level with him. "It took a lot for me to come up here, Wallace. I'm not mad about it or about how it was handled. And I'm not holding anything against you. I want you to know that."

He leaned back in his chair and rubbed his hands together like he was trying to warm them.

"We've always had one thing in common, Tammy Tyler. We both know how to get what we want. You'll figure it out."

Tammy left the facility and trudged out to her car. She would gas up, grab a snack, and drive three and a half hours back to Derby. And then she would do it again next week. With cookies. And batter. She would shore up her courage and be more flirty if she had to. This was going to take some finessing.

As Tammy crossed into Derby County and passed by the turn off for the Hole in the Woods, she wondered how long she could keep this up and still survive the recurring nightmares that had started to rattle her awake and steal her sleeping hours.

Chapter 36

RILEY ST. JAMES

Asleep on the living room couch, I can feel the beads of sweat forming on my forehead and the rush of heat through my core. But I'm helpless to open my eyes, sunken deep into a dream state that finds myself once again in the forest by my university.

Once again, the dark shadow catches up to me in my periphery. Soon, it envelops me. I struggle to free from its grip, but it wraps and wraps and wraps me with a pink satin ribbon constricting me from the feet … up the legs… and binding my arms to my torso. I try to expand myself, but it works its way up to my neck and around my head so that only my eyes and forehead are exposed.

I gasp for air as the shadow pulls tight on the ribbon constricting my chest. The air in my lungs seeps out. I expel it in small puffs while trying to cry out. A squeak emerges, breathless and weak. As I sip air for my last breath, the pink satin ribbon dances in front of my eyes, about to seal my fate. A loud BANG! jolts me from the nightmare.

I pant awake, sweat dripping down my spine, and attempt to stand from the couch, but I find the afghan twisted up around my neck. A second blanket is in a tangle around my legs. I tear at them but they only get tighter.

BANG!

I place the sound. Heavy metal crashing down from somewhere in the back of the house.

I roll off the couch to the floor, pulling at the afghan as my eyes search for my gun on the coffee table. It's there, under the stack of mail where I slid it before nodding off. I snatch it, keeping low and am able to thwart off my shrouds to the floor. Crawling towards the back door, my senses are on high alert. My pulse is a runner's rate and a flush of heat flashes through me. I crouch by the back door listening for any movement and trying to steady my shaking hands. I can hear two sets of footsteps stealing across the gravel driveway. I crane my neck to the paned window of the back door. A long, white lace curtain provides me with a protective view and I focus my gaze through one of the eyelets in the lace as I scan the yard and driveway.

But they're gone. Nothing. No one. I listen with full attention.

No footsteps.

I crack the door and on all fours creep out with my gun drawn. I position myself behind a patio chair and listen again. The metal cellar doors are raised at an angle to provide an entrance from the ground into the basement. I notice the latch is undone.

I pull my phone from my back pocket and text Grable through shaking hands. I manage to press the voice activation button and whisper a text for Grable to come to my house.

I draw in a deep breath then hold it for six counts before exhaling. It's a technique I learned in therapy to slow the pulse and calm the nervous system. I do it two more times.

In my squatting position, I waddle towards the edge of the deck, weapon still trained and scan my yard. I move with cautious precision down the porch steps into the yard, searching behind bushes and trees for the shooter. Finding all clear, I proceed to the detached garage, checking the perimeter first. Clear. Same with the interior of the garage. I even check the crawl space off to the side of the garage. It's here I notice a set of boot prints in my gravel driveway. I mark them with a circle of stones and head to the front yard. I check behind the front bushes and under the stoop.

A couple blocks down the street, I can hear a truck speeding past houses, pausing at stop signs with little squeals of the brake. In seconds Grable's truck appears. He parks on the street and jumps out, his gun pulled. He rushes to me with fervor in his eyes.

"I checked the area," I say quietly as Grable approaches.

"What did the suspect look like?"

"I don't know. The slamming of the cellar doors woke me up. I didn't see anyone."

"You okay?"

"Yeah. I'm fine."

"Do you think it's the twins?" he asks.

I shrug. "Maybe. But what would have triggered an attack like that?"

He shrugs. "Let's search the house together."

We start with the house and work our way into the basement cellar. From here we proceed out from the cellar doors, dusting everything for prints. From here we move around the perimeter of the house, yard, and garage until we are sure the area is clear.

We make a circular search of the vehicle, spiraling out towards the yard. I find a single set of boot prints in the driveway and grab my scene investigation kit. I want to get molds of the shoeprints.

"Maybe it was only one of them," says Grable. "Otherwise, we would see two sets of prints."

"Unless they wear the same kind of boots."

I prep the dental stone powder for the cast. I pour the wet stone mixture into the first print.

I allow my casting to dry and remove it at a snail's pace. Castings are fragile. I need to preserve all possible lines and groves of the sole of the boot to get the most accurate reproduction.

"I'll get those down to the lab tomorrow," Grable says taking the castings from me.

"Maye it's a kind of warning," I say.

Grable nods. "You've created a pressure cooker situation. People in the town are talking. And the twins aren't stupid. They have to be feeling the pressure."

"Coming here was ballsy," I say trying to steady my shaking hands. My mouth is so dry. I click my tongue on the roof of my mouth to activate my salivary glands. "Leakage. They're starting to leak." It was a term we used when criminals involuntarily or voluntarily started to release their guilt in visibly noticeable ways. Sometimes it was physical, like sweating or turning red, nervous twitching. Sometimes leakage was verbal if a criminal started to talk to close friends. Rarely was it the kind of bold action the twins had just taken.

I look up to see Grable wiping sweat off his forehead.

"Hey, you okay? You want something to drink?" I ask.

"Yeah. Yeah."

He follows me into the kitchen and I grab two ice tea glasses from the cupboard. I fill each glass and shut off the faucet as the moon pokes out from behind the clouds, throwing beams of moonlight through the kitchen window.

"The kitchen window," I exclaim. "They would have been able to see me from there, sleeping on the couch. They could have done anything and I was entirely defenseless."

I pace the kitchen, unspooling inside, as water sloshes out of my glass. Grable takes his down in three large gulps and pours himself another glass.

"But they didn't. And they won't," says Grable. "They're not that stupid."

"Don't be so sure." I bolt from the back kitchen door into the back yard. Grable follows me and we trek through the grass looking for any more clues in the lawn.

As I tread through the grass in a zig zag pattern, my reserves of calm and control begin to expire. The pressure squeezes around my chest and I gasp for snippets of air. The anxiety attack is ramping up and my thoughts are blurring back to the woods near my college.

"Hey, you okay?" He sidles up alongside me. I turn to him and see his penetrating look.

Then, the shaking starts and I can't control it. Grable takes me by the shoulders. I let him. He steadies me as he seats me on the lawn. "Breathe. Just breathe," he commands, sitting crossed legged in front of me. "Don't go there, Riley. Stay with me."

I struggle to release of the images of being thrust onto the ground. I can smell the wet earth, wormy, as my face is pressed against the cool soil.

"Riley. Get out of there. Look at me. Study my face." His sharp tone rips me from the memory and I do what he says, locking my eyes on his. Breathing. In and out. In and out until the breaths become less shallow, finally reaching down to the bottom of my lungs and filling my diaphragm. The whole time, he never lets go of my hands.

After my college attack, I vowed I would never be a victim again. Three days after I left campus, I signed up for the police academy. I trained and trained and trained for self-defense. Hand to hand combat. Marital arts. Firearms.

I am determined to rewrite that moment in my history. And here it comes. Chasing me down in my backyard. On my doorstep. Hunting me as I knew it would.

Chapter 37

RILEY ST. JAMES

I show up at Ray's front door the next morning, after I agree to let Grable spend the night in my house. On the couch downstairs.

Ray is dressed in work clothes and has already been down to his hives. He welcomes me in. He's eating his morning oatmeal and egg and asks if I'll join him. Yes. I will. I haven't eaten a meal in over twenty-four hours, nor have I had much of an appetite. But now, smelling those eggs on the stove. Yeah, I'm starving.

I take a place at the kitchen table and while Ray finishes preparing the simple meal, I explain the events from the day before.

"I'm very sorry to hear that happened to you," says Ray cracking eggs into a fry pan. They sizzle when they hit the hot butter. "But not entirely surprised."

"Part of the job?" I try to brush off my concern. But Ray sends me a look. I can tell that he knows I'm shaken. He doesn't belabor the point.

"It means you've successfully attracted bees to your hive."

"I'm just glad one of the bees left a shoeprint," I say. "At least it's something to track."

"I suppose you have a plan for finding the known sample," says Ray as he plates the eggs.

"Grable's gonna send one of his guys to follow the twins and get their prints."

"Good." Ray gives the eggs a dash of salt and pepper. "You take anything in your oatmeal?"

"I don't usually eat oatmeal."

"You should. Low fat. Sticks to the ribs." He places a bowl of steaming oats in front of her. "Put a tablespoon of honey in it," he says pointing to a glass honey jar on the lazy Susan in the middle of the table. I spin it to reach the honey and I dip my clean spoon into the jar, pulling out the measured amount. It drips a string of honey across the table as I transfer it from the jar to the bowl. "Sorry." I scoop it up with my index finger. "Couldn't help it. So good!"

Ray dips a clean teaspoon into his jar of honey and I notice a sallowness come over his visage.

"Take another."

Ray hands me a clean teaspoon and I extract the gooey, amber medicine from the jar. It spreads over my tongue and roof of my mouth, liquefying its sweetness down the back of my throat. It has an odd calming effect. Since my first visit with Ray, I've studied up on honey and had learned that it has healing properties. It alleviates allergy symptoms, dandruff, skin irritation, aids with sleep, boosts memory, and heals wounds.

I like that I feel so safe with Ray. He's that grandfather who always says the right things and lets you be yourself without any judgment.

"I'm sure you know I didn't come here for eggs and oatmeal," I say.

His warm smile gives me permission to smile. My stiff face muscles release from their long-held scowl. "What can I do to help?"

"I'm in the process of writing up a report for my Commander. I'm asking to be released from this case. Especially after last night."

"I see." he says calmly. "One little snag and you're running?"

I see what he's doing. "I'm not the best person for this case."

"That's not how I see it." He is patient, but persistent.

"Health reasons. I have panic attacks. They're becoming more frequent. And I think they're going to affect my judgement here."

"We all have dark thoughts, Detective St. James," he says. "It's nothing to be ashamed of. It's part of being human. In fact, if you didn't I might question that even more. It's only when we give into the temptation and act upon those ideas that we cross the line."

He has cut right to the crux of me. "But I'm afraid one of these days, I will do just that," I say. "Or I will completely shut down and end up... like Nina."

There. I admitted it. Like a priest, Ray would never betray my confession. No. someone like Ray would give me absolution and then I could go on my way back to Detroit. I wait for my pardon. Ray eats the rest of his oatmeal before responding.

"It's okay to have a physical reaction to evil. I would even argue that it's a healthy reaction. I know exactly how you feel. I lived with it for thirty years. Their evilness haunts me every time I cross paths with them in town. My throat gets tight, my heartbeat ignites, and my blood pressure shoots up. And it brings up my own evil thoughts."

"How do you deal with that? How do you go on living here in peace and tranquility with your bees when you know they're still out there?"

"Evil wants evil to be both feared and lauded. Don't give evil it's due," says Ray.

"Ignore them? They could have killed me," I can't cover my frustration.

"You've made good headway. Keep going. Face them. Face *it*, Riley. And conquer it. Isn't this what you've prepared for? Perhaps… even hoped for."

"I thought I was prepared," I say with confidence slipping. "But my body completely shuts down."

"If you quit this case now, how will that ever improve?" He poses to me. "Do you want to be paralyzed forever?"

"I'm so tired," I say quietly.

"Close your eyes." I do. "Follow them in your mind. What do you see?"

I imagine myself in my kitchen. It's night. I see the twins trekking up my driveway, into my back yard, my back porch. Looking at me through my kitchen window.

"They want you to be afraid," says Ray off to my side. "To over-power you."

My blood pressure rises. My anger flows from that well of anguish in my own woods. I am pinched by the impulse to raise my gun. I aim it at Silas' forehead and I squeeze the trigger.

My eyes pop open and I look into Ray's calm grey ones. He knows what I've done in there. And doesn't judge it.

He waits for me to reset before getting up from the table and clears their plates. He sets them into the sink and runs the water for a moment. I wait. I don't want to rush the conversation because I sense he's about to guide me into something important.

"Have you ever thought about getting a dog?"

I laugh at the suggestion. "A dog?"

"Yes. A big dog." Ray hands me a jar of honey.

Chapter 38

SILAS & SOLOMON

Solomon poured gasoline into a fifty-five gallon drum set in the back of in his five-acre, wooded property. He lit a match and threw it in. He let the fire roar. Flames leapt six feet up then died down. He threw in two white plastic bags of kitchen trash. When he was satisfied with the size of the fire, he picked up a paper grocery bag and threw it into the flames. Soon, thick, black smoke rose from the melting rubber. He fanned it away from him, thinning the smoke into the air so it wouldn't draw attention. After a few minutes, sooty, dark curls of black evidence rose and dissipated into the air. It took about ten minutes before the flames died down, turning to embers. Satisfied, Solomon headed back up to the house.

Chapter 39

RILEY ST. JAMES

After my experience with Ray Polland, I delete my report to my Commander and resolve to wait, listen, and keep busy at my hive. I ramp up my security system and take extra precautions like leaving lights on and adding more dead bolt locks to each door. I set up more video cameras to surround my home, yard, driveway, and street. I practice my martial arts and find a firing range. I do whatever I can to silence the ticking time bomb.

During the daylight hours, I troll around town, patronizing the local establishments, and keeping tabs on Misty Beckett's Facebook page to see if the chatter has died down or the legends have changed. There doesn't seem to anything new related to the case and I become particularly annoyed by memes that keep popping up from a Facebook page called Cornucopia of Hope, toting online inspirational products like plaques, note cards, and jewelry.

Forgiveness is a way of opening up the doors again and moving forward.

Forgiveness doesn't excuse their actions. Forgiveness stops their actions from destroying your heart.

Forgiveness doesn't diminish justice, it just entrusts it to God.

Wrong. Forgiveness is entrusted to us detectives. No victim really believes some great source of love or divine being will magically serve up a killer's confession or put a murderer in prison. No, it's up to people like me to wallow into the gutters and snatch up the dregs of society.

I keep scrolling the page until I tire of running into the pithy affirmations of false hope. I stop. And listen. Quiet. So very quiet. I yawn and lean back into my couch, slapping my laptop closed. I allow myself to slouch over into a fetal position and pull an afghan over my shoulders. Maybe I can sneak in a quick nap, if my mind will let me. I'm drifting off when a dog barks down the street and jolts me awake.

Get a dog.

Get a dog.

Ray's suggestion has woven itself into me.

A dog might be good company. And protection. Maybe I could even get a good night's sleep?

I rock myself back to a seated position and open up my laptop. I type "dog adoption" in the search engine. How long does it take to get a dog? Could I go home with one today? I scan profile after profile until my heart patters at the image of a young, retired police shepherd. His current home is only an hour's drive. I quickly dial the number.

Andre, the owner, answers and I learn that he is still available. I tell Andre a little bit about myself and direct him to the profile page I've created under "Adoptive Parents." He takes a moment to glance over it while they are on the phone, asks me a few questions. He tells me he likes my profile and thinks the shepherd might be a good match. He wonders if I can be there by six.

***

Andre's home is a new two-story construction on five-acre lot. To the side is a newly installed playground set and children's toys scattered around the yard. I park in the drive, get out, and head to the front door. I hear what sounds like twenty children shrieking, laughing, and running around inside. I have to ring the doorbell again to get someone's attention. Finally, Andre answers with a friendly smile and a small child wrapped around each leg.

"You must be Miss Riley?" he says.

"Yes, Riley St. James. Andre?"

"Come in, please. This is Jalissa and Klara. My twins. Jalissa and Klara, this is the nice lady who's here to see Zikmund," says Andre, making no attempt to peel the children from his body as they lumber through the house towards a laundry area off the kitchen. "Okay, kids. Daddy needs you to hop off so I can introduce Miss Riley to Zik."

They both let go, dropping dramatically to the floor in a burst of laughter.

"Off you go. To the play room. Or outside. Where I can see you."

They scamper off as I stand outside the laundry room wondering if I should follow Andre or just stay put as he puts on his work boots.

"Just stay where you are," says Andre answering my thoughts as he disappears into the garage. I can hear him whispering something to the animal. It doesn't sound like English. After a moment, the door opens and a dog appears into the laundry room. He saunters up to me, sitting at my feet, his blue eyes looking at mine, waiting for a command.

"This is Zikmund. Means, victorious protector," says Andre looking on from the laundry room doorway.

I like that.

"Hello, Zikmund," I say holding out my palm for him to sniff. Which he does, but oddly never allows his eyes to leave mine.

"He was trained in Czech. So, you'll have to learn the commands," says Andre.

"Not a problem," My eyes locked with Zik's.

"Oh, you speak Czech?" he seems surprised.

"No, but I'm a fast learner." There was something old and wise in Zikmund's unwavering expression. "He's seen a lot, hasn't he?"

"His last assignment was in Afghanistan. He was there eighteen months sniffing for bodies and bombs. Highly stressful situation. He has a hard time relaxing. It's not good for him to be in a home with children or loud noises. That's the only reason I can't adopt. It's too noisy here. I'm fostering him for now. What's your living situation like?"

"Quiet. Very quiet. I'm single. I live alone in a small town. He'll have a yard and a big house. I work close by and I'm pretty sure he can come to the office with me during my shifts," I reassure Andre.

"That should check out fine," he says. "I'll have the pet adoption agency stop by to do a house inspection."

I nod. Zikmund continues to stare at me. I like the way his ears prick up at the slightest sound, but that he doesn't turn in a distracted look. He knows how to distinguish normal sounds from those that threaten. I like his icy blue eyes and the way his pink tongue hangs out between his white fang teeth. They've been cleaned recently. No brown tartar. And I like that he doesn't drool like a lot of dogs I've known. His coat is thick and groomed. His legs and paws are more petite than the average German shepherd. I like his lithe gait. I noticed it when he first approached me. There was no hesitancy or concern in accepting me.

"Do you have time to train me now?"

"Ano," says Andre. "That means 'yes' in Czech. First lesson."

I smile at Zikmund and lean over to scratch under his chin. "Ano, Zikmund, we are going to be family."

Chapter 39

GRABLE

After the cadet cop returns from his mission of covertly capturing the boot print castings from both Silas and Solomon from the muddy driveway at the rear of a feed store, Grable guides him through all the steps of processing physical evidence. He then drives the two of them and the prints to the state lab a couple hour's south of Derby. Thanks to St. James' connection, Maria, at the state lab, they are able to meet up in person and put a rush on the evidence examination. Maria is very welcoming and invites the cadet to see how the prints are analyzed and categorized in their database. She explains that it will be a long shot to make an exact match, but at least assist in narrowing down to boot maker and model number. Perhaps even a seller location.

Grable asks if he can take Maria to lunch and she is happy to extend teaching opportunity over a lunch of burgers, fries, and shakes.

She also takes a lot of interest in Grable; his job in Derby, hobbies, the Laramie case. She even gives him her mobile number, just in case they have more questions later. Grable likes her and finds himself texting her from the car to thank her.

They leave the crime lab with the information they need on the boot prints. But not the information Grable was hoping for. The prints collected from the feed store are not a match to the boot prints found in Riley's driveway. They come from two different brands manufactured by two entirely different boot companies. The cadet is devastated, having been very much a CSI fan and influenced by the CSI effect. Grable has to explain to him that this is real life, not a television episode. More often than not, evidence cannot be identified to an individual source. More often than not, physical evidence is not integral in bringing an arrest, or a case to trial, or a criminal conviction. The crushed cadet stays quiet on the ride back to Derby and Grable can read the cadet's thoughts as if they were tattooed across his forearm. He's had the same ones. Many times since graduation from the police academy, Grable has wondered if anything he is doing is mounting to a hill of beans. His thoughts are often seeded with doubts on the value of becoming a police officer especially in one's own hometown. There are the proud moments –a thank you from parents of a suicidal teen, a successful car rescue from a flooded river, or the well-timed arrest of a burglar.

Grable lets the silence and unspoken questions fill the space between them. There is no advice or encouragement he can give this cadet cop that would help. It's something he needs to sort out within himself. And it may take a life time.

They are about thirty minutes from Derby when Grable gets a call from dispatch. Could he drive up to the hospital and take a statement from Jacob Zachary? A statement about what? What had happened? Burglary? Domestic abuse?

No, the old man had called for an ambulance because he was feeling light headed and dizzy. After he was admitted at the hospital they couldn't seem to get his blood pressure to come down. His wife, in a panic about her husband's declining health, insisted that it wasn't medicine he needed. He needed to get something off his chest.

The cadet cop perks up. "Finally, some action," he says.

Grable shakes his head. The kid's gonna hold on tight to notions they are part of a TV crime show.

Chapter 40

GRABLE

G rable and the cadet are taken up to Jacob Zachary's hospital floor by the nurse on duty.

"You stay at the back of the room. Don't make a peep. Not even a sneeze. I want you to pretend like you're not even there. Listen. Take notes. Observe. You got it?" Grable says to the cadet.

The cadet nods.

"You got a pen? Pad of paper?" asks Grable.

"No."

"You need to carry your own," Grable says.

"I can take notes on my phone."

"Don't rely on your phone." Grable shakes his head and looks to the nurse with an embarrassed nod. "Ask her."

A nurse procures one from the nurse's station and leads the two to Jacob's room. When they enter Grable points to the spot where he wants the cadet to plant himself. The cadet moves into position like a soldier. The nurse approaches Jacob Zachary and touches his shoulder. "Mr. Zachary, Detective Grable is here to speak with you. Can you hear me? Mr. Zachary?"

His droopy eyelids unfold around his eye sockets and he looks up at the nurse. "What's that now?"

"It's okay, Jacob," says his wife Genny close at his side. "The Detective is here to speak with you. Do you want to sit up?"

"Ah, yes. Yes," he says groaning to lift his skeleton frame. The nurse presses the left button on the bed and helps him to a sitting position.

"How's that?" Genny tucks the sheets up around his waist and then turns to Grable. "I'm Genny Zachary, Jacob's wife. How do you do?"

"Just fine, ma'am," says Grable extending his hand to Genny. "Is he feeling well enough to talk right now?"

"He'll talk. You being here is the best medicine for him," she says.

"I'm sure he's getting great care here."

"Not the kind that can really heal him."

"Not sure I understand, ma'am."

"Now, what'd you say your name was?" Jacob looks up at Grable who is standing at the foot of the bed.

"I'm Detective Kevin Grable with the Derby County Police. What can I do for you?"

"Jacob, tell him what you been bottling up. Get it off your chest so your heart can get back to getting healthy," says Genny.

"Did something happen to you, sir?" says Grable, glancing back at the cadet to make sure he is paying attention. He is met with disappointment when he sees the kid staring at the screen of his phone. Grable clears his throat and the cadet looks up. Busted. He sheepishly slides his phone away and puts pen to paper.

"It was a late summer night when they came over. And they had been drinking," says Jacob.

"Who is they?" asks Grable.

"My nephews. Silas and Solomon Newton."

"When was this?"

"I dunno... they was only seventeen or eighteen at the time."

"Okay. So about thirty years ago."

"I'd say. At least."

"They were drunk when they came over?" asks Grable.

"Yeah. And high. I had 'em sit down at the kitchen table and Genny made some sandwiches for us."

"I didn't like the way there were acting. I wanted them to leave," pipes in Genny.

Grable isn't sure where all of this is leading. Or how lucid Jacob Zachary is at the moment. He should remember to ask the nurse about the side effects of Jacob's medications.

"What did you talk about during their visit?" asks Grable.

"Lotta small talk. Mostly I let them do the talking. Asking them about family and their jobs. What they'd been up to all summer. I hadn't seen them in months. Then the topic came up about that girl who was missing."

"Who brought it up?" Grable asks.

"I believe I did. She was about their age and I wondered if they knew anything about her."

"Did they mention her by name?"

"Yeah, they said it was Nina Laramie," says Genny crossing her arms over her chest.

"And did they know Nina?" asks Grable.

"That's the thing. They said they didn't know her that well. But then as we talked some more one of them said they had been with her."

"With her how? When?" asks Grable.

"Sounded like they were hanging out together. Silas said she had been in his car and he thought she was pretty," says Jacob.

Grable's mind flashes to an image of Nina smiling and getting into a Mustang at the Argo. He can still feel his urgency and helplessness as he scrambles to find gas money between the seat cushions so Nina would stay and ride with him.

Jacob readjusts his position. Genny hands him a water glass with a straw and he takes a sip.

"Was there something more?" Grable asks.

"You need to tell him the rest, Jacob," says Genny.

"I don't wanna testify against my own family," says Jacob. "I'm done talking Genny. I don't want no harm to come to you."

"Testify? What do you mean? Why would you use that word?" says Grable.

"He's afraid his statement is gonna get those boys in trouble. And if you don't take him seriously, those boys are gonna retaliate on us," says Genny with her gaze locked onto Grable. "So we gotta know we have some protection from you. Can you do that?"

"Well, I don't even know what we're dealing with here, so until I have Mr. Zachary's statement, I can't exactly make that call," says Grable.

"Jacob neglected to tell you that along with those sandwiches, they had a few rounds of hard liquor. Smoked some pot. Weed loosens lips. They said some things to Jacob about that Nina girl," says Genny. "Go on, Jacob. Tell him what they said."

"I was just half paying attention because Genny was watching TV in the other room," says Jacob.

"Stop making excuses. You know what you heard," Genny insists.

"One of them said they was in the clear because the cops had already talked to them and exonerated them." Jacob stops for another sip of water.

"And what else?" Genny demands.

Jacob goes into a coughing fit and when he comes out, his voice is gravely. The words have trouble coming out at first. He clears his throat and takes a deep breath.

"They said maybe we shouldn't have hit her so hard. And then the other one said, well, maybe she shoulda given us what we wanted." He pulls his lips in and his eyes bounce down to his lap. The room is quiet except for the beeping of the heart monitor.

Grable notices Genny take Jacob's hand. The corners of her eyes are wet with tears.

"And do you think they were talking about Nina Laramie?" says Grable.

"Yes," he says looking straight forward at Grable. "I have no doubts."

Grable takes in Jacob's sallow eyes. This is a huge piece of testimony that has laid fallow for two decades. Why hadn't Jacob said anything until now? Or Genny? Was it fear holding them back? Had the twins threatened them? Or was it familial loyalty? Had Jacob ever mentioned this conversation to the twins? Since they had both been three sheets to wind, maybe they hadn't even remembered they spoke these words in front of their uncle? Perhaps it was one of those family skeletons in the closet?

"I know those boys had something to do with Nina's death. And I just couldn't keep it in anymore," Jacob's voice is scratchy. Genny lifts the straw to his lips. He takes two sips.

"You're not gonna tell them we said anything, are you?" asks Genny.

"No, of course not. It doesn't work like that."

"Did we do the right thing?" asks Jacob.

"Yes. You did," says Grable.

"So what do we do now? Do we get some sort of police protection or something?"

"You just go on living like normal. You take care of yourselves and you, Mr. Zachary, try to get well soon. Okay?" Grable manages a half smile. "Don't worry. What you said today was a good thing. And I hope it helps getting it off your conscience."

Jacob looks to his wife and nods slightly.

"I just have one question. Why did you wait so long? Why now?"

"We saw in the paper that a new detective is looking into her case again after all these years," says Genny. "I guess it jogged our memories."

"Nonsense. I went to the police back then. They didn't believe me," says Jacob.

"Who didn't?" asks Grable.

"That retired guy, Polland."

"Detective Polland? You talked to him about this?"

"Yeah, right after it happened. I went down to the station. But Polland told me they had questioned the twins and there was nothing linking them to Nina's disappearance."

Grable tries to recall anything from Nina's case file about Jacob Zachary's visiting Polland and making this statement. He is sure he would have remembered something like this in the files.

"Did Polland take your statement?"

"I met with him in his office. But I don't think he wrote anything down officially. I was only in there about five or so minutes... and I had alcohol on my breath." He lowers his head. "I wasn't all together myself back then."

"Thank you for your statements, Mr. and Mrs. Zachary," says Grable.

Grable steps out of the room and wanders the hall until he finds the nurse who had showed them in. He pulls her to the side of the nurse's station. "Is Mr. Zachary on any medications that would affect his judgment or memory?"

"You know I can't breach patient confidentiality, Detective Grable."

"I know. And I'm not asking you to," Grable says and adds gently. "Let me put it this way. If I were to subpoena you about Mr. Zachary's medical records, would there be anything there that would raise doubt as to his ability to testify?"

The nurse smiles and pulls him away from the nurse's station so no one can hear their conversation.

"Genny brought her husband in because he was experiencing shortness of breath and pain in his stomach. But once we stabilized him and ran some tests we found the underlying cause is that Jacob Zachary has stage four stomach cancer. We had to put him on a strong dose of pain killers."

Grable stands frozen for a moment. "How long does he have?"

The nurse shrugs. "Each case is different. But generally we see two to four months average life span on a case this advanced."

Even if they can arrest Silas and Solomon today, Jacob Zachary wouldn't last long enough to testify at trial. Grable sighs and thanks the nurse. He walks the hall to the elevator and is about to enter when he hears footsteps running up to him.

"Hey, detective Grable? Are we done here?" It's the fresh-faced cadet.

Grable has completely forgotten about the cadet in Jacob's room. He has been waiting in stealth mode back in Jacob's room. He motions for the young cadet to climb into the elevator.

"Yes, we're ready to go. You get good notes?" he asks.

"I think so," he says with a proud lilt to his tone. "I recorded everything on my phone."

Grable can barely hold back his anger. He takes a deep breath and tries in his most steady voice to explain that since they didn't ask for permission, technically none of that recording can be used in court. The cadet's face sinks.

"When we get back to the station, sit down immediately, before you do anything. Even before you take a piss or get a snack. Write down everything you remember from that conversation. Got it? And then come to my office and we'll go over it together. I'll help you fill in any holes."

"Can I use the recording?"

Grable doesn't justify the question with an audible answer. He holds the cadet in an insolent stare until the elevator doors open.

Chapter 41

TAMMY

T ammy slid a tin to Wallace. He pried open the lid and looked inside where the perfectly round discs of chocolate chip cookie dough were stacked between layers of wax paper.

"You didn't bake them?" Wallace asked lifting one to his lips.

"You said you liked the batter better."

He popped a dough disc into his mouth.

"Don't eat too many. You'll upset your stomach," she said.

He grabbed another one from the top layer. "You think this is gonna get me to talk, don't ya?"

"Wallace, do you know what's been going on back in Derby? Has anyone told you?"

He shook his head. "You're the only one's come to visit me all year."

"You ever check the news?"

"Why?" He ate another disc.

"There's a new cold case detective working up in Derby to--"

"Damn, these are good!"

His loud praise drew the attention of other visitors and inmates. Wallace reached for another raw cookie and Tammy snapped the lid shut on the box.

"You're gonna be out of here in five years. You ever think about what you're going to do then?" she said.

Wallace shrugged. "It's a long ways off."

"Time goes fast." She strummed her fingers on top of the metal lid. "You ever think about finding a woman, settling down? Kids?"

"What are you saying Tammy Tyler?" He sent her a sly smile. "I know you always had a crush on me."

She leaned in as close as she felt comfortable while the guards were watching.

"I wanna talk about that night in the woods," she said.

He pulled back. "Why? We don't know nothing about it."

"I need to get it off my chest."

"Then go see a therapist."

"Why can't we talk about it?" Tammy snapped.

"Because there ain't nothing to talk about." He pushed his chair back an inch and crossed his arms in front of his chest. Tammy ignored the body language.

"I feel responsible."

"You do, huh? Well, don't. We done nothing wrong."

"We saw her that night," Tammy said in a hushed voice.

"Saw who?"

"The dead girl. Nina Laramie."

"I don't know who that is or what that has to do with me or you?" said Wallace hissing back at her.

"Yes, you do. Don't play dumb."

Wallace wagged his head back and forth. "You're losing it, Tammy."

"We saw a girl being dragged on the ground. You remember. I know you do."

"I was too fucked up to remember," said Wallace.

"No, you weren't. You almost got the shit beat out of you. We barely made it outta there alive." She felt the tone of her voice rising and the room quieted in one of those odd communal conversation lulls that makes everyone suddenly feel self-aware.

"Why are you bringing this up now? Ain't gonna do no one, no good."

"Because what if… I wanna be clear about what we saw that night, Wallace? I can't get it outta my brain. I'm having nightmares about it and I don't know if it's my mind making shit up or what I actually saw. I just need to talk about it with you so I can make sense of this."

"So you can go to the cops and be a hero. Fuck that!"

"No! I just want some peace. I can't get any decent sleep."

Wallace palmed the sides of the tin and slid it from under Tammy's tap, tap, tapping fingers. She let him open the tin and he ate a fourth dough disc while his eyes wandered the perimeter of the visiting room. Tammy knew this look. Wallace was processing. After he swallowed the last bite of cookie, he cocked his head at her and his tone was less agitated when he spoke again.

"They gettin' close to solving this case down there in Derby?" he asked.

"I don't know. Lots of rumors."

"They have a suspect?"

"I don't know. But if we can help--"

"We. Weren't. Involved." His voice punctuated without a flicker of anger. Was it supposed to intimidate her? It didn't. She was more driven than ever.

"But I think we were there. We were, weren't we? Wasn't that her we saw on the ground?"

"How the hell do I know? I don't know nothing about this case or this girl. I never even heard of her before. I think your imagination is working overtime, Tammy."

"From what I've been reading, Nina Laramie disappeared on a summer night in August. Late. After midnight. In the Oconee Forest. That lines up exactly when we were there. It was the night Nina disappeared. We saw those guys with her dead body. Didn't we?"

Wallace crossed his arms and leaned back on his chair until the front two legs were off the ground. He was wagging his head slightly and staring at her with a clenched jaw. She knew if they were alone he would have grabbed her by the shoulders and "shaken some sense" into her. Like he had that night. It wasn't that he was violent towards women. No. Never had been. Tammy knew he would never hit her or throw her. A raised voice and a firm grasp was as far as he would go to make his point. But Wallace was a cop-hater with a lot of pent up anger.

"Four on the floor, Wallace!" yelled the nearby guard. Wallace slammed the legs to the cement.

"You open this can of worms and things could go to shit for you. And your kid. They'll do it again. Don't think they won't. That's why I threatened to kill you. Not cause I would, but because I knew they would."

"So you do remember. I knew it." She almost wept from sheer relief.

"No. You listen, here. I am not willing to talk about this. Don't you drag me into this. Things don't go well in prison for snitches." Wallace said under his breath.

"I'm scared, Wallace. Scared if I don't say something. Scared if I do. It haunts me."

"We're done with this conversation. You got it? You even try to tell the cops about this and I'll deny everything. It's your word against mine, Tammy. And no proof to back it up." His eyes went steely cold and he motioned to the guard that he was ready to leave. "Don't you come back here to visit me. Don't you call me. Don't you write me.

Don't you fucking dare go running to the cops about this. And don't you dare coming looking for me in five years."

The guard came over and escorted Wallace out of the room. Tammy picked up her tin of cookie dough and walked out the visitor's door. Once she was outside she drove twenty minutes sobbing down the two lane highway. Then, she caught her breath and rolled down the window giving the tin box of cookies a heave into the ditch.

Chapter 43

RILEY ST. JAMES

D
r. Berlyn Hardenberg, the medical examiner, calls me to his home. He's made a discovery and he wants to tell me in person, not over phone or email. When I arrive I see that there is a large team of roofers, like bees swarming a hive atop of his roof. Dr. Hardenberg is standing outside watching them with scrutiny written all over his face.

"Detective St. James, have you ever hired roofers before?" he says glancing at me, and then back to the hive of activity on his roof.

"I can't say that I have." His gaze is back on the roof again.

"It's incredible the speed at which they work. Two days ago they came and stripped the tiles, down to bare bones. Yesterday they laid fresh paper. Today the new tiles. They'll be done by six, they tell me."

"That's incredible. How many square feet is that?" I say looking at the expansive roof of his mid-century home.

"Two thousand. I've been standing here the better of three days just watching. It's better than television." He laughs.

In just the few minutes I had been there they had moved a full foot down the roof, covering it with the black asphalt looking roof shingles.

"What made you decide to redo your roof? Was it leaking?" I ask.

"Heavens no. A tragic event. After the wind the other day, one of the older maples from the back yard fell onto the kitchen side of the house. Landed smack dab into our oldest son's bedroom. Of course, he's off at college, thank God."

"Oh, wow. Was anyone hurt?"

"No, thankfully. And my wife and I were out to dinner."

"I'm so grateful."

"I told Melinda last fall that I needed to cut that tree down."

"You're very lucky," I say.

"Luck has nothing to do with it. Just wasn't our time to go."

That certainly is one way to look at it. I watch the busy bee roofing team, mesmerized by their efficiency. "Is there something else you wanted to show me?"

"Of course. Yes." He motions for me to follow him inside. "This whole disaster has yielded a very important discovery. There are no coincidences in life, St. James."

He is lithe and excited as he leads me into his office where we can hear the roofers' nail guns zapping like artillery two stories overhead.

"It was the first day they were here when I saw it. Each one of them had one. There were dozens of them. But I didn't know what I was looking at until they took their first break and one of them set the tool down on the ground near where I was standing to watch."

Dr. Hardenberg had raised his voice to combat the rapid fire from above. He sits at his computer, logs in and starts clicking.

"What was the tool?"

"It's used to remove the old singles. It's simply called, 'a roofing tool'. But I had never seen one before. Have you?"

"No. Never." I am completely drawn into his mystery and enthusiasm. I can't wait to see where he's going with this.

"And that's when it all came together. A roofing tool has four small prongs that grab the edge of the shingles so they can peel them off the roof. The size of each prong and the space apart from each other exactly match the wound marks on Nina."

I can't believe it. He's pulling up images of roofing tools and Nina's autopsy photographs. He's even had time in the past two day to create a little slide show that overlaps the tool to the wound marks. I almost gasp when he overlays the two. They are an exact match.

"It's undeniable. Don't you see?" He looks to me for my reaction.

I nod. Speechless.

"Of course, I'm aware the police never found anything like this in the twins' possession. They searched their car, house. Nothing. But I'm not surprised. They had plenty of time and opportunity to rid themselves of their roofing tool before the cops came calling."

Dr. Hardenberg is almost vibrating. He jumps up from his desk and starts to pace. "But it's here, it's all here! Thirty years and it drops into my lap. I can't believe it."

"It's an incredible discovery. It's wonderful information to have," I say as I continue to study the screen. I feel like I'm watching something out of NCIS. It's that perfect. That exact. But, unlike the show, I don't have a lot of hope this will give us a lead to anything.

"You can't go public with this. You know that, right? We have to keep it under wraps just in case..."

"I know that." I don't mean to cut him off.

"I mean... maybe there's a chance it's in their barn? Or basement... or a bedroom under a mattress. I don't know. Sometimes criminals keep murder weapons as souvenirs or talisman," he says. "It's possible, I guess."

"Dr. Hardenberg, you've done amazing work here. Can I get a copy for Nina's file? I'll be sure to bring this to light with the rest of the team ASAP. I hope it leads us to something valuable."

"Yes, yes." He leaps back to his computer, throws in a flash drive and makes me a copy. All the while the rat-a-tat-tat goes on upstairs. And then, a chain saw starts up. Dr. Hardenberg hands me the flash drive as he rises.

"Oh, good. The tree trimmer is finally here. He said I may be able to get some good logs outta that old maple. If it's not too rotted. I was thinking of making Melinda a picnic table."

"That's really nice of you," I say. "Is there anything you don't do?"

"Melinda says I'm not very good at relaxing."

I laugh. "I think she may be hinting at a vacation."

"I'm pretty sure it's more than a hint," he says as he walks me to my car. "Slow down and you die. I've seen it over and over again." He turns his attention back to the roof work.

I head back to the station and into my office. Seconds later, Grable finds me, enthusiastic about a conversation with Jacob Zachary. I am stunned as I read the cadet's report. More legend surfacing. We agree that this could be admissible in court and we need to get an official statement from Mr. Zachary as soon as possible. Grable says he will arrange to go to the hospital for a witness statement.

I show Grable Hardenberg's file, he tells me about a conversation he had with Misty claiming that she overhead the twins say the murder weapon was a roofing tool.

"Why didn't you mention that to me before?" I ask.

Grable shrugs. "Misty says a lot of things when she's drunk."

"Everything counts. I need everything right now. Do you understand that?" I'm so annoyed. "Is there anything else you're keeping from me?"

"Chill out. You know everything."

"Do I?"

Grable clucks at me. "It's gone, St. James. We're never going to find the murder weapon." He pivots out of my office.

Despite Grable's pessimism, hope has alighted my spirit for a change. There is a very nice path of evidence and corroboration lining up. Especially given the timing of Dr. Hardenberg figuring it out. Laura's statement. The tool identification. Jacob Zachary's admission. I'm not ready to give up on finding a murder weapon just yet.

I sink into my desk chair feeling the intimation of relief. These recent findings have shown me that I am not forgotten. Nina is not forgotten. And I only hope justice will not be forgotten.

Queen bee must stay in her hive. The swarm is coming. I sense it. I don't know how or when. But the crack in the code of silence is widening. I'm going to fight through this and I'm not going to let Ray Polland down.

Chapter 44

NINA, 1989

We had driven all over the county for several hours and land-ed at a gas station a good deal south of Derby. Rich got gas and some snacks while I waited in the car with Solomon and Silas. We all pulled out, Rich first. And Silas tailgated Rich's car all twenty miles back to Derby. I know it pissed off Rich. He was flipping us off the whole time. We all had a good laugh about it.

I told the guys I was ready to go home. I was tired of riding around. I wanted to see Tucker. He probably needed to go out and I didn't want to clean up any more messes. I told them they could drop me off before they went on to Rich's house. They were staying the night there because they didn't want to drive all the way back to their home in Brantwood in the middle of the night.

"Do you live by Rich?" asked Solomon.

"Downtown Derby. It's right on your way."

Silas laid off Rich's tail and pretty soon Rich was a good quarter mile ahead and gaining distance from us.

"You're lettin' him get away," I joked.

Silas smiled. Solomon tried to light a cigarette with the window down. It wasn't working so he rolled it up half way and finally got the match to stay lit long enough to ignite it. He drew in a long breath and the tip glowed red.

"You wanna go to a bonfire?" asked Solomon. They made a right turn just before we got into Derby city limits.

"Not really. Just home," I said. "There's a back way to my house if you turn left at the next street."

"Come on. Just for a little while," coaxed Solomon.

"No, I'm done for the night. Just turn left up here and bring me home."

I didn't like it that Rich's car was outta sight. In fact, there were no cars on the road. It had to be past midnight. Derby's a ghost town after 8 P.M. on a weekday. They sailed past the street I asked them to take.

Solomon took my right hand and lifted it up, looking at my class ring.

"Nice ring," said Solomon.

"Can you turn around please and take me home?"

"What birthstone is that?"

I didn't answer. I was not having fun anymore and I'm annoyed they won't take me home.

"Can I see it up close?" said Solomon.

I felt him start to wiggle the ring off my finger. I tried to stop him, but the ring had always been slightly oversized and it came right off.

"Hey, gimme that back," I said cupping my hand out in front of him to catch it.

"Just wanna see what you put on it. What were you, a cheerleader? Band? Volleyball?" he asked.

"I wasn't in anything."

"Then why'd you get one?" asked Silas.

Dad had saved up and bought me that ring sophomore year. He said it was important that I graduate from high school and hoped a class ring would be some incentive to try. I quit second semester junior year. He made me get my GED in the fall. It's the only piece of jewelry he ever gave me.

"Give that back to me. Now."

"Whatcha getting' so worked up about? I ain't gonna steal it." He chuckled and flicked his cigarette butt out the window. Then, he faked like he was going to toss the ring out, too.

I lurched to grab it and he pulled back his fist. Opened it. No ring.

"Shit! What did you do, you jerk!" I punched his arm.

"Hey, ow. You hit hard for a girl," said Solomon.

"Silas, stop this car. Turn around. Now!"

"Relax," said Solomon opening his other fist to show me my ring.

I tried to pluck it from his palm, but he was too quick. He laughed.

He pulled away and then unclasped a silver stud chain he was wearing. He slipped my class ring onto the chain and slipped it around his neck.

"What are you doing?"

"Isn't this what guys do when they're dating a girl?" said Solomon.

"We're not dating. I have a boyfriend. A serious one," I informed them.

"Yeah, well, where is Mr. Serious tonight then?" taunted Silas in a tone that sent a sharp twinge to the center of my stomach. He and Solomon laughed.

Without a second thought, I reached up and yanked that chain right off his neck. It left a red welt on Solomon's neck, almost as red as his face.

"What the fuck? You bitch!" He rubbed his neck.

I pushed the ring back on my finger. "Head back to Derby and drop me home."

Neither one said anything more as Silas slowed the car off the shoulder. I thought he was gonna do a U-turn. But then, he turned the car onto the dirt two-track that lead to the Hole in the Woods.

Chapter 45

WALLACE

Wallace almost didn't go to visiting hour when he heard he had a visitor. He knew it would be Tammy and he was pissed she came back. He would see her and tell her she should never return. And then he would end the visit. After that he would head to the gym to get in another half hour because it wouldn't be busy now.

He made an audible gasp when he saw his father, Paul, sitting in the chair at the visitor's table. His sagging jeans were cinched by a brown leather belt with three homemade holes beyond the original manufacturer's. It was the same one he used to whip Wallace's backside when he was on drunken rages. His skin looked gray and his eyes were sunken into dark sockets. He rose to his feet when Wallace approached.

"Hello, son."

"You don't have to get up," Wallace said. Paul gripped the side of the table as he steadied himself into his chair. Wallace sat too.

"How are you?" Paul asked with rattle in voice.

"Never better," said Wallace.

"You spoke to your brother recently?"

"No. You?"

"He calls now and again," said Paul. "What do you got here? Another five?"

"Five."

"Be nice if you set up down there after this. Maybe find a wife. Start a family."

"Sure. I'll get a two-story with a dog and boat. Dream life," Wallace flung his sarcasm.

"I hear it, son. The bitterness. The anger."

"You said you were never coming to visit. So--?"

"I know."

"You don't look so good," said Wallace. He saw the insides of his arms torn up by IV track marks. "What've you been doing?"

Paul saw Wallace looking at his arms. "It ain't what you're thinking."

"Oh yeah. What am I thinking?"

"It's from the hospital."

"You sick?"

"I've got liver cancer. Probably only a couple more months on this earth."

Wallace was quiet as his dad took out a hanky and wiped away the saliva forming around his mouth. "I can't help the drooling. Awful side effect from one of these experimental drugs they put me on."

He couldn't say he was sorry to hear it. He had been praying for his dad to die since the beatings started at age seven. The old man was finally getting what was coming to him. "You got someone taking care of you?"

"Your aunt. She comes by a couple times a week."

Wallace nodded. She was yet another family member who had disowned him after Wallace's third arrest for armed robbery and assault.

"So you came here to tell me you're dying. What am I supposed to do with that?"

"There ain't nothing to do. I just wanted to see you one last time."

"Well, lucky for you I'm a captive audience."

"Life is shorter than we think it's going to be."

Was he really going to start offering advice? Wallace had no patience for this.

"Why are you really here, old man?" Wallace asked him.

"I wish I woulda spent more time helping people than hurting them. You included."

His shame forces Paul to set his gaze to the floor.

"I can't offer you my forgiveness just like that. On the spot. So if that's what you really came for, you best leave now."

Paul cleared the phlegm from his throat. The awful guttural sound drew the probing eyes of those around him. He dabbed away more saliva oozing from the crusty corner of his mouth.

"Maybe you can forgive me, maybe you can't. That'll be up to you. And God. Not my business. Just hope you can live your life better than I did. You understand? You still have time to make things right with people."

"What people? Who sent you up here?" It seemed like a cheap trick to use his cancer as a calling card. How was dad trying to manipulate him this time?

"I don't know, son. I don't know where you been in your life or what you've really done. But I recognize the discontent. That peace you're craving. And I know you do. Crave it. I know your restless soul, son. Am I'm part to blame for it."

"Maybe all to blame," said Wallace.

His father nodded. "I know I didn't always treat you the best. You can either keep blaming me and find no peace or go about seeing how you can make this crooked trail you've created, straight."

"My father, the death bed philosopher," Wallace sneered.

"Can't tell you what weights have been lifted off me. I wish I woulda known all this thirty years ago."

"Oh yeah. How would that have made things any better for me and my brother?" asked Wallace rhetorically.

"I wish I woulda treated you better. Maybe you wouldn't have ended up here." Paul's hand drifted down to his belt buckle knowing this was the source of their pain. "I'm sorry. For everything."

The silence hung between like a thick marine layer, growing more opaque. Wallace shuffled his feet under the table and cocked his head to the right as if trying to see through it.

"I don't know what you want me say?" Wallace blurted out.

"There's no words, son," said Paul. "Only actions. I want you to do something. Just one thing. Promise me before I leave here to die."

Wallace shrugged. He was willing to hear it, but the word promise would never slip through his lips.

"Just start with one person," said Paul, looking up at Wallace, his head quivering under the compulsion of the meds and disease.

"And do what?" asked Wallace dryly.

"You'll know what." Paul clutched the table and used all his strength to stand. Wallace instinctively stood, too. "Good bye, son. I love you."

Then, Paul shuffled off and Wallace saw a glimpse of his aunt behind the door waiting for him. She glanced up, glowering at Wallace. Disdain poured from her tight lips and furrowed brow. The feeling was mutual. She knew what was going on in their home back then. She saw the welts and bruises. She knew how Wallace had really broken his arm summer after fifth grade. And she had stayed silent. He couldn't forgive her for that.

She reached out for Paul and took his arm. His father never looked back and Wallace felt the ache rise from the pit of his stomach up into his esophagus and pinching at his pharynx. He felt he may pass out. He willed himself to draw in a sip of air as if through a drinking straw and his lungs inflated enough to ward off the dizzy feeling. Emotions churned his insides like a wash tub.

Wallace thought about his dad's request. Help one person. For what gain? He had always done what was best for Wallace. He was used to a world where he was in control. That's what felt safe to him. He had never felt peace. He couldn't think of one time, even as a kid. The real question was, how many people did he need to help until he felt complete peace? And would he even recognize that feeling once it came? One selfless act in exchange for an ounce of peace. It seemed like a fleeting bargain.

The guard returned Wallace to the gym, but he had lost the desire. He lay awake on his bed the rest of the day and all night thinking about his past. His father. Their past. His heart was too hard to reach out to family. They didn't deserve it. He knew that wasn't the point. But he wasn't ready. So what if his dad was dying. He would never hear the words "I forgive you" from Wallace. Never.

As he meditated on his father's final appearance, Wallace started to see into the crack in his abusive personality. The rage wasn't there. And beyond his sallow, sickly appearance, his father held a calm about him that was new to Wallace. The way dad looked at him as he left. The only word Wallace could muster up, was love. It was the first time he saw it in his father and he loathed to admit that his father had just shown him love. Wallace recognized it as such because he had seen it in just a few others who had loved him like that. His mother.

His brother. Tammy. And then it struck him, is that perhaps what peace looked like? Were peace and love the same? If that were true, Wallace would like to have some. Wasn't he entitled?

As Wallace turned onto his side, he felt the tension and the tight knots in his neck and shoulders that no amount of massaging or pain pills could dull away. He would consider about his father's suggestion. But only because he didn't want his father to be the only one who got to be free. In fact, he would make it a goal to be even freer than his father. His father had lived a small, sheltered, selfish life. In that instant, Wallace became aware that this was his own. Only he was literally in prison. A despondency blanketed Wallace. His life was much worse and even more pathetic than his father's.

No more.

Something inside him broke like a rope that had been rubbing itself raw for years over and over a roughly hewn wooden beam. The weight sprung off his body, as he left the dense beam of resentment and anger behind. His churning, exhausted mental state settled into that semi-conscious state of being awake yet being asleep. In his mind's eye, he ran and ran. Skipping, leaping, flinging his arms about. He was lithe and light.

Finally, Wallace drifted into a deep sleep where dreams come. Wallace saw a flash of a Mustang on a dirt two-track. Then a limp-bodied girl being dragged across the forest floor. He turned around and headlights blinded him. Wallace's eye blinked open and he found he was staring into the bright bulb on the ceiling of his cell. It was morning already.

Chapter 46

RILEY ST. JAMES

The dream begins again in a place just after the incident. I can feel the cold and shiver back to consciousness, but my body does not try to wake. I am paralyzed by an achy stiffness....

I see the dark sky overhead and when I lower my gaze to the horizon, I can see the bottom edges of the sky start to mellow with light. I roll a little to my left side. Pain twinges through my back and shoulders. A twig cracks under my weight. I pause to regain my balance.

I see the reason I am so, so cold. My legs are bare. My bottom is bare. I touch myself, searching for my panties. Gone. Where? How? Why? I see my pants down by my ankles. And I feel wet in my crotch. I touch between my legs lightly and my fingers wet with something light and sticky. I smell it. Blood. It's not my time of the month.

I try to get my sluggish brain to rewind the events of the past few hours and why I am lying on the floor of the woods. I yank up my pants. My fingers fumble to close the zipper. I can't manage to get the button looped into the button-hole and give up as I crawl to my knees. My entire head throbs in pain and I let it hang between my arms.

Questions ping through my sluggish brain. Why does the back of my head hurt so badly? I reach to the throbbing spot and feel a goose egg. Hot tears well from my eyes as a memory flashes across the screen of my brain. I remember crunchy footsteps over dry leaves and brittle twigs.

I'm on my hunches retching, but nothing comes out. My mouth is dry. So dry. Water. I crawl a few paces and try to gain balance to stand. Gripping a nearby tree it takes every ounce of my strength to stand. Once I do, a sharp pain jabs at my crotch. I double over, breathing heavily as fear grips me and squeezes my lungs. I struggle to breath.

What happened to me? Who was with me in the woods? Where was he? Was he going to attack again? Was he still in the woods? What if he's hiding? Waiting to take me down again?

I have to get out of here. Run. Run. Go. Go. Get out! Go! My pupils, full and dark, search the woods. I can't see anyone.Grabbing at tree branches, I manage to move my cement legs, one foot in front of another. Adrenaline shoots through my body, releasing the hold of fear and replacing it with a flutter in my stomach. I ignore the pain as I pump my legs down the well-worn path towards the college campus.

The sky's soft blue and orange hues breaking at the horizon provide the light I need to find my way out of the woods. The path dumps me into the nearly empty parking lot at the far end of the campus. No one parks here except the commuters during the day. I race across the asphalt, through the sleepy campus.

No one is out. No one to see me. What if someone does see me? I don't want anyone to see me. I dive behind the buildings, slinking my way towards the dorm. Wait. The dorm doesn't open its doors until 6am. What time is it? Has anyone noticed I've been gone all night?

The gym. The gym will be open for early morning athlete workouts. I make a sharp turn and head away from the dorm. I can hide out there for a bit until I figure out what to do. I can't face roommates. I can't face anyone.

I slip into the side door of the gym, keeping my head down, and dart to the women's locker room. Thankfully, it's empty, although I can see that it's recently been in use. Without thinking I wander into a shower stall and turn on the water. Hot. Hair, clothes, shoes, and all are soon soaked. I have no strength or wherewithal to take of my clothes. I stand there as the steam fills the stall and wafts out into the locker room. After a few minutes I hear someone enter and use the toilet. Then leave. The weight of my soaking clothes makes me feel suffocated so I step out of my shoes and begin to peel the layers of clothing off my body. I let the water wash down my naked skin. And I cry and cry. I can't look down there. I can't spread my legs to clean down there. I can't move.

The locker room door opens again and I muffle my sobs in the palms of my hands. Two females enter, get something from their lockers, use the sink, and then leave again. I realize I have to get out of here before more people come. I have no towel or fresh clothes, so I begin to search for an open locker. For articles of clothes someone has left behind. After the fourth try, I find an open locker. No towel, but a set of workout clothes that look like they'll fit. I take them and use paper towel from the dispenser to dry off. Pulling the clothes onto my damp body, I notice a line of bruises along my left leg. Those weren't there before. Those are from... him.

I need shoes. I try a couple more lockers. Nothing. I hear more female voices approaching outside the locker room and grab the wet clothes from my shower stall. I stuff them into the garbage bin as a pack of four basketball players enter with their oversized duffle bags. I leap into a bathroom stall and wait. The girls change quickly because they are late for practice. I hear them carelessly slam their duffle bags into lockers and trot out. When the door closes and silence fills the room, I emerge. I see one of the duffle straps wedged between the locker door. I yank on the strap and the locker door pops open. Inside the duffle is a pair of slip-on athletic sandals. I swipe those, too. They're two sizes too big. My toes clutch at the thong strap as I flip-flop out of the locker room, down the tiled hallway, and out the side door that leads to the soccer practice fields. Beyond the fields is... just somewhere that's not here. I can never go back. I don't know where to go or who to go to. I can't tell anyone what has happened. It's not that they wouldn't under-stand... it's just that... A twinge in my crotch sends a wave of nausea. I double up. Breathe. Breathe. It intensifies and I throw up, heaving only liquid contents of my stomach now. I smell garlic and it triggers the memory of him. I keep heaving until there is nothing but a gag-ging sound.

I haven't been able to eat anything with garlic in it since this. The restaurant I was coming from that night was Valentino's, a high-end Italian restaurant where I worked part time. When I thought it through later, I determined that I actually worked with my attacker. Hence the garlic breath and garlic hands. Valentino's puts garlic in everything! It was their signature. Sauce. Bread. Pasta. Pizza. Even the ice cream. Their novelty item. I went back to work at my wait job the next weekend, head held high, smile pasted on. And I watched the wait staff, busboys, dishwashers, valets, bartenders. Who was snitching a garlic roll on the side? Or sneaking in bites of garlic ice cream? After working there for one week, no one could stand the taste of garlic. We all steered clear of it.

Except one. I noted a bartender named Clinton. Handsome. Well-liked. Charismatic.

Why had I never noticed before that he always ordered a basket of garlic rolls to keep under the bar?

During my first shift back, I went to pick up a drink order at the bar. There was a mistake in the order and when I let Clinton know, he refused to make eye contact and asked another bartender to make the correction.

That had never happened before. The mistake or the deflection.

I cross the practice field and come out on the other side, where a narrow drive leads off campus and into the neighborhood. I've been told... we, the prey, we've all been told... that if something like this happens, go to the emergency room and request a sexual assault exam.

A rape kit. Rape. Vile. Vile word. A word happened to me. I will *never* tell anyone about this vile word.

I walk and walk… down the neighborhood streets at dawn. Several blocks down, a garbage truck jerks from house to house picking up the weekly trash. I keep walking, ignoring the soreness between my legs.

A dog barks from behind a fence as I pass. It stirs up the other dogs in the neighborhood, triggering an outburst of barking dogs. Soon, the only thing I can hear is a cacophony of barking dogs… growing louder, meaner. The world is now a loud, mean, frightful place. The gnashing of teeth. The nipping at your heels. No peace. No more peace ever. I find myself running through the forest again. The dream on a repeating loop. More barking.

My eyes pop open just as my garlic-breathed attacker is about to pummel me to the floor of the forest. My hair is damp and sticking to my forehead. My t-shirt and boxers are soaked in sweat. My armpits smell like rotten eggs. I check my heart rate. It's at 130, like I've literally been running a race in my sleep. This isn't good for my heart health. I know that. And I avoid medical checkups because I don't want to be forced to take a leave of absence from my job.

Barking!

Zikmund!

Chapter 47

RILEY ST. JAMES

I bolt from bed and rush into the living room to find Zikmund on the couch, saliva from his hot breath on the window wetting the glass. He has two paws up against the window and the fur along his spine is standing on end. I look beyond the window to the outside where I see the taillights of a black Ford 150 disappear around the corner. I collapse to the couch, heart pounding, flutter in my belly.

Zikmund's barking turns into a low growl and he comes down off his hunches. He shakes off, sending a spray of loose fur into the air. He sits on the couch so that he still has a view of any outside activity.

I stroke Zikmund's back. "Good boy, good boy. Good boy."

I sit there for a long time thinking. Zikmund never leaves my side, his gaze glancing back and forth between me and the outside.

I refuse to live under the gnashing of teeth and nipping at my heels.

I can no longer be a sitting target.

The daylight hours bring no relief as my frustrated mind immediately shifts to Nina's rape and murder. We are so close, but it's not close enough or fast enough for me. The Newtons' second attack leaves me cold and angry. I watch my surveillance video footage of Solomon's truck trolling in front of my house. I'm tired of cowering behind the scenes while they are getting away with it. I can only imagine this is a fraction of what Jim Laramie feels every single day of his life.

Retaliation has to be met. And now. Enough of being stalked.

Because God only knows what they might do to their uncle, once they find out he's made a statement or to Jim, who is looking more fragile now than when I met him weeks ago.

As I stew in all this, drinking coffee on my back porch with Zikmund laying in the sun next to me, I find my push point. I will go looking for that roofing tool. I know it's a long, long, long shot. But I'm aching for the tangible, solid evidence that will provide a concrete, undeniable link to place them at Nina's murder. I know what Misty heard them say. But I am not going to rely on drunken gossip. No stone unturned. My gut tells me that there's a good possibility that the chatter about a roofing tool and the foundry is planted.

Enough of all the secrets and kowtowing around them. I will not be prey. I will not let anyone else become prey.

I will face my enemy and show I am not afraid. I don't even bother to finish my coffee. I grab my keys and Zikmund follows me to the truck. He jumps in shotgun and off we go.

Chapter 48

RILEY ST. JAMES

S olomon's house, if you can call it that, is a doublewide trailer on a two-acre lot set off a side street just outside of Derby. It's not remote. But it's not in plain view. I know I should contact Grable, but I don't want to. I know what I'm doing defies rational thought and conventional wisdom. It could even be argued that I'm reaching outside bounds of law. But none of this stops me from pulling into Solomon's driveway. Behind the trailer is a pole barn that's probably twice the size of his living quarters. And probably where Solomon spends more of his time anyhow.

I don't see his truck and I brazenly park at the end of the driveway. The impulse to confront him, to get him to confess, rages within me heating my spine all the way up to my neck and cheeks. I step out of the truck and Zikmund bounces out after me. He stays by my side. His formidable presence offers me reassurance. Poor thing has no idea what he's followed me into. He can sense my anxiousness and stays at my heels, glancing up at me every couple of seconds.

I go right up to the front door and find it locked, which doesn't surprise me. Most folks in Derby don't lock their doors, I've learned. But Solomon has secrets to hide. I head for the pole barn. Zikmund and I enter easily through the unlocked side door. It's a typical man's world cluttered with tools, machinery parts, and a dismantled car. I tread carefully so as not to disturb anything and begin my hunt for the roofing tool. I decide to use a grid search technique and imagine the pole barn squared into nine even blocks. I begin with the top corner block located on the east facing side of the barn. I place the obedient Zikmund to guard the door. Once inside my first block, I take to the corner against the wall and walk slowly in a straight line to the end of the imaginary block line. I turn, step one foot over, and walk back. All the while I'm scanning every inch of space so I don't miss a single detail. I realize, even as I'm doing it, how ludicrous this is!

My next line takes me to the corner of the barn where I see a standing toolbox. I slip a glove over my right hand and open each drawer, examining the mess of tools collected here. I'm about to open the bottom drawer, my concentration laser focused, when Zikmund whimpers and cocks his head toward the door. I look up. Nothing is there.

"What is it buddy?" I whisper.

His head is stiffly locked and pointed at the open barn door. I listen for a moment.

"It's nothing. Just some leaves blowing in." I tell him and quickly resume my search, opening the bottom drawer. Kneeling down to take a closer look, I see the jagged edge of the head of a roofing tool with its four prongs sticking face up from under a hand saw. A guttural sound gurgles from the back of my throat. Part gasp, part groan. I fumble for my phone to snap a picture when Zikmund's deep bark jerks me up. He sprints toward the door causing me to jump up.

I reach for my gun but it's not there. Shock waves flash from my gut to brain reminding me that in my haste, I left it at home.

Zikmund is holding Solomon hostage at the doorway, barking and growling with teeth bared inches from Solomon's thigh.

"What the hell are you doing here?" Solomon shouts at me from across the pole barn.

I don't answer. I march my way towards Solomon and my gaze never leaves his.

"I said, what the fuck are you doing here?" He swings to hit Zikmund and Zikmund sends him a warning snap. "Get this dog under control!"

I do no such thing. "One more word and I'll command him to attack." I'm now behind Zikmund about twenty feet's distance. "You kept it, huh?"

"What are you talking about?" Solomon does a poor job of playing dumb.

"Does it make you feel good? Strong?"

"You're crazy. You need to leave."

"Who actually struck Nina with the roofing tool? You or your brother?" I say with undefiled confidence, realizing in that sinking moment that I had just given away that I knew about the murder weapon. Damn it. Rage was taking over reason. And I couldn't help myself unspool on him.

Solomon's face twists and he snarls back. "You need to leave... or I'll…. I'm…"

"Gonna call the police?" I taunt. "I have video footage of you at my house this morning."

"Fuck you!" His brilliant response. I know I've rattled him.

"Did you take turns hitting her?" The adrenaline rush is in high gear and I'm starting to feel that heat radiating into my legs. I get a whiff of sulfur from under my arms. "Who dealt the final blow?"

Zikmund senses our danger. The hair on his back raises. He takes a small step towards Solomon. Solomon instinctively backs up. Zikmund growls.

"Seriously, lady. Tell this dog to back off."

I shake my head. "You didn't back down when Nina was crying for mercy, did you?"

I take a step forward. Zikmund steps forward too with a low growl. Solomon scoots out the door backwards.

Zik and I immediately follow him out and find him climbing into the back of his pickup truck for higher ground. At that moment, it occurs to me that he probably has a gun in that pick up. What am I thinking? What am I doing here? Trespassing! Threatening an inno-cent-until-proven-guilty citizen! Ruining everything I have done to build this case. What has come over me? I command Zikmund to my side. I stride up to the truck and look Solomon in the eye. It doesn't appear he has a gun or any object with which to strike me. I whistle and Zikmund puts his front paws up on the bed of the truck. He could clear it in one jump. But I make him wait and I decide I have to just go for it.

"Did you kill Nina Laramie?" I say, drawing out each word.

"You're fucking crazy, lady."

I shrug. "I am. I am!" I'm batshit crazy right now! And I don't back down. But that doesn't make my action any less imprudent. And in the back of my mind, I am very aware of that, too.

"We're getting close, Solomon," I use his name, making the space between us more intimate. "But there's still time to claim your part. Are you killer or accomplice?"

Solomon's look tells me he's trying to wrap his head around everything that's transpired in the last three minutes of his life.

"You wouldn't have found what you're looking for in there anyhow," he finally says to me.

"Don't be so sure." My adrenaline is crashing.

There are so many things I want to express at this moment. But I have to get out of here. I walk backwards to my truck so I can keep him in view. Zikmund trots at my side. Solomon doesn't make any attempt to get out of the truck bed until I open the door for Zikmund and he jumps in. I get in after him, locked the doors out of habit, and take off. I know I have to report myself to Grable. Oh God, what have I just done?

Chapter 49

RILEY ST. JAMES

I lock myself into the house, turn on all the security systems, and check the cameras. I do not call Grable. I do not eat. I do not watch television or get on my phone. I do not open my computer. I do not sleep. I rattle around the house doing little odds and ends while Zikmund watches me and then curls up in his bed and yawns. In a few minutes he is asleep.

Finally, I try to incorporate some sleep habits that a therapist taught me. No blue lights. Essential oils. Hot water bottle. None of it works.

I lay down on the couch and try to find something to watch. I settle on a documentary about food production, but it only depresses me and made me more upset with humanity. Why are we killing each other over nothing? I click off the channel and put on some soft classical music for background noise. I grab my YA novel, pull a blanket around me, and read the same page four times before I give up.

I get up and pace to the kitchen. I open the fridge and an odor wafts out, causing me to clap my hand over my mouth. With my free hand I dig and search for the foul item. My search yields nothing fetid. In fact, every item is sealed and fresh. I check the crisper. There's no way I would have bought it. I take out every item. There is only a bag of celery, several carrots, and a single potato. I remove everything and bleach wash each shelf and drawer.

But I still smell garlic.

Chapter 50

SILAS & SOLOMON

S ilas drove up to his brother's house and hopped out of his pickup. The door to the pole barn was open so Silas figured he was working in there. As he wandered over he saw that Solomon had parked his truck off to the side of the pole barn and not in front of his house like usual. And now he realized that was why he had such a perfect angle from Solomon's dash cam. There were also tire tracks in the drive that were not from Solomon's truck. It was undeniable that Solomon had had a visitor that day. Silas had recognized the guest vehicle immediately and jumped into his truck.

"Saw you had a visitor," Silas said as he entered the barn and saw his brother jump.

"Huh?" Solomon tried not to look up from his workbench.

"Why was she here?" Silas asked.

"Ain't nobody been here," said Solomon.

"You ain't never been able to lie to me," Silas gave him a toothy grin and turned up his nose, sniffing the place like a hound on the hunt "I smell her."

"All you smell is your own shit," said Solomon. "Why'd you come over here anyhow?"

Solomon glanced at his brother whose face was growing hard. Silas stepped up to his twin and whispered in his ear. "You left the dash cam running on your truck. I saw her truck. What the hell's going on, Solomon?"

Solomon wiped down a power drill with a shaky hand. Yes, he had given Silas access to his dash cam app password. Big mistake. He was always spying on Solomon.

"Bitch scared the living shit outta me. Almost sic'd that dog on me," protested Solomon.

"What was she doing in here?" said Silas calmly.

"Snooping around."

"Trespassing. That's bold." Silas said.

"What are we gonna do, Si?"

Silas sighed. "Maybe we gotta get rid of her."

"Why would you say that? We ain't done nothing. That she can prove," said Solomon.

"What did she say to you?" asked Silas.

"She flat out asked me if we killed Nina Laramie," said Solomon.

"I don't want to hear you say that name out loud. Ever. You got that."

"We gonna report this to Grable?" said Solomon.

"Shit no," said Silas. "She didn't find anything? Take anything?"

Solomon paused. If he told his brother the truth, there would be hell to pay. "I don't think so. What are we gonna do."

Silas shook his head. "We're not gonna do nothing."

"Okay. You sure?" said Solomon.

"It was a non-incident. Don't you see? It's your word against hers. So, we're not gonna say anything," said Silas.

"But what if she..." said Solomon. "She was pissed off. She woulda had that dog kill me."

"Big picture, brother. Our plan is working. Cat and mouse. We're getting under her skin. As far as I'm concerned, you did the right thing staying calm," Silas said. "Let's get outta here and get something to eat."

"We could do it, Si. She's just a little bitty thing. Smaller than that girl we did up north. And ain't nobody even, ever found her body yet," said Solomon.

"And they never will." Silas' words came through gritted teeth. "Don't be a jackass. We're not doing anything."

"She knew about the roofing tool!" Solomon belted out. "How did she know about that? Huh?" Solomon wiped away beads of sweat on his forehead. "How did she know?" Solomon asked again, calmer as he clasped his hands together to stop them from quivering.

"Because you've been blabbering all over town how you melded it at the foundry. That's how, jack ass," said Silas. "What do you have to worry about anyhow?"

"I only said that to throw people off track," Solomon defended.

"What?" said Silas.

Solomon wagged his head for Silas to follow him as he unlocked his standing tool chest. He opened the bottom drawer and pointed. Silas looked down disbelieving.

"You kept it?! You fucking fool!"

"There was nothing wrong with it. I still use it," said Solomon.

"Holy shit. Get rid of it," said Silas with calm tone. "Got it? You're fucking lucky she didn't find it."

Solomon nodded over and over as his shaky hands locked up the tool chest.

"Okay. So, let's go eat. Huh? Play some pool?" said Silas.

"You get a head start. I wanna clean up a second," said Solomon.

Silas marched out of the garage and Solomon waited in the barn until he heard Silas' engine rev up and take off down the drive.

It took a minute for Solomon to gather his wits. He straightened a few things up on his workbench and wiped down the power drill for a third time. He liked to keep things neat and tidy. Then he locked the pole barn, wrenching hard on the double bolted door which always stuck at the threshold. He scuffed his knuckle on the door as he locked it and it started to bleed.

Once he was in his truck, Solomon ripped out the dash cam.

Silas hadn't faced her. Silas hadn't felt her rage. Silas hadn't felt the hot, wet saliva of her beastly dog on his thigh about to bare down.

But now. Now that she had seen it, there was no choice. He would have to get rid of her and he didn't need his brother's blessing. In fact, he would be protecting him.

Chapter 51

RILEY ST. JAMES

I don't know what to do with my shame and rage and fear. So, I pretend like nothing happened and show up at Pub Griffin for dinner. I can't sit at home. I can't drive anywhere. I can't face Grable. I walk over from my house with Zikmund. Joyce lets me take him in the bar, even though it's against health code.

"He's a police dog, right?" she says with a wink. Zik sits at my side by the bar, head up. On alert. "That's what you tell anyone if they ask." She starts to prepare my club soda and lime. I know I should keep my wits about me right now, but instinctively I call out, "Stella, please."

Joyce glances at me to make sure. I nod. "You got it."

I notice another young gal with flaming auburn hair in a messy ponytail, tight tank and leggings sitting opposite end of the bar. We're the only two at the counter.

"You know Misty?" Joyce reads my glance.

"Not formally." I really don't care for a new friend at the moment. Especially Misty and her overflowing cleavage and peppy smirk.

"I know who you are," says Misty sliding off her stool to come sit closer. "You're that detective from Detroit."

"I am." But I don't announce my name. Joyce hands me my Stella.

"What are you eating? It's on me," says Joyce.

"Burger, please. No mustard or onions."

"You got it. Misty, anything? It's not on me."

"Nah, just another Cosmo. With two cherries," says Misty as she swirls the last sip of her pink liquid in the martini glass and swishes it down. Then, she licks the last of the sugar on the rim. "God, I love these things. Like candy."

I give her a polite smile. I wouldn't know. Joyce shakes Misty's Cosmo into a fresh glass and hands it to her, some of it sloshes over the rim.

"Careful. Don't waste a drop. You charge enough for these," says Misty, slurping from the cocktail glass. Joyce disappears into the kitchen.

"I've always wondered why you never brought me in to get my statement," she says to me as she licks the sugar off the rim.

"You're not on the list," I tell her dryly.

"I know a lot about this case."

"I'm sure you do. And I've read most of it on Facebook," I tell her.

"So when are you gonna arrest those bastard Newton twins?"

"I can't really talk about the case. Sorry." I lean over to pet Zik and hope she'll take the hint to go back to her end of the bar.

"Kev won't talk about it either. And we've been friends since high school. Personally, I don't think he wants to arrest them." Kev. First name basis. Everybody connected. Everybody keeping their secrets.

I barely glance at her but it's enough to prompt Misty to continue. "You know I told him about that roofing tool. And he didn't do squat."

"There's nothing to be done. It's just hearsay."

"It's real, all right. I know what I heard."

I turn to Misty and don't even try to hide my judgement. "Why do you hang around those guys anyhow?"

She pushes a lock of fallen hair out of her eye and sips her drink, ignoring my question.

Joyce comes back to the bar with napkins and silverware and sets them at my place.

"Joyce used to date Solomon. You should talk to her," Misty says.

Joyce wipes down the bar where she had spilled some of Misty's drink.

"Misty wants to single handedly solve the Nina Laramie case," Joyce says.

Misty rolls her eyes. "So what if I give a damn and the rest of you don't! Especially the people who have the power to. Like Kevin Grable." She turns to me with an exaggerated look.

"It's better if you leave it up to the police," I say.

Misty leans over to feed Zik one of the cherries from her drink.

"Please don't give him that," I say and put my hand up over his snout. She pops it into her mouth instead.

"If you wanna learn some stuff, you should try hanging out there. Over by the pool tables," she says.

"Don't believe everything you hear," I say knowing what I saw.

I can't shake the sick gnawing at my insides. My gut is getting the better of me on this one. How am I going to explain this to my commander in Detroit? Have the Newtons won because of my impulsiveness? If I self-report, I'll damn well be off this case by morning.

"Your burger should be up. Be right back," says Joyce heading for the kitchen. This gives Misty a chance to swipe a cherry from the garnish tray. She gives me a wink, signaling me not to tell. *Why do I care?* I take another sip of my Stella when the back doors open and two men enter.

"Oh, speak of the devils," said Misty, laying eyes on Silas and Solomon Newton. "Ain't there something you can do, as a cop, you know? Kick 'em out?" She straightens up in her seat. She won't be intimidated. Three cosmos give her courage.

"They have a right to be here," I say quietly.

"I can't stand breathing the same air as them. I'm telling Joyce. She don't want 'em here either. I hope you get those fucking bastards soon." Misty marches behind the bar and disappears into the kitchen.

My spine stiffens into an icicle, paralyzing me. They have stopped short of the bar and have selected a booth at the back near the pool tables. Silas has his back to me. Solomon faces me. I glance at him and see in his pupils that the Evil has a new and dangerous plan. And I am its target. It chills me and sends me sliding off my bar stool. Zik immediately stands at attention. I don't want my burger anymore. I slap down a ten spot and take off out the front entrance.

I jog all the way home with Zik at my side. It's only a mile and at the pace I run, I quickly work up a sweat. Zik stays in stride with me. Good dog. When I arrive home I enter through the back yard. I want Zik to take his bathroom break before we go in. As I turn to round the corner of the house and open the back gate, I see a female figure sitting on the back stoop. The figure rises. My guess she's in her late thirties. A little rotund and dressed in a simple sweater and jeans. Nothing about her seems particularly dangerous. Zik barks once and growls.

"I'm sorry to startle you," the woman says. "I didn't want to wait in the front."

"Who are you?" I plant myself a safe distance from her and reach for my gun.

"Tammy Tyler."

Zik barks again.

"It's okay," I command in Czech. The hair on his back is on end. She sees my gun aimed at her and reaches her arm above her head.

"I'm not armed. Please, don't shoot me. I just want to talk."

Tammy Tyler. I racked my brain. Her name isn't in any of the records or transcripts. She is an unknown entity in this case. No one had ever mentioned her name to me. Grable had never talked about her. Nor Ray Polland.

"Who are you exactly?"

"I'm sorry, I didn't mean to scare you. I didn't know where else to go."

"Ms. Tyler, would you rise and remove yourself from my back yard, please," I say with steady voice. I examine her top to bottom. Her jeans are tight. No weapons bulging. But the sweater is baggy. And she's carrying an oversized handbag. I can't trust what's in there to be just credit cards and tampons. "And can you please keep your hands where I can see them?"

She keeps her arms above her head in compliance as she starts to walk towards the gate that leads out of the yard. I open the chain linked gate door for her.

Once she's on my driveway, I escort her towards the sidewalk with Zik between us. She's clearly not comfortable with him and takes several quick strides to remove herself from his reach. I look to the street and realize there's no cars parked in front of my house. How did she get here?

"You're the detective in charge of the Nina Laramie case, right?"

"Yes."

"I want to report a tip," she says, lowering her arms.

"There's a tip line, you know. You didn't have to camp out in my back yard." We've reached the sidewalk and the sun has gone behind the trees darkening the street. I keep both hands on my gun and lower it a few inches.

"I know. But I need to talk to someone in person. You. I need you."

"You would do better to call the police station and make an appointment."

"I can't wait that long."

"Are you in danger?" I ask with an irony twisting my gut. I'm the one in danger. I should be alerting Grable, but I'm not ready to face losing my job.

"In danger of losing my mind," her voice is desperate and shaky. "My stomach's in knots all the time and I can't sleep, eat. I'm losing it. I don't know where else to turn."

"Do you need to see a doctor?" I worry a mental patient has found her way to my home.

"No. I don't need a doctor," she says breathlessly.

"Are you suicidal?" I return my gun to its holster. She doesn't seem like a physical threat, but I certainly am concerned for her mental ability.

"No. I'm fine. Well, not completely fine. I have this constant pain in my chest."

Was she having a heart attack? I take one hand off my gun to reach for my phone. "I'm calling you an ambulance."

"No. Don't. I know who killed Nina Laramie."

"What?" My fingers hover over the nine on my dial pad.

"I know it sounds crazy. I feel crazy. But I'm not. Please believe me." Tammy Tyler's shoulder sag and she tears up.

"How do you know this?" I ask calmly.

"Because I saw her right after she was killed. And I saw who killed her. And I'm not the only one."

Chapter 52

TAMMY

T ammy Tyler followed Detective Riley St. James back into her back yard. She offered her a seat at the patio set and Tammy sat down. St. James took out her phone and set up the video to record.

"With your permission I'm going to record our conversation. I need a verbal yes," said St. James.

"Yes," said Tammy.

Tammy watched as St. James spoke into the camera, "I am Riley St. James with the Michigan State Police interviewing Tammy...? What's your last name again?"

"Tyler. This is Tammy Tyler." Tammy pointed to herself. She didn't know why she had done that. It was obvious on camera she was talking about herself.

"Tammy, just start from the beginning, what you remember about that night at the Hole in the Woods," said St. James.

"My grandma actually lived across the street from Nina when I was little. I kinda remember her, but she was a couple years older than me. I don't remember playing with her or anything. Just seeing her around. I think after I was ten I never saw her again because grandma passed away and we didn't go around to her neighborhood anymore. I didn't even think of her until I saw those billboards they put up about her being missing."

"I see. But I'm a little confused, Tammy. You told me you saw her right after she was killed?" The detective's calm voice lured her to unleash the heap of pent up presentiments that were piling on top of her.

"Yeah. I mean, that… yeah, but I didn't really know that's who I was seeing until just a couple weeks ago when Misty told me about the Oconee National Forest being here in Derby County and that the Hole in the Woods is part of the Oconee National Forest. And then I guess I started to put it all together."

"Put what together?" St. James asked her in a soft voice that made her feel protected. She couldn't wait to release all this emotion that had been bottling up.

"That the girl I had seen that night at the Hole in the Woods was Nina Laramie."

"What night?"

"Somewhere in early August. I was fourteen. So about thirty years ago."

St. James nodded and her gentle eyes never left Tammy's face. She poured more water into Tammy's glass and Tammy drank from it. Anxiety had parched her throat and the cool water opened it.

"But you weren't sure it was Nina?" St. James asked her when she finished drinking.

Tammy shook her head. "I was pretty sure, but I wanted to confirm it."

"How did you do that?"

"Wallace Gunter. He was with me that night."

"Who's Wallace Gunter?"

"He was my neighbor growing up. I've known him since I was like seven. He's about five years older than me."

St. James nodded again. Tammy almost broke down in a sob. It felt so good to release this. There was a quality about St. James that she trusted, like an old friend. Not a friend like Misty, who just wanted your gossip so she could make social currency out of it. No, she knew she could tell St. James anything and it would be safe. So she did. She let the whole story spew from her, barely taking breaths between thoughts.

"I snuck out of the house one summer night when I was fourteen and I went over to Wallace's. His parents were gone and he had been drinking. A lot. He was bitching about Wendy, his girlfriend. Well, I think she was an ex-girlfriend. He wanted to find her and was getting ready to head out to look for her at some of the party spots around Derby. I begged to go with him. He didn't want me to come at first, but I kept at him and finally he just told me to get in the car."

"We drove for hours around the county, two-tracks, lakes, the river. His girlfriend wasn't anywhere. There were no parties. Wallace was doing hard drugs, whiskey. He didn't see this really rutted area and he got his bumper stuck in a dip in the road."

"A dip?" St. James asked.

"Like a dip in the road. It was a sandy single track with lots of little hills. Dips. So the bumper got stuck and he was trying to move the car forward and backward to get us out of it when this other car came up the road head on. But it's a one-lane so the car stopped and this guy got out. Wallace got out. And they were talking, you know, in between the two cars and I could see them in the headlights."

"Was it a friendly conversation?" Tammy asked.

"I guess. The other guy was closer to Wallace's age. There was someone else in the car, but I couldn't see who. A guy."

"Could you hear what they were talking about?"

"The one guy introduced himself. Gave his last name."

"What name did he give? Do you remember?"

"They looked alike. Twins."

"They talk about anything else?" asked the detective.

"This guy, Newton, asked Wallace if he had seen a girl around there."

"In the woods?"

"Yeah. Out roaming in the woods," said Tammy.

"Did you find that odd?"

"I don't know? It was a party spot. I don't really know because then the guy asked who was in the car."

"Meaning your car?" asked the detective.

"Yeah, meaning me. And Wallace said none of his fucking business and blocked the guy's view so he couldn't see me."

"How did you feel about that?"

"I get it, you know. Wallace was nineteen and I was a minor and he didn't want people knowing he was out with me. Plus the drinking, the drugs. It did not look good for him, you know? And he was already in trouble with the law."

"How so?" asked the detective.

"He had been arrested for assault. Spent a month in jail right after his eighteenth birthday."

With each moment the knot in Tammy's stomach unfurled its grip. She felt like she could breathe deeper, think clearer for the first time in weeks.

"What about the girl? The girl you say was Nina. When did you see her?" the detective asked, helping Tammy to focus again on her story.

"We kept driving around and Wallace keeps drinking. And he's getting more and more spooled up about Wendy and I'm trying to calm him down. He could be really threatening and intimidating."

"Did he ever try to harm you?" St. James asked.

"Oh no. Never. I just mean his attitude towards things. Hot headed."

"He ever threaten you?"

Tammy paused. St. James nodded again at her. "It's okay." St. James understood things, Tammy sensed. She understood what it was like to fear.

Tammy nodded.

"What kind of threats?" asked the detective.

"To kill me. If I told."

"And you never did?"

Tammy shook her head.

"Continue."

"We were going along this one track that leads by the power lines. I think it was a couple hours later and we come across this same car again. And it looked like an accident. At least that's what Wallace said. He said, 'oh my god, there's been an accident.' And he slammed on the brakes and jumped outta the car. But first he told me to 'stay the fuck in the car.' His exact words."

"Did you?" asked the detective.

"Oh hell yeah."

"What kind of accident? What did you see?"

Tammy paused for a moment as the images formulated in her mind. She looked past St. James and used her hands to place the people in the scene she was envisioning.

"There were the two guys. The one I had seen before and the other one who was in the car. And they were leaning over this body. This girl. And the girl was not moving. I thought maybe she was passed out. And I'm seeing all this through the headlights cause, you know, it's the middle of the night, and it's really, really dark. And I could see her bare legs. And her head. There was a lot of blood on her face and in her hair."

Tammy's voice halted by the impact of the violent image planted in her memory.

"Do you remember what she was wearing?" the detective asked her softly.

Tammy's thoughts shifted to the girl's outfit. She remembered it in detail because of the blouse. "She was wearing jeans. Tennis shoes. Like those Ked's we all used to wear. And a blue top. With flouncy, ruffled sleeves. The kind with the elastic that you can wear up or pulled over your shoulders."

Tammy was very certain about the blouse because she had asked for a similar one in pink that summer and her mother refused to buy it for her. Said she wasn't old enough for that kind of outfit.

"What happened next, Tammy?" said St. James.

"Wallace jumped out of the car and he was in such a rush to get to them that he tripped. Well, he was also pretty wasted so maybe that had something to do with it, too."

"Too drunk enough to remember what he saw?"

"He sobered up pretty fast after he got kicked in the face."

"Why did that happen?"

"These guys didn't like him there. But Wallace wouldn't leave. He kept asking them what was happening? Did they need some help?"

"And they didn't like that?" says the detective.

"No. One of them punched Wallace. He went down. And when he was on his knees the other twin came up and shoved his boot in Wallace's face. I screamed and laid on the horn. I swear he was gonna get the shit kicked outta him. Wallace jumped up and he was getting ready to swing at the guy, but then I honked the horn again and he came back and got into the car."

"Did you hear anything they were saying?"

"I couldn't hear anything. I was sobbing at this point. Scared shitless."

"I imagine you were. That's a lot for a young girl to take in."

"Wallace was bleeding from above his eyebrow."

"And the girl? What happened to her?" asked the detective.

Tammy looked down at her hands and picked at a cracked nail, tearing off the fingernail in a jagged edge.

"She wasn't moving. They… each took an arm. She didn't struggle or resist. They just dragged her behind the car. I couldn't see anything after that. And before I knew it we were racing backwards down the two-track until we were out of sight of them."

Tammy pulled a nail file from her purse and began filing the ripped fingernail. She was embarrassed by the shape of her nails. Normally she had them done every week. But she had been biting them to jagged nubs.

"What happened next?" St. James said.

"I was screaming, like a typical fourteen year old, and Wallace had to calm me down. He kept telling me that everything was going to be okay. And I was like, 'what's wrong with that girl?' And he assured me over and over that they were taking her to the hospital. He said it was an accident."

"And you believed him."

Tammy nodded. She didn't want to discuss what Wallace was capable of. "Wallace made me believe it was an accident. In my mind, it was an accident. End of story. He dropped me off at the cemetery, which was a couple blocks from my house and I walked home and snuck back in."

"When did you see Wallace next?"

She didn't. "He avoided me. I didn't see him the rest of the summer."

"And life went on?" asked the detective. "Did you ever hear about the girl you saw at the Hole in the Woods?"

"No. I never did."

"Why speak out now?"

"I can't sleep."

"What are you afraid of?" asked the detective.

"He threatened back then. And he has the means to deliver on that threat."

"Even from prison?"

She nodded.

"You're very brave to come forward with this. Thank you, Tammy."

"Do you think Nina will stop visiting me in my dreams now?" It was the first time she had used the girl's name out loud and the sound of it suddenly gave Nina humanity. A wave of nausea overtook her. Tammy looked up into the detective's face hoping to feel a connection or some warmth that would promise her things would be all right. But the corners of St. James' mouth turned up into an unnatural smile, sending goose bumps up Tammy's arms. That familiar sharp pain jabbed Tammy in the gut, assuring she had just done a very dangerous thing.

"I wish I knew the secret of how to control dreams," said the detective. "The only thing we can control is how we react to it. You've done a good thing here by telling me your story."

"I'm sorry... just so sorry I didn't do it sooner. Everything would be different." Even this moment. Her fear. Her uncertain future. Tammy broke down in a wash of tears. This awful code she had shared with Wallace would no longer hold her... or Nina, captive.

Chapter 53

RILEY ST. JAMES

I escort Tammy home in my truck. I'm nearly shaking from her confession and thoughts are racing through my head. It takes a huge
effort on my part to make a calm and graceful exit. I thank her for her
testimony and instruct her to lay low.

"Talk to no one. Not your mother. Your sons. Your best friend.
Don't let anyone know what you told me," I say.

"Okay, I won't."

"You haven't told anyone already have you?"

"No. I... I almost told Misty."

"But you didn't?"

"No. You're the first person I've told," Tammy tells me.

"And I should be the only person you tell." God, please don't say
anything to that gossipy woman, I plead silently. "Don't tell Misty."

"No way. She would blab it all over the place."

"That's right, Tammy. She would. And it would put you and your kids in danger? You understand that, right?"

"Perfectly." But I can see her hands trembling as she clutches her purse.

"It's going to be okay. You've done the right thing."

She nods, but there's doubt and fear in her frown lines. "What's gonna happen now? When will you arrest them?"

"I have a little more work to do before that can happen. Can you hang in there for me and just pretend like everything's normal."

"But I don't feel normal... I feel scared all the time. Wallace says he knows people on the outside who can... get to me."

"There's no reason to feel scared. Right now, it's just you and me. Wallace doesn't know you told me. It's our secret."

"And the twins. They know. They saw me."

"But they don't know that I know. And they don't know you personally, right?"

Tammy nods.

"We have that to our advantage. And as long as we do, there's nothing to fear."

She shakes her head, but I know that now that the seal's been broken. Tammy's aching for more relief. She will want to confide in someone. I know the feeling. And I know the toll stress takes to keep a secret.

"How long?" she presses.

"I can't say. But I'll be in touch. I won't leave you hanging. I promise." I look Tammy in the eyes and give her a small, reassuring smile. "What you've done tonight is very good, Tammy. And very brave."

"Will it put them behind bars?"

"Don't worry about that right now. That's for me to worry about. Just go on like everything is normal." I didn't want to give her any false hope. Plus, I needed to corroborate her story with Wallace and who knows if he will cooperate.

"Okay, well. I'll just wait to hear from you," she reaches for the door handle.

"Just pretend like we never had this conversation."

She says nothing and gets out. I watch her scurry to her front door and slip inside. She shuts it and I can hear the deadbolt latching. Good girl, Tammy.

As I pull out of Tammy's driveway, I pass a driver with flaming red hair and music blaring from the open windows. Misty. I slow and watch as her taillights turn into Tammy's driveway. All my faith in my pep talk with Tammy drains. There's no way that fragile woman will be able to hold out in the presence of Misty's plucky persistence. The ticking clock on Tammy's safety has started.

Grable's phone goes straight to voicemail. He's probably fly fishing. Damn it. *Grable, you have horrible timing.* I head the truck down to the river road in search of his favorite spots. He's at none of them. So I keep heading down river on the frontage road thinking maybe he's decided to try a new locale. A half hour sails by and no sign of Grable. I phone again. Right to voicemail. I leave a message for him to call me.

No specifics. Then, I text him the same message. No response. I can't play this game of hide and seek any longer. I spin the truck around, making a U-turn on the river road and speed back towards the Derby county road that leads to the main interstate heading north. I'm on a countdown.

Chapter 54

GRABLE

G rable sits alone at the bank of the river, a bucket of fresh catch and his fly-fishing gear at his side. He had driven an hour up river to try a new spot that local fisherman had been bragging about on a local fly fishing group chat. It's dark now and he should head home. To what though? An empty house? Books and magazines he's already read? A DVR queue he's exhausted? A Netflix account that sends him into decision paralysis?

Grable's hand reaches into his tackle box. From the back of one of the little drawers he removes Nina's class ring. He slips it on the tip of his index finger and turns it round and round just above his first knuckle as if he's trying to wind up his thoughts like an old wrist watch.

Except that his thoughts are going in rewind, stopping on September 27, 1989.

He was drunk and high, partying out at the Hole in the Woods with a couple dozen people, randoms from high school. He can see faces, but names allude him. Conversations that night didn't stick. He didn't even know how he arrived or how he got home. But he does remember having to take a leak. Badly.

He wandered from the clearing where they had set up a large bonfire and headed into the woods. After a safe enough distance, Grable unzipped his pants and leaned one arm against a tree to steady himself. The world around him was spinning as sweet relief came.

As Grable zipped up his pants, a little breeze whispered through the forest and the foul stench of decay went straight up his nostrils. Grable gagged and plugged his nose. He tried to breathe through his mouth, but he could taste it on the back of his tongue. He gagged again. Gasping for large inhales of breath, Grable realized the smell had left as the breezed died down.

He took a few staggered steps back towards the clearing, when an odd idea swept over him. He wanted to find the source of the smell. It was gut instinct driving him. Why? Maybe he had thought some poacher shot an animal and left the parts to rot? Or maybe it was just boyhood curiosity taking over.

Before he knew it, Grable was using the tall old pine trees, which had been planted in straight lines in a re-forestry effort decades before, to guide him deeper and deeper in the direction of the decay. Small breezes pointed him left or right as the smell grew more and more pungent. Grable pulled the cuff of his t-shirt over his nose and mouth, but it did little to mask the malodor.

A few more steps and the fetid tang overpowered him. He stopped abruptly, searching out the area for an animal carcass. Instead, his gaze landed on a blackened human body laying a few feet ahead of him between two trees.

It was exposed. Small. Female. Long hair spread on the forest floor. On her tiny feet were white Ked tennis shoes. He didn't have to study the corpse any longer to know that this was Nina.

Grable backed away a few steps, sucking in large sips of decomp-infused air that soured his stomach. Nausea and alcohol had slowed his thinking and reaction time. He wobbled in place, feeling light-headed and trying to figure out what to do. Something stirred out of the corner of his eye and Grable pivoted in alarm.

Nearby, a small fox was eyeing something on the ground. In the reflected light of the moon, Grable could make out the object of the fox's desire. It was Nina's hand, detached from her body and laying a good twelve feet from her torso.

He waved his arms, shooing the fox away. Then, stepping up to the dismembered hand, Grable recognized her class ring on her fourth finger. His eyes locked on it and his mind scrambled. Should he pick it up? Put it back with the body? Take it with him? Tell someone? Then, a single thought surfaced above the rest. Take the ring. If he didn't, he reasoned, the fox would return for the hand and it'd be gone.

Grable bent over Nina's hand. Using a stick to hold it down, he managed to slide the class ring off her finger with his own thumb and index finger. But when her skin loosened due to the advanced stages of decomposition and slipped off the bone, Grable rocked to one side as the rush of an entire fifth of vodka projected itself from his stomach. For some time, he knelt on the forest floor emptying himself to the point of dry heaving.

Crawling up to a crooked standing position, Grable wiped off his mouth and turned from the body. He shoved Nina's class ring into his front jeans pocket and miraculously stumbled his way back to the bonfire where he drank to the point of blacking out and woke up in his bedroom the next afternoon, stripped down to his underwear.

After the hangover subsided, Grable convinced himself that what he experienced during his trip to the forest bathroom was just his own foggy, drunken imagination. A week later, an early snow blanketed the county and he didn't bother to return to the woods to see if his mind had played tricks on him.

A month later, Grable found the jeans with the ring wadded up in the back of his closet. But by then, a hunter had already discovered the corpse. He learned later, much later, through the autopsy reports that all of Nina's body had been recovered, except for one hand.

Chapter 55

RILEY ST. JAMES

I arrive five hours later at the Northern Michigan Correctional Facility. It's just before midnight. I have called ahead to request a private visit with Wallace Gunter and it is granted. They place us in an interrogation room. Wallace handcuffed to the table with an officer outside the door. I enter and sit down across from him. His orange jumpsuit is snug around his chest and biceps. Lots of gym time, this one. His stature is squatty and he can't be more than an inch taller than me. His large round head bobbles slightly at me atop his body making him look like a cartoon character. The sandy blonde hair has flecks of gray on the sides and is thinning on top. He's not a bad looking dude. I'm sure he could score with some less choosy woman if he were on the other side.

"I'm Detective Riley St. James, with the Michigan State Police," I say clearly and without emotion.

"Pretty late for a social call," says Wallace with a flat look that tells me he knows the justice system ropes and he's not flustered by detectives and cops. In fact, his arrogant smirk communicates a great dislike for me. Wallace is in prison for armed robbery, assault, and home invasion. Crimes that have landed him his fifteen-year sentence. But one good look at his dull, bluish gray eyes and I know there is no true evil behind them.

"I'm sorry to bother you so late. I want to talk with you about a woman you know. Tammy Tyler."

He shakes his head slightly. "Who?"

I see how it's going to be. "She was your neighbor growing up."

"I guess so. That was a while ago."

"Prison visitation records show she was here not too long ago. A couple times."

"I sure the fuck didn't ask her to come. What do you want anyway, lady cop."

"Detective, St. James," I correct. "I just want to know what the two of you talked about."

"Why?"

"She recently brought some things to my attention about a case I'm working on," I say. "And your name came up."

"Then that's between her and you. I ain't got nothing to do with whatever she's been talking to you about."

I fold my hands on the table in front of me and keep my eyes on his. I'm unflappable. And I want him to see that I'm not going anywhere.

And I know that eventually he will come around and he will let me in because he's not innately seeded with the evil. Which means there's still a touch of humanity in the deep well of his mistreated heart.

"That's not what she says."

"Oh yeah, what does Tammy Tyler say?" He spits back at me. I don't so much as flinch a muscle on my entire body.

"You tell me. What was she doing up here?" I want Wallace to know that I am not leaving without some answer. "Was it a social visit?"

"Aren't they all?" he sneers.

"Why now?"

"That's what I asked her," he says.

"And what was her answer?"

"She missed me." Wallace laughs.

I nod. I see where he is turning this. "When was the last time you saw Tammy before recently?"

"We were neighbors. She was just a kid last time I saw her."

We are taking baby steps.

"What'd you two talk about when she came?"

"Politics. Religion. Philosophy."

I leap over his snark. "Did you discuss your time together during the summer when Tammy was fourteen?"

"How do I know when that was? I don't know how old the fuck she is."

I back off. I'm leading too strongly.

"You discuss family?" I ask.

"Yes."

"How is your family, Wallace?"

"The best." More snark. I let the moment rest. Silence. Silence is a great conversation starter. Especially uncomfortable silence, which this room is brimming with. I wait a full sixty seconds. It doesn't sound like much. But you try staring in silence at someone for that long.

Wallace had no problem with it. Another minute passes. I keep my eyes trained on him and my face expressionless. I breath steadily in and out of my nostrils, calming my nervous system. I refold my fingers in the opposite position. And keep staring. Neutral. No judgment behind my eyes. The whole time Tammy's story runs a loop in my brain. If Tammy was right, Wallace had seen Nina's body up close. He had seen her killers, too. Talked to them. Fought with them. What details would he remember? Would they corroborate with the other evidence in the case file? *Please, let me in.* The faint buzz of the overhead fluorescent bulbs is a subtle but straining torture to the eardrums. Still, I remain quiet. As does he. And then he shifts in his chair.

"I was with my girlfriend Wendy," he says breaking the cavity of silence.

"You were with Wendy when?" I ask.

"That whole goddamn summer," Wallace chuckles.

"What whole summer?" I need him to be specific.

"That summer Tammy's talking about."

"Which summer was that?" I know I'm annoying him, but I want him to say it.

"When she was fourteen."

"Why do you think that summer is so important to Tammy?" I ask.

He laughs and throws his head back a little. "Shit. Tammy wanted so bad for me to like her. She was always trying to be with me. Silly teenage crush thing. I just saw her as like a kid sister, you know?"

I nod.

"Why do you think she remembers that summer in particular?" I ask with constrained calmness.

"I don't know.

I remain guarded in my questioning.

"Did she come here asking you for something?"

"Aren't women always asking for something," Wallace says.

I smile. Touché. "What was it she wanted this time?"

"She's still in love with me," he says and his mouth twitches.

"She loves you, huh?" His lie is almost comical. I nod, pretending to take it in. "She loves you. How sweet. Have your feelings for her changed in thirty years?"

"She's a drama queen, Detective. Do yourself a favor. Whatever she said to you, she's lying."

I select my next words carefully. I want to purposefully pack on the emotion. "Attention is the last thing Tammy Tyler wants. Trust me. She's scared, Wallace. She's terrified right now. She did a brave thing coming to me with her story."

Wallace glanced up at the ceiling and back at me. "Her story. Yeah, Tammy loves to tell stories."

"Maybe you and she share the same story?" I suggest.

More silence. I wait. His expression doesn't change. "It's horrible being in here," Wallace says in a lower voice. "I wouldn't want to put anyone in this place."

I'm not sure if that's an indictment on my profession or a general statement.

"How long you got left?" I ask.

"Another five."

"Another five," I repeat. "If you have something to tell me, maybe I can help you?"

"I'm made for this." His biceps flexed voluntarily under his shirt.

"You're made for prison?"

"I'm a good convict. I'm no snitch."

"You said before it was horrible here."

The door opens and the prison guard announces our time is up.

There's nothing more than can be done tonight. I rise as the officer helps Wallace from his chair.

"I'm Detective Riley St. James," I say again, my eyes never leaving his. "I'm working a cold case right now of a girl, Nina Laramie. She was found murdered in the Oconee National Forest thirty years ago."

I see Wallace's left eyebrow rise and fall. "If you have any information about this case, let the officers here know to give me a call."

I leave the room and feel his eyes trace my exit. It's an okay first meeting. His body language and his rhetorical deflection give me exactly what I need to know right now. It's just going to take a bit to crack his shell.

I jump into my truck and head back to the lower peninsula. I keep the window rolled down all five hours back to Derby. It's almost light when I arrive home. Zikmund! I had forgotten about him. I should have arranged for someone to take him out while I was gone. *What a horrible dog mom I am!* I chastise myself until I see him dashing from his bed to greet me with licks and wagging tails. I apologize a million times in Czech as I burrow my face into his. I open the door for him to run out and do his business. I then prepare his breakfast and call for him to come inside. No response. Very odd. Then, a bark. I run to the door and see he's sniffing and circling at something in the driveway.

I wander out with my gun holstered, a force of habit, and a flashlight at my side. Panning my light where Zikmund is sniffing, I see a set of shoeprints that I know are not my own. They are large and formed in the shape of a boot. He sniffs towards the garage shed and I follow him with wary steps. Gravel turns to grass. The boot prints disappear, but the grass is matted in a footpath pattern towards the back of the garage, but off to the side near a wood pile. Why here? I turn to look at the house. All the kitchen lights are on. A vulnerable view. I notice that branches that once hung over the wood pile have been snapped off, leaving frayed twigs hanging above my head about a foot.

I lean over the woodpile, which is about waist height and lean over. I pretend to rest a rifle on the logs. I squint through my imaginary site and discover that this gives me a direct eye line into the kitchen. Somebody has created the perfect sniper's post.

Chapter 56

RILEY ST. JAMES

While Zik is licking the bottom of his bowl, I call Grable. He's already been up for an hour when his phone started to blow up. Dozens of calls and texts from friends informing him about Misty's newest Facebook post. He's been reading through it and was getting ready to phone me when I called. I tell him about my talk with Tammy and I tell him I want to give him the interview audio file so we can get it transcribed. He's excited. Very excited.

He agrees that the integrity of evidence in Nina's case is in danger and he's going to get a court order for Facebook to retract Misty's post ASAP.

"No," I tell him. "We have to let on like normal. Ignore it like you do every other post. If you pull it now, it will put out the signal that it's real information. Dismiss it. It's unsubstantiated."

"You sound paranoid," says Grable.

"I'm just being cautious. Get one of your men to keep an eye on Tammy and her boys."

"Why?" he asks me. "The twins don't know who she is."

"I know. But, Grable… I did something I'm not proud of," I say.

"Does it relate to the case?" he says.

"It's a fireable offense." The words catch in my throat. "I need to tell you in person."

"Bring the interview file. Come over. I'll put the coffee on."

Chapter 57

SILAS & SOLOMON

"You on Facebook?" Solomon asks his brother over the phone as he paces the perimeter of his pole barn with the roofing tool in his left hand swinging at his side.

"Why are you calling me so early?" grunts Silas.

"Have you seen Facebook?"

"I don't waste time on that trash," Silas' curt response comes over the phone line.

"Misty Beckett's saying there's a woman who has evidence that we killed Nina Laramie."

"Don't you say that name out loud to me. Especially not over the phone," says Silas. "What kinda evidence?"

"The post doesn't say specifically. Just that *some woman's* been to the police about it. Do you think it's her?

Silas is silent on the other end. Solomon can hear him take a swig from his Coors' bottle.

"What kind of evidence?" Silas asks.

"Doesn't say."

"Then it doesn't sound like anything to get your feathers ruffled over."

"She says here we're finally gonna get what's coming to us," says Solomon.

"It ain't nothing but Misty running her mouth," responds Silas.

"What are we gonna do about it?" asks Solomon running his fingers over his short cut.

"Nothing." Silas sighs. "It's stupid social media."

Solomon is too wound up to let this go. "What are you doing right now?"

"Chores," says Silas. "Unless you got something to get me out of it."

"I think we should shut her up about it."

"Who?" says Silas.

"Misty," says his twin.

"That's a shitty idea. She's trying to stir things up. It'll blow over."

"I'm going into town," says Solomon.

"Do not talk to Misty," Silas' voice warns.

"She's spreading lies."

"She doesn't know shit," Silas says and Solomon can hear his wife in the background calling for him to clean out the chest freezer in the garage.

"She needs to know that she can't keep doing this," says Solomon.

"We'll talk about it later. Okay?"

"Okay." But Silas can sense that Solomon is forming a plan in his mind.

"Tell me what you're gonna do in town," asks Silas in a demanding tone.

"I jest got errands to run."

"That's all you better be doing. Call me later."

"You call me when you're free." Solomon hangs up before Silas. He expected support. He expected a reaction. He did not like being left to hang. Silas had left him hanging all his life. Silas called the shots. Silas got him into all this. He's the one who spent time in prison for the stuff they'd done.

Solomon launches from his work shed and hops into this truck. He can't let this go. It's not going to blow over. One hundred and seventy-eight comments. Most of them pointing to him and Silas. Misty has to be stopped. He'll rip that cell phone where she does all her posting right from her hands and crush it with his boot. He'll threaten her, if he needs to. He'll stalk her day and night. The little twat. He'll shut her up all right and he'll find out who *this woman* is.

Solomon drives straight to Misty's house. He barrels up the driveway, throws it in park, and keeps the engine running. With no plan in place, he hurls himself towards her front door, pounding on it with the fleshy part of his fist. After several minutes, Solomon stomps back to his truck and pulls down the street to wait. He spends the next two hours nursing from his Smirnoff bottle before Misty shows up.

He watches as Misty parks her car in the drive and heads inside. Lights come on. It's time to jump. Solomon reaches under the back seat for duct tape, rope, and lubricating jelly. He can't wait to put that gossiping bitch in her place. But first he will get her to talk.

Chapter 58

RILEY ST. JAMES

"It was stupid. I don't know what came over me. But you deserve to know. It's the ethical thing to do," I admit blurting out the story about trespassing at Solomon's house. Grable just stares at me wide-eyed. I'm not sure what I would say to me either if someone delivered me this kind of news. I feel all my misgivings surfacing. This is the beginning of the end of my career in law enforcement.

"I'm sorry. I'm just so shocked," quips Grable. "I mean, there's no way we'll ever get that weapon now. And worse, you've set the trap."

"I know what I did was reprehensible," I say. "And if you have to report me, I understand."

"I don't know yet. The case, that's one thing. But what--- what have you unleashed on yourself, St. James?"

"I'm fine. I'll be fine." I have left out the part about the sniper's post in my woodpile.

"You are not fine. This little retaliation of yours was triggered by that demon you're still dealing with from your past," says Grable in a calm voice. "You can see that, can't you?"

"Don't. Shame. Me." I hiss at him.

He backs down and sighs, squeezing his hands together over his forehead, as if trying to press out an answer from his brain.

"Okay, let's just focus on what we need to do right now. We need to get a warrant to arrest the twins," says Grable. "How do we do that?"

"We need Wallace to testify so we can get an investigative subpoena," I say. "We need him to admit what he saw that night."

"How? It's clear Wallace isn't going to talk to you," says Grable.

"I know. I know. All the way back to Derby I was thinking about how to unblunder this," I say. "And I have an idea."

When I tell him, Grable's not in favor at first, but I insist that this is the best way to handle it.

"Do you have a better idea?" I give him a blank stare.

He shakes his head. "I could go up there and try."

Now, I shake my head. But before I can put up an argument, we get interrupted by police dispatch. There's been a distress call from Misty Beckett's place. Panic surges through me. What else have I unleashed?

"I'm putting my plan into place. We can't sit on this," I tell him as Grable gathers his gun and cell phone.

"I always believed this case was unsolvable. Don't screw this up," he says. "I'm actually hopeful for the first time."

As Grable dashes out, I grab my phone and dial.

Chapter 59

RILEY ST. JAMES

M y voice has an edge to it when Ray Polland picks up just before eight a.m.

"I hope I didn't wake you?" I say.

"I answered the phone, didn't I?" says Polland and I feel the warm smile behind it.

"Can I come over right now?"

"Of course. Everything okay?"

"It's swarming season, Ray. Time to harvest." I hang up.

Zik and I hop into my truck. I'm not leaving him behind this time.

Ray Polland is, predictably, in his yard with his bees. I barely have the truck in park as I unlatch the door and Zik springs out. I dart after him leaving the door open and the keys in the ignition. I sprint down the half-acre lot to Ray's bee boxes, paying no heed to the swarm of bees buzzing around his bee suit. I stop a few feet short of him when

I realize the bees are starting to fly my direction. I duck and bob, back tracking and calling out.

"Ray!" The shrill of my voice surprises him. But given his situation, he finishes what he is doing and moves calmly from the bee box. He motions for me to move slowly towards the house. I take a couple steps backwards, twisting around too fast, I can feel myself begin to lose footing. I put my arms back to catch myself and butt-side down land on the grass. I scramble to my feet. I'm so flustered and I must look ridiculous, because Ray yanks off his hat and veil and I read his concerned expression before I hear him say it. "Detective, are you okay?"

"Ray... the code of silence... I cracked it."

Ray rushes up. I refrain from telling him how badly I may have messed things up with my trespassing stunt.

"But we have to move fast."

He slips off his glove and reaches to help me up. "Come. Let's sit on the back patio."

He leads me to the table where we had our first conversation. But I don't sit down.

I pace the patio telling him about Tammy Tyler and how she blabbed to Misty and it's all over the internet. Time is running out. Wallace won't talk to me. Something bad has already happened to Misty. My briefing to Ray is more of a babbling and as he presses me for more, I confess my trespassing mishap and the sniper's stand in my back yard.

Ray doesn't blame or shame. Ray is worried for me. Really worried. He doesn't want me staying at home until we can make an arrest. I tell him it won't be a problem. I'll be fine. But he insists that I stay at his house. There will be no more discussion about it. I file it away. I don't want to stay at Ray's. What I want is to arrest these bastards and get a good night's sleep in my own bed. Ray looks at me with questions growing in his brow.

"That's all fine and well if you have a good plan. Do you and Grable have a plan?" he asks.

"We do," I say. "Will you take a drive with me?"

Chapter 60

SOLOMON

J oyce greets Solomon with her usual glare from behind the bar of the Pub Griffin. It's just before noon.

"What are you doing here so early?" she says. "I didn't think you got up before noon."

"Whiskey." Solomon slaps his hands onto the wooden bar top. "Now."

"You look like crap," Joyce snarls back.

"Just give me the drink."

Joyce grabs a rocks glass and pours, her eyes never leaving Solomon. "Six dollars. Pay me now."

Solomon puts a ten on the counter. She slides the drink to him. He downs it in one swig.

"You see what Misty wrote on Facebook?" Solomon can't help himself.

"I did." She continues her stare down. She makes change and takes two dollars for her tip. "Are you worried?"

"What do I got to be worried about?" Solomon turns his nervous gaze to meet her cold one.

"You think you'd never get caught?"

"I ain't done nothing."

Joyce leans in towards him. "Sure."

"You owe me four dollars," he growls. "Gimme those other two back."

Solomon pounds a fist on the bar. Joyce doesn't even flinch. She keeps her eyes on him as she takes the clean rocks glasses and begins stacking them behind the bar.

"Whatever it is you think you know, it's not true. Tammy's lying."

Four glasses nearly slip out of Joyce's hands. "How do you know about Tammy?"

"So, Misty was telling the truth?" It slips out.

"Did you talk to Misty?" Joyce demands.

"No," Solomon looks away. Joyce knows he's lying.

"When did you talk to Misty?" Joyce spotlights him with a hostile look. "Were you over there?"

She pulls her cell phone from the front pocket of her apron.

"If I called Misty right now, would she answer?"

"How the hell would I know?"

"Solomon Newton, what did you do to Misty Beckett?"

Solomon wants to jump up behind the bar and belt Joyce one. Hard.

Just then police sirens scream by and Solomon's insides fragment. He bolts from the bar leaving the other two dollars on the counter.

Chapter 61

RILEY ST. JAMES

R ay Polland and I arrive at the prison by early afternoon and I take Zikmund out to relieve himself. I settle him back into the truck with windows cracked. It's a cool day so I'm not worried he'll get too hot. I give him a handful of treats and promise I'll be back soon.

Ray and I ask for an interrogation room with a two-way glass so that I can stay out of view and observe. I don't want Wallace to know I'm here. Although I'm sure it won't take him long to put it together why Ray is here.

Ray stands comfortably leaning against one wall of the room and checking his mobile, when Wallace arrives. I know he's not really looking at anything on that phone. You can't get reception behind those brick walls. The guards lock Wallace's cuffs to the table. Ray motions for them to unlock Wallace. They do and Wallace shakes out his hands.

"I'm Ray Polland. Nice to meet you," Ray extends his hand to shake Wallace's. Wallace doesn't return the gesture. Ray responds calmly when Wallace asks who the fuck he is. Ray doesn't explain right away what he's doing there or anything about the current status of Nina's case. He just tells his story with a quiet and reflective tone. A man looking back on the past, and so desperately wanting to repair it.

"There are few things I regret in my life. Getting a divorce. Not spending enough time with my daughters. And dismissing the disappearance of Nina Laramie," says Ray.

Wallace's glance shoots to Ray's face. Ray still doesn't identify himself.

"You are a fucking cop," says Wallace. "Fucking figures. What the fuck do you want with me? I'm missing my yard time."

Ray lifts the corners of his mouth into a half smile and continues. "I told Jim Laramie that she probably just ran away to find her mom up north. Because she had done that earlier that spring. I didn't believe him. I thought she was hiding from her dad and I didn't want my precious few police resources going to waste on a 'wild, little Indian.' That's what the kids at school called her, my daughter said. Because she was just like her mom."

Ray pauses right here. He draws in a few breaths and his eyes bounce to the ceiling and back to Wallace. Then, he shoves the chair back and takes a seat at the table.

"But Jim insisted she hadn't run away. She didn't take anything with her, he said. And she would have never left her dog Tucker behind. I placated him. I said we'd keep an eye out if we heard anything. And

I asked him to take a trip up north to his ex-wife's and investigate for himself."

"Which he did. But she had never turned up at her mom's. And her dad came back to me and said, 'Please, something's really wrong. She's gone missing.' And he has this hand written description of his daughter on a sheet of notebook paper. And several photographs. In this one photo, Jim points out that Nina's wearing this slim chained necklace with three pearls. He tells me her mother gave it to her and she never took it off. Finally, a month later, I agree to put out the missing person's alert. A few days later we get a tip. Someone had seen a girl with a description a lot like Nina in a hardware store next county over. I spend another month tracking this girl. Turns out it wasn't Nina. But sure enough, she did look a lot like Nina. Another month wasted."

I expect Wallace to pipe up and say something belligerent at this point. My mark is spot on.

"You say your name's Ray?" grunts Wallace.

"That's right."

"Why are you telling me all this shit? I don't know this Nina girl."

Ray doesn't address this directly. He just continues on.

"Three months later my station gets a call from a local hunter. He's found human remains near his hunting site. I head out there and he leads me to the Hole in the Woods. You know the place?"

Wallace gives a small nod.

"I'm out there and I crouch down over these bones to get a better look and that's when I saw that pretty necklace twisted around her finger bones." Ray lets out a sigh. "And I knew it was Jim's daughter. I knew that if we had gone searching right away, we would have found more of her. And more of her would mean more evidence. And more evidence means a better trail to her killer or killers..." Ray pauses. Let it sink in. "But instead, I waited and waited and that wait cost me over thirty years of peace."

By this point in the conversation, I notice Wallace has angled his body square to Ray's, a sign that he is opening up to Ray.

"That afternoon I returned to the police station and I sat in my office and picked up the phone. I dialed Jim Laramie. Jim wasn't there. So I called the pub where I knew he often spent his time. The bartender answered and put Jim on the line."

Wallace uncrossed his arms and placed his hands atop his thighs. His upper torso had moved toward Ray at a slight angle. Ray has successfully snagged Wallace into his story web.

"I said, 'Jim, I have some news about Nina's case. I'd like for you to come down to the police station so I can talk to you about it.' Jim said one word, 'okay' and hung up the phone. Ten minutes later he was in my office, sitting in the chair across from my desk. He was wringing his hands like dish rags to keep them from shaking," says Ray.

"I think he already knew that Nina was dead. He thanked me and asked about Nina's body. He wanted to have a funeral as soon as possible. I told him we were going to get an autopsy first. We weren't able to release the body for four months. When Jim was finally able to bury his daughter, he had her wrapped in pink satin."

Ray stops. Wallace's eyebrows rise and fall. He cocks his head to one side and glances around the room, then back at Ray.

"That was three decades ago," says Ray. "Jim's been waitin' all these years to catch who killed his only child. His daughter."

"That's a long time," says Wallace.

My inner dialogue is begging Wallace to break. I realize I'm holding my breath and feeling dizzy. I slowly sip air into my lungs.

"Tammy send you up here? Or was it that girl cop?" he says. I exhale with an audible sigh. Thank God they can't hear me in here.

"Doesn't matter. All that matters is what you know and if you're willing to help?" says Ray.

"What the fuck do I get outta this?" Wallace's face hardens. We're right back to square one.

Ray's look holds no judgment. "What if the tables were turned and it was your mother or sister or daughter who was murdered?"

"I ain't got no daughter. Or sister. And my mom's dead," says Wallace.

He's playing hard ball. But Ray still has the reigns and I am confident he can get him to crack.

"I'm sorry to hear that," says Ray. "You good with your old man?"

"Shit, no." Wallace bursts into a laugh, then after a moment, he adds, "He's dying anyhow."

"I'm sorry to hear that." Ray locks his eyes on Wallace. "Is your dad proud of you?"

Wallace laughs. "I'm sittin' in fucking prison. What do you think?"

"You can change that, you know. Do something to make him proud." Ray states simply. Confidently. Compassionately.

This must have struck something raw inside Wallace because his face turns gloomy and he glances off Ray's shoulder to the wall behind him, training his focus there as if he's calculating his next move. Ray doesn't so much as blink or flinch. He lets the game play out in Wallace's court.

"There's a few things I'd like," said Wallace, his gaze returning to Ray. "I want my sentence shortened. And I want to be transferred. Further northwest in the UP."

I know why he's requesting this penitentiary. It's far removed from any local news sources. He would be pretty much out of danger from anyone knowing that he had testified. Wallace wouldn't want anyone in prison to know he had snitched. It might be the death of him.

Ray repeats these requests back to Wallace just to make sure he's clear. They both stare at one another, the negotiations now on the table.

"I can make those requests known," says Ray simply. I know he can't promise Wallace a single thing. He has no control over this. The prosecutor, judge, and prison board will have to work that out. There are never guarantees.

"I need to be assured."

Ray shrugs. "It's not up to me."

"Then, I'm not gonna fucking tell you anything."

Ray shrugs again and leans back into his chair. His ever present, ever calm expression never waivers. He knows his one regret as a career detective could be redeemed in this moment. He wants it, but he's not forcing it. It must come from Wallace, an honest vulnerability. Or it will be no good to him or Jim or Nina or me.

"Maybe this time it's not about you," coos Ray in that grandfather tone. Watch the undercurrent. Step carefully now. Stabilize yourself so you don't get swept under. "This case. This thing you witnessed is not of your doing. There's no shame in it. No judgment."

"What do I get?" insisted Wallace between his teeth.

"Yeah. What would make things better for Wallace? That's all you care about, isn't it?" says Ray.

Wallace doesn't respond. I think Ray's stumped him.

"You're in here because all your life you lived life for Wallace and only Wallace. You've boxed yourself into a very lonely place. No family. No friends. You've built your own prison. A prison of loneliness. Because you've only ever served yourself. How'd you like freedom from all that garbage that eats at you every day. How would you like a little taste of peace?"

Ray waits a moment to study Wallace's reaction. Wallace has cocked his head again and his gaze drifts down. He is mulling all of this over carefully. I can feel Ray penetrating Wallace's blocked emotional energies. Will Wallace let him in?

"You were witness to a young woman's death. I know you don't see this as a gift, but it can be. You will be giving Jim Laramie the gift of justice he deserves. It will lift a dark veil on a community that has been living in grief and fear. And it will give you a gift. You can start to shed light and redemption on the horrifying, dark memories you have. It will release you, Wallace."

Ray draws in a breath. His face is softened with eagerness and compassion. But Wallace refuses to look at him.

Wallace stretches his arms back as far as he can. He rolls his head back, moving it side to side as if working out some kink in his neck. I am sure this is the end of the interview. Worry shoots through me when I see this. What if Wallace isn't getting it all? His next words will tell us if he's done with this conversation or ready to cooperate. My shoulders drop and I close my notebook. I am vibrating with enough tension to blow these brick walls apart.

"I told Tammy it was an accident. Those guys were helping her… that they were putting her into their car to take her to the hospital," he said with his eyes glazing back into that horrifying memory. "I believed that for a long time, too… I can see her limp body. She wasn't breathing. Her eyes weren't open. There was blood coming from her ears. They were dragging her like she was a bag of garbage." His voice trails off and his eyes return to the wall behind Ray. I feel a cold bristle on my skin followed by an intense flush of heat that makes my back break out in perspiration.

His testimony has just shattered the silence and clenched our case. I glance to Ray, who has his hands folded in his lap. Three decades. Over. His watery eyes tell me he is resonating with everything that I am feeling right now. Ray's gentle look coaxes Wallace on.

"I got outta the car to help and… I tripped cause you know, it was dark and the ground was all uneven and shit. And this one he just pounced on me. Kicked me in the face. Then the other one jumped out from behind the front of the car and came after me. He had this thing in his hand. I thought it was a hammer or hatchet. I was just so focused on getting my ass off the ground… And I could hear Tammy screaming from the car."

Wallace paused for a moment, his look directed beyond us to an imaginary object on the wall.

"Did he hit you with it?" said Ray.

Wallace shakes his head. "But I got a good look at it though. It wasn't a hammer. It was a tool I had seen earlier that summer. My cousin was using it to tear off the shingles on his barn roof."

I almost gulp out loud. He had seen the roofing tool! This was epic testimony. We have them! I want to scream and run up and down the corridors of that prison. We have them! We have them!

I look up from the notes I'm jotting down furiously and notice Wallace. I almost gasp again at the man transforming before my eyes. The crinkles around his eyes and across his forehead, his pursed lips… all soften. His eyes are brighter. Bluer. There is nothing hard about him in this moment. His expression now is that of a little boy who just felt, for the first time, the crack of the ball on the bat… the steadiness of two wheels on the sidewalk… the tug of the fish on the end of his line… the victory of crossing a rushing undercurrent. He looks at Ray like he would at his proud father, desperate for the love and approval he longs for. Ray returns the look. And it is for real.

I marvel at the miracle unfolding in that square, gray, block room. Inside that orange jump suit yet lies a nugget of childlike purity. If Wallace, who had done so much wrong, caused so much pain, held so much hurt, and kept so many secrets, acted his whole life out of selfishness... if he could get a second chance at redemption and forgiveness and love, was it not possible there might be some left for me, too?

Chapter 62

SOLOMON

S olomon pulls away from Pub Griffin. He glances behind him making sure his rifle is still on the back seat of his extended cab. He drives around the county all day until his gas tank empties and he uses the last few fumes to find his way to Detective St. James' house.

He coasts past Riley's house, observing. Her truck is gone. That huge dog is gone. A few of the neighbors' porch lights flicker on as dusk settles in, but there's no one outside anywhere in the neighborhood. She's gotta come home sometime. He'll wait all night.

The engine dies as he steers the truck into a parking spot on the street a few blocks from her house. Only two cars go past him in the whole time he waits. Now under the deep cover of dark, he gets out and roams back towards Riley's house via the street. His boots slap-slap, slap-slap the asphalt and he slows to quiet them.

Solomon's mind wanders, as it often does, into attack thoughts on Silas. Silas, the one who had suggested they drive to the Hole in the Woods; Silas, who got them drunk and stoned; Silas, who reached for the tool to give to him and he had delivered the fatal blows. Now, every time he hears a large branch snap it sends him right back to the sound of her skull cracking as he made impact.

Solomon's guilt had festered and grown. His docile personality had turned angry and easily agitated. He became loathsome of anyone who didn't like him. Especially women.

Solomon and Silas never talked about her final moments. The gasp she let out at the end. The languid silence that followed. How heavy a hundred-and-five-pound body felt lifting it into their trunk.

The headlights shining into the cherry red Chevy Nova that pulled up. That young, blonde girl screaming her fool head off from the passenger seat as Silas kicked the girl's boyfriend in the head.

Silas must remember. He has to.

They never found out who those two were. They had waited on pins and needles for years afterwards, wondering if they would squeal. After a while, when nothing happened, they forgot about them.

Silas grew into his comfortable life, all tucked away in his two-story home with his wife and kids. A Newton in college. That was a Newton family first. Solomon tried to settle down. He had a string of girlfriends, his house, his hobbies. Later a wife. Then an ex-wife. And a son.

He had worked hard to quell the torment and put it in the past; and he didn't want anything to risk their good lives now. No one was going to take this away from them.

Hidden under the shadows of nightfall, Solomon checks his surroundings and hikes up Riley's driveway, his rifle clinging tight to his side to conceal it.

He walks right into the backyard and finds his way to the woodpile near the back fence. He shoulda popped her off the other night when he had the chance.

Chapter 63

RILEY ST. JAMES

I call Grable on the way home so we can download Wallace's testimony with him tonight and he can prepare the proper paperwork for an arrest warrant in the morning. I am grieved to find out the rough details of Misty's distress call. As Grable gives me the bullet points, they are too horrible for me to process at the moment. Solomon forced his way into her home, tied her up, and tortured her until she gave up Tammy's name. A neighbor recognized something was off and went to Misty's house. He saw them through the window and called for help. But not before Solomon caught on and fled. Knowing Tammy would be his next victim, Grable was able to set up police security for Tammy and her kids. The whole county has been unsuccessfully trying to track Solomon down. Sickening.

I shake it off and rest on more positive thoughts for the moment. In the morning we will secure arrest warrants for Silas and Solomon from the judge. They will be in custody before lunch time.

Near midnight, I pull into Ray's driveway. He continues to insist that I should spend the night at his home until the Newton brothers are behind bars. He cajoles me relentlessly and refuses to get out of the truck until I agree. I tell him that I need to get a few things from home. Like, Zik's dinner for one. A toothbrush and change of clothes would also be nice. He says he'll go inside to prep my room and wait up for me. If I'm not back in thirty minutes, he's coming to drag me out of my house. After all, he knows it doesn't take more than a few minutes to grab a couple things. He says it with a smile, but I know he's dead serious.

I pull out of his driveway and roll the windows down to let the cool air wake me. Zik joins me in the passenger seat as I take the main road to Derby to my house, purposefully driving under the speed limit so I can unwind. There are few cars and the fresh air clears my mind. I picture Ray on the drive back to Derby. Radiant and relieved. I think I even saw him wipe away a tear or two that escaped from those weathered lines around his eyes. I smile at the strange and illuminating string of events.

As I pull in the drive ten minutes later, Zikmund sits up and sticks his nose out the passenger side window. His snout twitches. Sniff, sniff, sniff, sniff in a circular motion. I turn the truck off. Zik puts his paws up onto the window sill.

"What is it?" I whisper and listen. A choir of crickets serenade predawn. Twigs snap under the weight of some small critter running through the trees in the back.

Zik scratches and scratches at the door wanting to get out. The hair on his back stands up. He lets out a low growl. Something is off.

I reached for the door handle and Zik bounces over onto my lap to leap out. All eighty pounds of him lands in my gut. "Uufff. What are you---?" He gently nips at my hand and I draw it back into my chest.

"Zik, what's going on? It's just a squirrel. Stop that." I swing the door open with my left foot while trying to yank him back by the collar. He growls and with a strong thrust, breaks from my grasp and scrambles off my lap. He jumps to the ground and spins around barking incessantly and lunging at me. He absolutely won't let me out of the truck.

I command him to stop. But he plants his front two paws on the running board so I can't get out. Another low growl.

"Okay. Okay," I mouth, taking his cue.

I reach into the console for my gun with my right hand and dial my cell with my left. Ray's number. Something tells me I can't and shouldn't wait for Ray to just show up as promised.

I pet Zik's head and try again to push him aside and slide down out of my truck. He takes a powerful jump onto my chest, wedging me back into the driver's seat. Ray's line is on the second ring.

"Hey, buddy. I get it," I whisper to him and he licks my cheek and lets out another low growl of warning. "I need to check it out. Let me out. Come on."

Zik dances in circles, blocking the door as I try to step forward again. This time I make it out of the truck. Third ring. Maybe Ray dozed off?

Just then Zik's large body goes between my legs and drops me to the ground. I land hard on my tailbone just as Ray answers on the fourth ring, stress already attached to his voice. "Riley? Everything okay?"

"I don't think so," I breathe through the pain zinging up my spine. "Zik's acting weird. He just knocked me to the ground. I'm lying outside my truck."

"Can you get up? Are you hurt?"

"I'm okay."

"Both of you, get back into the truck. Now. Take a drive around the neighborhood until I get over there."

Before I can answer, Ray has hung up. I get to my knees as Zik presses his weight against me, licking and uttering low growls.

"Okay buddy. Hop back into the truck. We're going for a ride."

But as I turn to usher him into the cab Zik's attention snaps to the yard and he sprints into the darkness. I'm about to chase after him when a loud BANG stops me in my tracks. It's followed by a single yelp and a soft THWUMP. In the moonlight I see Zik's body slump to the grass.

Instinct and training thrust me to the ground and I crawl on all fours for cover behind a nearby bush. I train my weapon towards the sound. From this perch, I am able to see across the lawn and I search for the shooter.

My thoughts are escorted by a blast of adrenaline that throbs in my neck and head.

Another BANG explodes over my head spraying a shower of leaves and twigs down on my head. I shake them out of my eyes with no time to overthink my next action. I point my gun in the direction of the shot and fire back in quick successive shots. POP! POP! POP!

It could be considered a risky move to shoot into the darkness, but there's no house behind mine. Very little chance of civilian presence. And I have no choice. This is self-defense and well within my law enforcement rights.

I wait motionless as the ringing deafens me. My eyes are pried wide open, scanning the yard for any movement. I pull on the bottoms of my ear lobes and cup my palms over my ears, still crunched to the ground. Equilibrium returns to my inner ear. The sounds of the night are restored as my hearing comes back. Sweat soaks my shirt.

I wait for another thirty seconds, which feels like an hour. I don't hear a single rustle from the back. I engaged the flashlight feature on my cell phone and point it in the direction where I fired. The body of a man is slumped over my woodpile, his arms tucked under his torso. I can't see his legs or his weapon. Dark, glistening fluid runs from underneath him and down the logs like sap. I take no chances and call out to him.

"Sir, put your hands up where I can see them."

I slowly rise to my feet calling out again. No response. I rest my flashlight beam on the victim and tread one careful step at a time across my lawn as I continue to call to him. "Can you hear me, sir? I need to see your hands up. This is Officer St. James of the Michigan state police. Hands up!"

My gun never leaves its target as I approach. I'm now less than ten feet from the man and I can see a cavity the size of a half dollar blown into the side of his head, brain matter exposed. I gasp at the damage I've caused another human being. The contents of my stomach shoot up my throat. And I reel back, sending them back down with sheer will power.

I take another look at the body, focusing on his clothes. I recognize the style—or rather lack of--- of his hair cut. I know immediately whom I've shot. But I have to be one hundred percent sure.

"Sir? Sir! I'm approaching you now."

I step up at arm's length. Flies have already begun to swarm and land on the open wounds. I watch for a rise and fall in his chest.

No movement. Not even the slightest rise of the chest.

Flies buzz away from their blood bath as I place my shaking index and middle fingers to the neck for a pulse.

In that one touch I know there will be no trial… no jail time… no time for some crazy deathbed conversion. I have just sent Solomon Newton to hell.

I lower my gun and look away as the vomit makes its way up my throat. I swallow it down and step away from Solomon's body.

Stay calm. Stabilize yourself. Push against the undercurrent. You can take this river.

I reach for my phone when a soft cry from the yard turns my attention to Zikmund. I rush away from Solomon's corpse and dive toward Zik. Scooping him up, I can feel a shallow panting. I hold onto him, warming his body with mine, as headlight beams illumine the driveway.

Chapter 64

GRABLE

Around 6 a.m., after Ray had notified him about the situation at the home of Riley St. James, Grable finds himself hunched behind a squad car facing the front door of Silas Newton's home, fresh arrest warrant burning a hole in his pant pocket. He cradles his cell phone in the palm of his hand, speaker function on. A dozen cops and a SWAT team from the next county over surround Silas' house in a standoff. Things have gone as expected... with a struggle.

Silas appears at the door with his semi-automatic rifle. Earlier that night, he marched his family out of the house, shut and locked the door behind them and then went radio silent. His wife and kids took off and the police are still trying to track them down. Now, Grable has managed to get Silas on the phone.

Grable speaks in a steady voice. "Silas. I want you to meet me at the front door. Just open the door. No guns. And just meet me there. I just wanna talk. Okay?"

Listening to Silas' breath on the other end, he waits for a response.

"Will you do it? There's something I need to tell you."

"Tell me over the phone," says Silas and Grable thinks he detects a slur in his voice.

"I can't do that. I'm going to come out from behind my car now. Don't shoot me. Got it?"

"I won't shoot you if you don't shoot me," says Silas.

Grable steps out from behind the squad car and edges his way to the front door, still holding his phone.

"You said no guns," says Silas from the phone. "You got a gun."

Grable lowers his gun, knowing that several dozen weapons are backing him up but it unnerves him. He stands there, trying to portray confidence.

"Toss it," says Silas.

Grable hesitates, then lays the gun on the ground and takes a step toward the house. "All right. Come on out now."

After a tense moment, the door swings open.

"Hey, Silas." Grable says simply taking another step toward the house.

Silas shuffles into view. Arms at his sides.

"Hands up."

Silas wobbles. Steadies himself on the door frame. And then, obeys.

Grable holds his hand up to signal to the officers, all clear.

"No one fire!" says Grable.

Grable moves in a few more steps.

"You better have some pretty damn good reason for all this, Kevin."

"It's Officer Grable."

"You said you had something to tell me."

"At the station."

"You tell me now. Here."

"I need to know you don't have a weapon on you. Raise your pant legs and take off your shirt."

"This is bullshit. What do you wanna say to me?"

"Show me you don't have a gun," Grables' voice commands.

Silas takes a step backwards into the house. Grable feared this and doesn't want things to get any uglier.

"Not another step, Silas."

"What's so important you gotta rush over here with all this fanfare?"

"Lift your shirt and turn around."

Silas finally relents, tugging his shirt up to his neck. He turns around to show Grable front and back.

"Thank you. And your pants?"

Silas hikes up his pant legs, left and right. He is clean.

"So? What you gotta tell me, Kev?"

"Solomon--" Grable's words get caught in his throat.

"Yeah. What about him? He in trouble again?"

"I'd really like for you to come out here with me," says Grable.

"What's this all about? I ain't done nothing." Silas starts to lower his arms.

"Arms up!" shouts Grable.

"Did Solomon tell you about how that detective came trespassing into his work shed?"

Grable locks eyes with Silas.

"Your brother is dead."

Silas chuckles. "You think that trick'll work to get me to go peacefully?"

"No. Solomon was killed."

"Nice try. He called me last night."

"He camped out at the home of Detective St. James. Tried to kill her."

"Nah. You're fooling."

Grable shakes his head. "He's gone, Silas."

"You're just saying that to get me to surrender."

"Your brother is dead."

Silas studies Grable as a smirk unfolds over his face.

"There's a reason we wanted to ditch you that night. Prick."

Silas steps over the threshold.

"Don't come any further." Grable trains him with a gruff look. "On your knees! Now!"

"You ain't fooling around, are you?"

"There's ten guns pointed at you, Silas."

"Okay. Okay." Silas drops to his knees.

"Hands on the back of your head." Silas moves them into place. Grable quickly rushes to him with handcuffs. Another cop jumps up from the rear, to cover Grable. Silas makes no attempt to retaliate.

"So, the Hardy Boys and Nancy Drew finally solved the case, huh?" says Silas, breaking in hysterical laughter.

Grable cuffs him and pulls him to his feet. It's finally over.

Chapter 65

RILEY ST. JAMES

"We've arrested Silas Newton," I say when Jim is able to look up at me. "And you probably heard about what happened to Solomon?"

He nods. "You okay?"

I nod.

"I heard he shot your dog."

"Zik's gonna be okay. Vet found the bullet. Patched him up. He's resting at home now."

Jim nods again.

"I can't really tell you much about the evidence we found. But I can tell you that the judge has ruled that it's sufficient to hold a trial."

Tears well up in the bottom of Jim's saggy eye lids.

"Doesn't change my pain, but at least there is justice coming." Each word is layered with hurt.

"Yes. There will be justice for Nina." I say with complete conviction in my tone. "I feel certain Silas will be locked away for the rest of his life."

Jim nods once. Maybe he believes me. Maybe he needs to see it for himself.

"How... how... have you done it all these years?" I have to know because even though I, too, have suffered, I truly believe his fate to be worse than mine. Now that I have seen redemption with my own eyes, I want it. I want to know the way out of my prison.

Jim lets out a long exhale. When I look at the man in the thread worn armchair in front of me to the one in the photographs, it's shocking to compare how much his frame has withered over the years since Nina's death. Skin sagging over skeleton.

"We have to forgive ourselves first. It frees us to love again," says Jim. "Took me forever to understand this."

"How?" I say in a whisper.

"It's a different process for everyone. But in the end, you just decide. It's a choice."

A lump in my throat stops me from responding.

"Your suffering must be great," he says.

I'm not surprised he sees the suffering in me. Jim knows a thing or two about what suffering looks like. I'm only surprised that he cares enough to notice.

"It is." I admit to someone for the first time.

"Your suffering is important. It's a gift. Did you know that, Riley?"

I've never heard him call me by my first name. I didn't even know he knew my first name.

"A gift? That's a terrible gift," I try to brush it off. Jim won't have it.

"Suffering is that place where love does its best work," says Jim barely moving in his chair.

"Have you ever gotten up really early in the morning and took a walk outside just before the sun comes up. That new light opening the sky, that's love." He sounds poetic when he speaks. Very unlike a blue-collar truck driver. "It's the peaceful breeze on a summer evening. It's the gentle nudging of your dog's nose to let you know he's there for you. It's the laughter of friends who sit with you late into the night when you can't find sleep. It's you, Riley St. James, an angel with a hard past from a crooked city, relentless for justice for a girl you've never known. You are love embodied."

I am love?

He takes my hand and squeezes it. I think of Wallace. Pure sacrifice for a family he's never met. A selfless love that in turn freed himself. How ironic. How mysterious. How freeing.

"I don't think it works that way for me," I say.

"The miracle of love belongs to everyone. Just have to ask for it."

My eyes flit from the floor to meet his.

"And when it comes, and it will, you must have the courage to give up that anger you're gripping so tightly. Let it slip from your fingers. You don't need it anymore."

He leans forward in his chair now. Veins in his neck pulsing with the hope and love and blood that have kept him alive the last thirty years.

Chapter 66

NINA

I went to the river again. That woman detective Riley St. James was there, wading thigh-deep into the rushing current and bracing herself upstream. I had never seen her at the river before. She held a fly rod and was struggling to get the line to cooperate. There was something familiar in the way she was trying to keep her arms stiff but her wrist was snapping just as she let the line out and messing up her cast. It was the same little quirk Adam used when he fished. He said Kevin Grable taught him. He said it was Kevin's signature move. The little snap at the end made for the longest line extension. Adam showed me once, but I kept laughing and he thought I wasn't taking it seriously. I just wanted to be with Adam. After a while he got kinda mad at me for acting silly. He pretended to ignore me as he plunged up stream about ten feet. I followed him with my line and stood a few feet from his side and started to cast the line. One-two-three-four-wrist snap-release thumb. Over and over the same rhythm. Over and over my line sailed out perfectly over the water. I smiled at Adam and he smiled back and shook his head. We fished all afternoon and then made love on the river bank when the sun was setting. Afterwards he asked me to marry him. Right there beside our stinky catch.

Riley wasn't getting it so I waded up next to her and breathed the mantra Adam taught me.

One-two-three-four-wrist snap-release thumb.

I wanted to hug this poor thing and tell her it would get better. I gently reached out, hoping the temporal would let me in. My hand hovered over her shoulder. I lay it down. I could feel the cloth of her coat under my fingers. I could feel the warmth radiating from her! With my other hand, I took a hold of her arm and she let me guide her. We cast the line back and then I moved her arm over her head, extending it in front of her and snapping her wrist at the right moment while lifting her thumb with a light flick of my forefinger. We did it again. And again.

One-two-three-four-wrist snap-release thumb.

One-two-three-four-wrist snap-release thumb.

One-two-three-four-wrist snap-release thumb.

A small smile curled Riley's lips as she watched the line sail out above the river, reaching almost all the way across. She held onto the line and when nothing bit on the other end, she took the line in and held it. She raised her arm again to cast and I reached out to assist, but then Riley stopped. She looked out over the river and she exploded in tears. Her wave of emotion surprised me. Wherever this was coming from was deep. Her whole body shook and she was having a hard time controlling her balance. I was afraid she was going to just end it all in the river. I've seen that too many times to count in the past twenty years.

Her heaves subsided to mournful whimpers and she tossed her rod into the water. After a few seconds, it bobbed out of view. Then, she dipped her body into the river up to her neck and lifted her feet off the river bottom, giving into the current. It swirled her towards the center of the river and downstream. I dove into the water towards her and floated alongside her, watching as she floated herself onto her back and lifted her eyes to the sky. She studied it as if she was expecting some one or some thing to suddenly appear.

We must have drifted at least a mile or more to where the river went shallow near a state park picnic area. Riley let her feet drag along the river bottom, anchoring her in place. She planted her feet and calmly walked to the river bank. Her wet clothes weighed her down as she plodded out of the river. She collapsed a few feet from shore and rolled onto her back, her gaze again pointed to the sky.

I sat next to her. I waited to see what she would do next. Her breathing restored itself to a resting rhythm. I reached for her hand and I squeezed it. At the touch of human skin her fingers hers curled around mine. And I whispered to her again.

"You are not alone. Can you feel that? You are very much loved by a spirit that's all around you. I don't know what hurt and anger you are struggling with. But it's nothing compared to... compared to this love. It's bigger than Adam's love. Bigger than Dad's love. Bigger even than Tucker's. Take it."

I wish I would have known this kind of love that night... I would have never left the house... never gotten into that car...never walked that path with evil...

I saw her lips moving as if she were talking silently to herself. And the whole time she didn't let go of my hand. I could have sworn she even squeezed it. She didn't look upset or troubled anymore. I recognized the face of peace. The face of love. It was the same for me the moment I left my body at the Hole in the Woods. No, she wasn't dead or anything. Riley was still living in the temporal world. And now, this love was hers, too.

Chapter 67

GRABLE

G rable slips Nina's class ring into Jim's hand. His fingers curl up around it and he holds it for a while in his fist. Grable looks away, lifting his glance to the pictures of Nina on the living room walls. Nina, Mom, and Dad, in happier, younger times. Nina and Dad, the pre-teen, braces years. Nina, Grandma, and Dad at Grandma's birthday party. Nina and Tucker as a puppy. Nina in her cap and gown. Nina and Adam, embracing on the day he left for Ohio.

"I don't know why I never gave it to you," says Grable. "I'm sorry."

"I know why." Jim says. "You needed it more than I did."

"But it wasn't mine to keep. The ring or the secret."

"What matters is that in the end, you did the right thing." With that, Grable knows there's no hard feelings. Jim slips the ring onto his pinky finger and sits back.

"Guess who wrote me a letter?" says Jim with a smile.

"I actually had no idea anybody wrote letters to anyone anymore," says Grable.

"Wallace."

"What! No way. What did he say?"

"That he's sorry."

"I could not be more shocked," says Grable. "What are you going to do?"

"I've already written him back."

"You did? What did you tell him?"

"That I forgive him."

Grable returns Jim's smile. They sit in comfortable silence for a bit until Grable's radio crackles. Suspicious person call. He rises to leave.

"You ever been fly fishing?" Grable asks him.

"Never have. Funny huh? Living this close to the river."

"You're missing out, old man. Why don't you come with me on Saturday."

"Yeah. Yeah. I'd like that," says Jim.

Chapter 68

RILEY ST. JAMES

F ind the criminal. Make the arrest. Attend the trial. Hope for fair sentencing. Life in prison. Satisfaction? Yes. Justice? Yes. Closure? Never.

I trace the deep lines on the brows on Jim's face. They've been there for thirty years, etching themselves permanently into his flesh the moment he got that call. Trawling deep, gnarled trenches across the forehead and around the eyes. They've grown more creviced with each year.

No amount of jail time will ever be enough retribution for the act committed against his daughter.

In the cool, rushing waters of the river, I have prayed and found relief from my burden. Solomon's death bed conversion is no longer my concern. It's not my journey. I've done my part. I have my own conversion to worry about.

I know there is no certainty in life. I know there is only surrender. Peace and mercy have kissed me. Love has visited me. And it planted itself into my soul. I can feel the pulse of it as surely as I can feel my own right now. In that moment down by the river, all the past, the pain, the bitterness, and the fear and the anger... oh, the anger... washed off and redeemed for me in ways I could never comprehend. I left it all there. And emerged clean.

The evening before I am supposed to return to Detroit, Zik and I meet Grable on the back patio of Pub Griffin at a table under a green patio umbrella. Joyce brings us two large burger plates and fries. And for me, a club soda with lime.

Zik rests on a blanket on the ground next to me. He gets up, shifts his weight and then tries to settle into a comfortable position.

"How's he doing?" asks Joyce.

"His spirits are great," I say petting him. "The vet says he may always have a bit of a limp, but he'll compensate."

Joyce leans over to scratch his head. "Good boy. You saved your mama's life. Good boy. Gonna miss you around here."

Zik's lips turn up and I know he's smiling which makes me smile.

"Gonna miss you, too" says Joyce. "Not gonna miss those Newton twins. You done good, St. James. Thank you."

"Don't worry. I'll be back. I'm gonna need some more of these burgers."

"That's right. Best in the north."

"Maybe all of Michigan," I say.

Joyce heads back into the pub and Grable turns to me.

"You look radiant. A little rest has been good for you, huh?"

"Yeah, something like that." It's been a much needed few days off-duty. "I've been at the river a lot, too."

"Really?"

"Yes. I've been practicing my fly fishing. And I'm getting pretty good at it." I laugh.

"Caught anything?"

"Working on my technique."

Grable laughs.

I laugh.

I realize that we've never actually laughed together.

"You found what you needed there," he says softly.

"And left a few things I don't." I hold his gaze with a deep, deep resonance.

Before things get too awkward, I slide a jar of honey from my purse and hand it to him. "Ray stopped by with a case of these and there's no way I should eat all of them."

He takes the jar and bobs his head away from me. I don't want to call him out on it, but I see him use the side of his sleeve to wipe away some wetness around his eyes.

We eat in silence for a few moments. I pull off a piece of bun for Zik and he snaps it from my fingers in a single gulp.

"I owe you an apology," says Grable.

"For what?" I stuff another bite into my face. Not being much of a cook, I've been existing on oatmeal, crackers, and fruit the last few days and I am ravenous for real food.

"I shouldn't have dug into your past. I shouldn't have pushed you. That was really inconsiderate of me. I should've known better. I've been there and...we're all on our own journeys. I didn't respect yours."

"No. It's good. You were part of my journey."

If Grable hadn't taken care of me after the woods incident... if Grable hadn't taken me flying fishing that one afternoon... if Grable hadn't come after the trespassing incident... if he hadn't been so open about his own past... if he hadn't... loved me... no strings attached.

"Kevin, I can't imagine what it's been like for you living under this cloud for so long. I'm glad it's finally over for you."

He nods. No words.

"What's next for Detective Riley St. James?" he asks.

"I've been assigned a new cold case in Detroit. So, it's back to the city..."

"You ready for that?"

"I'm ready to return to my old apartment. My old friends. My old office."

"You won't be returning as the old you."

"No, I'm not the old me."

A few moments slip between us and I'm trying to think of something to say that won't sound too trite or overly emotive. So much is stirring in me right now.

"Anytime you want to come up and do some fly fishing... I'd love to-"

"Yeah. Yeah. I'd love to. I'll be back for the trial. Let's pencil that in."

"Yeah. Let's do that. Definitely."

Grable dips a French fry into a pool of ketchup, pops it into his mouth. He turns to me with a smile.

"The river. It feels good, doesn't it?" he says.

I know exactly what he means. But I don't respond because his face is blurring through my gaze.

Chapter 69

NINA

After I saw that lady detective at the river, I hung out at my gravesite every day. I knew my Dad would show up and fill me in on everything. And he did. I learned that Kevin Grable had arrested Silas and that Riley St. James had killed Solomon in her back yard. Dad cried a little when he told me the whole story. Tears of relief, not sadness. I couldn't get my eyes off his face. All the stress had aged him in countless wrinkles, but his eyes… they were soft and full of relief. The purest blue reflecting off the blue sky. He told me I could continue my journey in peace.

He brought me two-dozen beautiful pink roses in a vase. The kind with the extra long stems. Then, he sat on the grave for a long time. I sat next to him. Of course, he couldn't see me. But just like Riley, I could feel his warmth, and every now and then I got a sweet whiff of the roses when the breeze blew the scent my way. That was the first time I was able to smell anything from the earth world since I died. I drank in that sweet smell, cupping my hands around my nose over the buds. It ran all the way through me.

It made my essence shiver with a tingly sensation from the tip of my head down through the tips of my toes, draining that lonely, tired feeling. In its place was just warmth. If I had to give it a name, I would call it, home.

Home. Those moments of home when Tucker was keeping me warm in bed while snow fell outside. Those moments when I sat down to eggs and toast and shared my day with Dad. Those moments when Dad kissed my cheek before he headed out to work for the night.

Something touched my hand. I glanced up quickly and saw a buttery soft hand reaching to pull me gently to my feet. The hand was attached to a beautiful, white creature. It was a face I had never seen, but yet was completely familiar to me. Not male. Not female. Just love. I knew in that instant, this was my spirit guide.

I followed the figure as it led me away from my grave… away from Dad… away from the scent of those roses.

I looked down at my Dad and saw that he was looking up at me. Or at least in the space where I was drifting away. Obviously he couldn't see me, but I think he must have sensed I was somewhere close. His lips form into a slight smile.

I wanted so badly to tell him thank you for never giving up the pursuit. And that I wasn't lonely anymore. Or tired. Or alone.

"You rest, now," I told him. And although I knew he couldn't actually hear the words, I believe he sensed their meaning. "I'm going to be taken care of. And no one and nothing can ever harm me again."

His image grew further from me. The last thing I saw was that he bent over and gave my gravestone a little kiss. Soon, we were rising over Derby, over the river, and into that purest blue sky I have ever seen. And I've seen a lot of blue sky.

I held on as we transitioned through the feathery shell of the atmosphere that separates the temporal from the eternal. Before my eyes could adjust to the brilliance of this new place, I heard a familiar bark and Tucker's soft coat brushed against my hand.

THE END

The True Crime Case of Shannon Siders

As summarized by John Hogan, Reporter, WZZM 13, Grand Rapids, Michigan, 2/10/17

In May, 2015, A Newaygo County jury convicted Matthew Wayne Jones, 46, of first-degree murder. His younger brother, 44-year-old Paul Michael Jones, was found guilty of second-degree murder of Shannon Siders, the only daughter of Bob Siders.

Matt and Paul were still teens when they killed Siders, 18, after she rejected their sexual advances, investigators said. A hunter found her mutilated, decomposing body in the Manistee National Forest near Newaygo three months later.

At the time, the brothers were interviewed, but no charges were filed because there was no evidence to link them to her murder. In 2011, a cold case team of investigators revisited the case, which some had called "unsolvable."

On the night Siders disappeared, investigators say the brothers spent several hours driving around "partying" with Siders and several other teens. The brothers eventually drove her to a secluded location and sought sexual favors from her.

The pair became enraged when she declined their advances. They took turns raping and beating her and eventually beat her to death, court records show.

At trial, several witnesses gave largely consistent testimony about what Siders was doing in the hours leading up to her disappearance. Most of the witnesses were drunk that night.

Siders at one point was seen in Paul Jones' red Mercury Cougar, seated between the two brothers. Several hours later, when the brothers pulled into a grocery store parking lot at the corner of M-37 and M-82, Siders was no longer with them. When asked where the victim was, Paul Jones said "we dropped her off at home," according to earlier testimony.

Siders' father the following morning called several of Shannon's friends and inquired about her whereabouts. Several days after her disappearance, Robert Siders reported her missing.

When police interviewed Paul Jones shortly after Siders' disappearance, he admitted Siders was with him "doing a lot of riding around," but said he dropped her off after midnight.

Police conducted roughly 476 witness interviews as part of the investigation; "no one ever reported seeing the victim alive after she was last seen with defendants," justices wrote.

One of the witnesses reported Paul Jones saying "just face it, she's dead." That statement was made a few days after Siders disappeared, court records show.

Three months later, a hunter found her body in the woods near M-82 and Thornapple Avenue east of Newaygo. The skull was found detached from the body, about 14 feet away. A pocket knife and a pair of table legs were found near the body.

In the months and years after her death, several incriminating statements attributed to the Jones brothers were made, according to testimony. Paul Jones said "the bitch got what she deserved," court records show.

Several years after the murder, while at a bachelor party, Matthew Jones grabbed a woman by the throat and threatened to "put her in the ground like the (expletive deleted) up north," according to testimony.

A year after the murder, the brothers were at a party, talking about Siders in a "bragging and cocky manner," another witness testified. "They can't pin it on us. They had us (and) they let us go," the brothers said, according to testimony.

Various other statements have been attributed to the pair, but the investigation went nowhere. In 2011, a cold case team was formed to investigate the case anew; roughly 300 people were interviewed, including numerous witnesses that were not interviewed as part of the original investigation.

Before trial, prosecutors asked that testimony of several witnesses, including Ronald King, be allowed at trial. King said he overheard one of the two brothers say "maybe we shouldn't have hit her so hard," "she should have give (sic) us what we wanted" and "I think we're in the clear."

Defense attorneys sought to have the statements kept out of trial. That bid was denied, and King's testimony was presented to jurors.

He testified that he heard the brothers talking about Siders, with one of the brothers saying "maybe they shouldn't have hit her so hard."

"They said she was looking good and said something about she should have given them what they wanted," King testified.

Investigators arrested and charged the brothers in June 2014.

Matthew Jones was sentenced in July 2015 to mandatory life in prison. He is at the Carson City Correctional Facility in Montcalm County.

Paul Jones was sentenced to between 30 and 75 years in prison for second-degree murder and is serving his time at the St. Louis Correctional Facility in Gratiot County.

A Word from Bob Siders,

Shannon Sider's father

After they found Shannon's body, the police were going door to door asking people if they had heard anything. And I remember asking one of the detectives, "How long does this go on?"

He said, "a few days."

This stuck in my mind and I talked to Detective Dick Miller about it. I knew that things were going to get pushed back and my daughter's case would get forgotten. I kept thinking, "what else can I do?"

One morning when I was coming home from work [Bob worked night shifts driving a truck], I was looking at those business signs, you know, those portable advertising signs. I thought, maybe I could get some of those businesses to put up: "Who Killed Shannon Siders" on those signs for her birthday on March 31. I started in Grant (a small town near Newaygo where Shannon lived) just asking people. Everyone was so cooperative. Almost everyone said yes. I kept asking all the way to White Cloud (the city north of Newaygo), Newaygo, and even into Fremont (a town west of Newaygo). Although I didn't get much cooperation there. So, I focused on the M37 North-South corridor. My friend, Stubby, and I took photographs of every one of them after they were up. Coincidentally, that weekend that everyone put up the signs was opening day of trout season. It was nice weather and the town was packed. I went to Sportsman (a local hangout) for lunch and I heard two different groups of people discussing those signs.

Yes, there were a couple of people that turned me down politely. They thought it looked bad for the community to point out that there was a murder. But I think it's better for the community to come together during times like these. The good thing was that there were people who didn't know me or Shannon, or who didn't even like us, who still wanted to help because they knew there was a murderer walking around. And because of the gruesomeness of her death, the medical examiner believed this killer was capable of doing it again.

The signs turned out to be a good thing because the prosecution used these photos as evidence in Shannon's trial to show that I was truly a sincere, grieving father.

My signs made the news, too.

Then, I thought, I wonder if I can do the same thing with billboards? I wonder if I could rent those? So, I called a guy who owned one and I met with the salesman and his supervisor and I told them what I wanted to do. They hadn't done anything like that before, but they leased me the billboard for a couple months. I paid for it in cash that day. They said they were gonna try it one time. After the lease was done, they wouldn't renew it, but they said they wouldn't take it down until they had another lease. It stayed up for a long time.

I also ran ads every year on her birthday or in July on the anniversary of her murder in the local paper. If some tip of interest came to me, I called the local TV station and tried to generate interest.

Those were some of the things I did because I knew that if anybody was to keep Shannon's case out there it had to be me. It wasn't going to be police or the news.

What would I tell others who have suffered this kind of loss?

Don't give up. Don't give up.

Sure, you start grasping a little bit. And you get mad at your kid. I still get mad at Shannon. She made some bad choices, and in her case, it cost her life.

You take it a day at a time. There's no pill that makes it feel better. It gets a little better but it's always there. The hole in your heart never really heals. You get some good days and then you get some bad days again. Most people understand that.

Sex can help. You need that union, that love. If that's available to you.

You need people who will talk to you when you wanna talk and leave you alone when you don't. I get days when I don't wanna talk about it.

After the funeral I got hundreds of sympathy cards. I appreciated every one of them cards. But the first good day I had after they found her is the day I went to the post box and there wasn't a single sympathy card. That was the first good day I had.

You learn as you go. A lot of people would call me trying to solve it. One woman called me convinced it was Satanism. She called me at least three times. There were other people that heard this and saw that and wanted to tell me. I would say, "Why are you calling me? Call Detective Miller. For you to tell me is heresay. It's not admissible in court."

The thing is, people call, but they don't wanna get involved. But it's too late! They are already involved because they called! I also had a couple of people calling just to learn about the reward money. When the first thing outta their mouth is how much is the reward? Well, that's kinda telling.

Before Shannon's funeral, I had the mortician take pictures of her remains and seal them up and keep them in case it ever went to court and I would need to view them in court. I wanted to be able to prepare myself. But I never did look at them or any other pictures in court. The last time I looked at Shannon she was eighteen and a half standing on the third step of the front porch.

After the funeral, people say, "let us know if we can help." Take them up on that! Because in a case like mine, it was such a large funeral and so many gifts and flowers and food. Get help with the thank you cards. Do the general ones first. Set those personal cards aside and do them when you can. If it starts to get to you, put them aside.

There's also all kinds of expenses you don't realize you'll have. With guests coming and going you have to spend on bedding, towels, extra gas, postage, and food. There's a lot of hidden expenses people don't think of. Even getting the death certificate takes time and a little gas money. I got some money from Victim's Rights. Parents of Murdered Children organization were at the funeral to help offer with counseling.

After the funeral, I stood at the door of the funeral home and shook hands and thanked everyone who came. I got down on my knees and hugged the kids.

It all happens so quickly. You don't reason things out when you're by yourself. It's good to have someone with you. Remember that well intentioned, well-meaning people do nice things, but they didn't always ask permission. They asked afterwards. And they don't understand that sometimes no means no. But people do things anyway.

Joining a support group helps. It does. Everybody there has suffered a loss. You can't go there and think you're different or better because your child was murdered. My loss is no greater than anyone else's. It's just the circumstances are different. Every loss is equally devastating. They need support from you, and you need support from them. You can also go and just say nothing and cry.

After the funeral I'd go to Shannon's grave almost daily. That tends to wean off over time. Time is the healer. And understanding. You wonder why. But I think it all gives you a little a more faith, too. You want to believe you'll see your child again. I always believed there was higher being and I hope there is. It makes you believe that there's something out there that exists beyond us.

--Bob Siders, father of Shannon Siders, June 11, 2020

Crime Writing for a Cause

Good news! I have partnered with The Cold Case Foundation. And if you bought this book, you helped support crime fighting efforts and solve cold cases!

As a crime fiction writer, I see crime first and foremost for its story and entertainment value. But as a citizen, I want to support crime fighters who are in the real crime fighting world. There is nothing more satisfying to me than giving back to the real-life crime fighting heroes who give us so much!

When I found the Cold Case Foundation, they drew an instant heart connection for me. Their mission mirrors my own: to shed hope and light into the darkest recesses of the human experience.

And they are doing this every day as they help solve cold cases from around the country, working closely with victim's families, and providing victim prevention services.

The CCF can take the remnants of a horrible, violent crime and, with their professional volunteer team, bring light to families who have walked in darkness, and breathe the hope of justice into seemingly impossible cases.

Cases like Shannon's.

We need the CCF because, unfortunately, Shannon's case is not uncommon. But why are there so many unsolved crimes?

First, law enforcement are focused on dealing with present crimes and preventing future crimes. Crimes in the past often do not take priority. Mostly, because the biggest obstacles facing police departments today are the lack of commitment to a case, manpower, and funds.

Additionally, only about 18 percent of the nation's 18,000-plus police agencies that have cold cases actually have a "cold case unit" to investigate these incidents.

This is where the Cold Case Foundation steps in to help!

CCF is a support arm for law enforcement agencies that takes on the hardest to solve, least funded cases. They assist by providing funding, expert consulting, training, networking, and victim support.

The CCF is currently run by an all-volunteer board and staff of law enforcement experts from the FBI, police branches, and investigators and forensic experts from around the country. Top notch service from seasoned professionals.

And all for free. There is no cost to police departments or victims and their families for the CCF support services.

Have a violent crime case you want help solving? The CCF is here for you.

Want to learn more about reducing your risk of becoming a victim of violent crime? The CCF offers victim prevention training to your group, school, business, or organization. www.coldcasefoundation.org

Thank you for reading.
JG Dornbush

A percentage of Hole in the Woods books sold will go to the Cold Case Foundation.

Acknowledgements

To Bob Siders, Shannon's dad, thank you for offering me your support and trust in telling this story. You have selflessly shared facts about the case and the people involved. You've told me stories about Shannon and shared your heart with me. One of the biggest blessings on this story journey has been getting to know you as a friend. I was so nervous when I sent you the first draft of the story for you to read. You picked it up from your mailbox on a Friday and spent the whole day and night reading it. Saturday morning you called me first thing to tell me your notes. They were few. You gave me your blessing on the manuscript and said you liked the way I had ended it. Thank you for letting me be a part of your life and your story. God bless you. You will see your beautiful daughter again and I bet her first words will be, "Thanks, Dad. You did a great job!"

To the tireless law enforcement, detectives, cold case team, attorneys, experts, witnesses, and countless others who helped bring this case to justice. Just to name a few who were key in bringing this case to justice: Michigan State Troopers Mike Stephens and John Forner, Michigan State Police Detective Sgt. Scott Rios, Newaygo County Detective Sgt. Adam Mercer, former Newaygo County Sheriff Pat Hedlund, Newaygo County Prosecutor Robert Springstead; God bless you all. Continue in excellence.

To my Dad, Dr. Ronald E. Graeser, D.O, the medical examiner assigned to Shannon's case in 1989. Your examination was thorough and professional. For twenty-three years you spent unnumbered hours trying to figure out what tool caused the injuries to Shannon, a piece of evidence that eventually proved highly influential in connecting the killers to Shannon's death.

To retired Michigan State Police Detective Sgt. Dick Miller, our longtime family friend and bee keeper extraordinaire. Everything has been redeemed and made whole. Thank you. God bless.

To Julie Gwinn, my tireless, positive, amazing literary agent. You believed in this project since the beginning and shepherded it to find a home and bring it to the world. Thank you for your unending support and encouragement. The journey continues and I'm so glad you are by my side!

To Shannon Siders, someday we will meet. And it will be an absolute treasure to get to know you better.